Praise for the novels of Nancy Kopp

"An exciting legal thriller . . . the characters are all top-rate." —Harriet Klausner, *Painted Rock Reviews*

"An admirable protrayal of the moral decisions that many of us may someday have to face . . . a satisfying read . . . will leave you wanting more chapters." —*Mystery News*

"A taut and intriguing thriller that combines the desperation of a hunt for a serial killer with the courtroom dramatics of a high profile lawsuit."
—*Romantic Times*

"Suspenseful. . . . What sets this book apart . . . is the strong development of the characters."
—*The Capital Times*

FINAL JUSTICE

NANCY KOPP

AN ONYX BOOK

ONYX
Published by New American Library, a division of
Penguin Putnam Inc., 375 Hudson Street,
New York, New York 10014, U.S.A.
Penguin Books Ltd, 80 Strand,
London WC2R 0RL, England
Penguin Books Australia Ltd, Ringwood,
Victoria, Australia
Penguin Books Canada Ltd, 10 Alcorn Avenue,
Toronto, Ontario, Canada M4V 3B2
Penguin Books (N.Z.) Ltd, 182–190 Wairau Road,
Auckland 10, New Zealand

Penguin Books Ltd, Registered Offices:
Harmondsworth, Middlesex, England

First published by Onyx, an imprint of New American Library,
a division of Penguin Putnam Inc.

First Printing, April 2002
10 9 8 7 6 5 4 3 2 1

Copyright © Nancy Kopp, 2002
All rights reserved

 REGISTERED TRADEMARK—MARCA REGISTRADA

Printed in the United States of America

Without limiting the rights under copyright reserved above, no part of
this publication may be reproduced, stored in or introduced into a
retrieval system, or transmitted, in any form, or by any means
(electronic, mechanical, photocopying, recording, or otherwise),
without the prior written permission of both the copyright owner and
the above publisher of this book.

PUBLISHER'S NOTE
This is a work of fiction. Names, characters, places, and incidents either
are the product of the author's imagination or are used fictitiously,
and any resemblance to actual persons, living or dead, business
establishments, events, or locales is entirely coincidental.

BOOKS ARE AVAILABLE AT QUANTITY DISCOUNTS WHEN USED TO PROMOTE
PRODUCTS OR SERVICES. FOR INFORMATION PLEASE WRITE TO PREMIUM
MARKETING DIVISION, PENGUIN PUTNAM INC., 375 HUDSON STREET, NEW YORK,
NEW YORK 10014.

If you purchased this book without a cover you should be aware that
this book is stolen property. It was reported as "unsold and
destroyed" to the publisher and neither the author nor the publisher
has received any payment for this "stripped book."

In memory of my grandmothers,
Elise Ingold Kopp
and
Martha Jegerlehner Stettler

ACKNOWLEDGMENTS

An author couldn't ask for better friends than Ann Muchin and Pat Grove. From the inception of my writing career they have unfailingly provided large doses of encourgement, humor, and inspiration—and if that weren't enough, they also know all the best restaurants in southern Wisconsin. It's amazing how many interesting plot lines can be worked out over a good meal.

My colleague Julie Rich (a.k.a. Mini-Me) is always willing to swap stories about the law, mysteries, and a variety of other topics, especially when the discussion is accompanied by a cold beer. Many thanks to everyone at the Orfordville, Wisconsin, public library for their continued support. Lorraine Gelly and everyone in the Fond du Lac mystery book club have helped keep me motivated.

For the record, the real Gary Carlson (who was named Wisconsin judge of the year for 2000) is quite a character, even if he didn't win a Pulitzer Prize.

For updates on my work, I invite everyone to visit my Web site, www.nancykopp.com, or contact me at nkmail@nancykopp.com.

PROLOGUE

Jesse Greer stood in the middle of a small storage room at the rear of a commercial building in downtown Madison, Wisconsin. It was midnight. Jesse's hands were encased in latex gloves. Shining a small flashlight beam around the room, he spotted a large cardboard box in a corner. Holding the pen-size flashlight between his knees, he reached into his jacket pocket and removed a utility knife, then deftly sliced the box open.

"Just what I was looking for!" the tall, dark-haired young man said aloud in a smooth Southern drawl as he saw that the box contained reams of copy machine paper. "This will do nicely." He tore open two of the reams and scattered loose sheets of paper around the room.

"Kowalski!" Jesse called in a louder voice. "Get your ass in here, *now*."

A moment later another small flashlight beam appeared from an adjoining room. The young man holding this light was barely one year out of high school. He, too, was wearing latex gloves. And he was also holding a red can containing gasoline.

"Did you shove rags under those shelves like I told you?" Jesse demanded.

"Yes," the youth replied. He sounded nervous.

"And did you splash gas around like I told you?"

"Yes." The youth's head bobbed up and down.

"Good. I'm glad to hear you can follow directions. Now give me that." Jesse reached out and yanked the gas can out of the young man's hand. He unscrewed the top, then liberally doused the sheets of paper strewn about the floor with the foul-smelling liquid.

"Don't you think that's enough?" the youth asked as Jesse continued to splash gasoline around the room.

"What's the matter, Benny?" Jesse asked. "You startin' to get cold feet?"

"Of course not," the youth replied. "I just thought maybe that was enough."

"And what would make you think that?" Jesse demanded.

"I don't know . . ." the young man stammered. "I was just thinking that there are houses on either side of here and people live in those houses and—you know—what if the fire spreads? Somebody could get hurt."

In an instant Jesse had dropped the can on the floor and was clutching the young man's throat with both hands. The youth's flashlight went flying. "What are you, Kowalski, some kind of fucking bleeding heart?" Jesse roared, squeezing Ben's throat as hard as he could. "Are you one of them fucking faggots? You know how much I hate faggots. Who are you to say what's enough? Who's in charge of this operation? *Answer me. Who is fucking in charge here?"*

Ben Kowalski's eyes bulged out from his lack of oxygen. He tried to push Jesse away but he was no match for the bigger and stronger attacker. Finally, when Ben felt himself starting to lose consciousness, Jesse relaxed his grip. Ben fell to his knees, gasping for air.

"Let me ask you again," Jesse said in a calmer tone. "Who is in charge of this operation?"

"You are, Jesse," the youth managed to choke out.

"Very good, son, " Jesse said, slapping Ben on the shoulder. "I might just make a worthy soldier out of you yet, boy." He pulled Ben to his feet and handed him the gas can. "Here, you go back to the truck and wait for me. I'll be there shortly, just as soon as I get the home fires burning here, so to speak." He laughed at his little joke, then shone the flashlight at his watch. "It's ten past twelve. We made real good time. We should be at our next stop in twenty minutes or so."

Jesse gave Ben a shove toward the door. "Get going. Don't let anybody see you. And don't even think about running away," he added menacingly. "Because if you run away, you know I'll find you."

Trembling with fear, Ben Kowalski eagerly fled the building.

Jesse reached into his pocket and pulled out a disposable lighter. A smile played about his handsome face as he flicked it on. "Take that, you godless murderers," he said. "May your filthy souls rot in hell." He leaned down and touched the flame to the gasoline-soaked paper. As the fire took hold and began to spread, Jesse retrieved Ben's flashlight from the floor and raced out into the dark night.

CHAPTER 1

The sun streamed brightly through the windows of Ann Monroe's office as the dark-haired middle-aged man seated across from her expressed his anger.

"The criminal trial was a joke!" Tom Robinson said. "Samuel Jenkins and Brad English nearly killed Bill, and they got off scot-free." Tom Robinson paused a moment and looked at the attractive thirty-something lawyer sitting across the desk from him before continuing. "We want those young punks held accountable for what they did to Bill. We want you to file a civil suit against them."

To Robinson's left his wife, Laurie, a slender redhead dressed in a brown pantsuit, nodded emphatically. To Robinson's right his son, Bill, who was dressed in jeans and a red sweatshirt, sat looking down at the floor, the toe of his right sneaker nervously digging into the carpet.

Ann pushed her shoulder-length brown hair behind her ears and collected her thoughts for a moment before commenting on Tom Robinson's request. She knew this family had been through hell, and she understood their anger.

Several weeks earlier, nineteen-year-old Bill Robinson had been at the center of one of Wisconsin's most closely watched trials. The previous fall, Bill, an openly gay student who attended the University of Wisconsin's Mount Pleasant campus, about an hour's drive from Madison, had been viciously assaulted by two seventeen-year-olds. The young men, Samuel Jenkins and Brad English, had been charged with causing great bodily harm.

The prosecution's theory was that Bill had been singled out because of his sexual orientation. If they had been convicted, the defendants' sentences could have been enhanced by up to five years under Wisconsin's new hate-crimes law, which applied to crimes committed against certain protected classes of people, including those victims selected on the basis of sexual preference.

Ann, a partner at Mishler and Stettler, a twelve-attorney Madison firm that exclusively handled plaintiffs' cases, had followed the trial closely and had hoped the jury would see fit to use the new law to enhance the penalty imposed on Bill's attackers. From what was reported in the media, it looked like the jury had plenty of evidence to find both defendants guilty. To Ann's dismay, both young men had been acquitted. Ann relished the idea of filing a civil suit against Bill Robinson's assailants.

Ann turned slightly in her chair so she could get a partial glimpse out one of her windows. The firm's

FINAL JUSTICE

offices on the fourth floor were at the top of a historic building on the east side of the capitol square in downtown Madison. It was late March, and the capitol grounds looked barren and forlorn. Ann knew, though, that in a matter of weeks the thousands of tulips the grounds crew had planted the previous fall would be forcing their way out of the cold soil. By early May the dazzling display of color would rival anything that existed in Holland.

Ann nodded sympathetically in response to Tom Robinson's comments. "Like many people who followed the case, I was surprised—and extremely disappointed—with the verdict."

"It was a disgrace!" Tom Robinson exclaimed. "I don't know how the people who served on that jury can sleep at night. And as for those young punks who tried to murder my son . . ." His voice trailed off. "That's why we want you to sue. It simply can't end like this."

Ann leaned back in her black leather chair and pulled down the sleeve of her red wool suit jacket. "What do you think about filing a civil suit, Bill?" she asked the victim of the assault. "Is that something you truly want to do, or is it just your parents' idea of how to achieve justice?"

For the first time in the ten minutes he had been in her office, the young man stopped his fidgeting and looked up at Ann. His ruggedly handsome looks were marred by a long, jagged scar that ran down his right cheek, a vivid reminder of the attack. "I want to do it," he said, his eyes bright with conviction. "The three of us have talked about it a lot over the past two weeks, and we all agree it's the right thing to do."

Ann nodded again. "I always like my clients to know exactly what they can expect when they're involved in a lawsuit, so let's talk a little bit about that. Then we'll discuss the pros and cons of filing a civil suit so we'll all be better able to decide how to proceed. Is that agreeable with everyone?"

All three Robinsons nodded.

"Good," Ann said, smiling. "I always say that a well-informed client is a satisfied client, so forgive me if I get a little long-winded in my explanation. Just bear with me for a few minutes and when I'm through you can ask me any questions you might have."

Ann had given the "Lawsuits 101" spiel so many times that she could do it in a manner approaching autopilot. "So that's the way the civil litigation process works, in a nutshell," Ann concluded her remarks some minutes later. "Now let's talk a little bit about the specifics of your particular case." She referred to the legal pad in front of her on which she had jotted some notes during the earlier part of their discussion and swiveled her chair around so she was squarely facing her clients. A huge framed poster from *The Wizard of Oz*, Ann's favorite film, dominated the back wall of the office.

Ann addressed Bill. "Are you absolutely certain that you want to go ahead with this?" she asked again. "I can certainly understand your disappointment with the verdict in the criminal case, but at least now that it's over you'll be able to go back to being a private citizen. If we file a civil suit, the media circus will start all over again. Are you positive that you're prepared emotionally to deal with that?"

The young man nodded emphatically. "I am," he said in a firm, strong voice. "I'm not doing this on a whim. Of course, I'd give anything to have my anonymity back. It's helped a lot that I've transferred to the university here in Madison. I'm doing well in school and I'm starting to feel like I fit in."

"Are you sure you want to disrupt all that?" Ann asked kindly.

Bill nodded. "The outcome of the criminal case left me feeling like the bad guys won," he said, his voice cracking a bit, "and I don't want to leave it like that. In the time since the trial ended I've come to realize that I'm not ready to give up. Maybe the first jury didn't believe me, but the next one might. So the answer to your question is, yes, I'm prepared to do whatever it takes to get through this."

Ann looked at Bill for a long moment. She considered herself to be a pretty good judge of character, and this young man seemed to be both resolute and sincere. "Okay," she said, nodding to signal her approval of the plan to go ahead with the suit. "Let me ask you a few questions about the facts of the case. In the criminal trial the defense attorney kept harping on the fact that Jenkins and English got rough with you only after you attacked them—"

"That's bullshit!" Bill exclaimed, cutting her off. "It was a setup from the word go. I was riding my bike down a country road a few miles from school, like I did at least three times a week. They were hiding behind some trees and jumped me as I came by. They knocked me off my bike and started beating the crap out of me. I was lucky enough to be able to get in some punches. I broke two of Jenkins's teeth and dislocated English's shoulder. I only wish I could've done more," he said bitterly, "but there were two of them and it didn't take long before they beat me unconscious and took off."

"How did they know you'd be riding your bike by that spot?"

Bill shook his head. "I don't know. They claimed they just happened to be there looking for soil samples for an agriculture class and that I stopped my bike and attacked English with no provocation. Jenkins did the most damage, and he claimed he was just coming to English's rescue. I figure the two of them must've followed me on an earlier bike ride, figured out my route, and then waited for me to ride by that day."

"How did they know you were gay?" Ann asked directly. "Had you met them before?"

Bill nodded. "I'd seen them a couple times at a coffee shop near campus, the Copper Kettle. Both times I was there with my partner, Terry Rukeyser. We don't hide the fact that we're gay, and we sometimes hold hands in public. The second time we saw them, Jenkins and English made fun of Terry and me and made some real nasty remarks like, 'Look at those queens over there.'"

"How long after they made that remark were you attacked?" Ann inquired.

"Five days," Bill replied. He paused a moment and gave an involuntary shudder, remembering the attack. "They broke three of my ribs, lacerated my liver, and gave me this nice little reminder on my face, all the while making terrible comments like, 'I hope you die, you stinking fag.'" He shook his head in disbelief. "If a farmer hadn't found me a half hour later, I probably would have died. I was in a coma for two days and in the hospital for twelve and still the jury chose to believe them instead of me. I suppose those jurors looked at me and thought a guy my size must've provoked things."

"You can't ever predict what a jury will do," Ann said. "I've tried cases where I would've sworn the jurors seemed to be hanging on my every word, and then they turned around and returned a verdict for my opponent. It's human nature for people to be fickle. Just because that jury didn't see things your way doesn't mean the next one won't."

"Does that mean you're willing to represent us?" Tom Robinson asked hopefully.

Ann smiled at the Robinsons and nodded. "If you want to go ahead with this, you've got yourselves a lawyer."

CHAPTER 2

After the Robinsons left, Ann dictated some letters on another one of her cases. Taking the tape out of her pocket-size Dictaphone, she gathered up her bag and black trench coat and left the office. "There's no hurry on these letters," she said as she set the tape on her assistant's desk. "Whenever you get to them is fine."

"I'll have them done by the end of the day," Kari Johnson replied cheerfully, looking up from her computer. "I'm almost done with the interrogatories in the Bushnell case."

"I don't know why you speed through everything like a house afire," Ann teased. "You can't possibly impress me more than you already have."

"You never know," Kari volleyed back. A tall, dark-haired woman in her late thirties who had worked for Ann for five years, Kari was ferociously loyal and protective of her boss, and her clerical skills were matched only by her fearlessness.

Kari had become the stuff of legend at Mishler and Stettler several years earlier, when a mentally imbalanced man who had been named as a defendant in one of the firm's lawsuits had suddenly burst into the office brandishing a knife. Kari, manning the reception desk, managed to talk the distraught man into relinquishing his weapon and then sat on the floor next to him talking soothingly until the authorities came to take him to a mental hospital for observation.

"I'm glad you're taking the Robinsons' case," Kari said. "They seem like nice people."

"I think so, too," Ann agreed. "They feel as though the legal system let them down. I hope we can do something to change that."

"Me, too. Going to lunch?" Kari asked, noticing that Ann had her coat in hand.

Ann nodded. "I'll probably be gone longer than usual. I'm meeting Georgia today."

Kari nodded knowingly. "Time to catch up on gossip."

Ann laughed. "Unfortunately we both spend so much time working that we can't keep up on gossip the way we used to. But we'll give it our best shot anyhow. See you later."

"Have fun," Kari said, waving with one hand as she turned back to her computer.

On her way toward the office's main entrance, Ann passed by Fred Stettler's corner office. Seeing both Fred and Mark Mishler, Ann stepped inside. "How's it going, guys?" she asked.

The firm's founding partners were seated in front of Fred's computer, staring intently at the screen. "Hi, Ann," Mark said. "Fred just heard about an upcoming IPO for a new software company, and we're doing a little due diligence to see if it's worth investing any of our hard-earned money in it."

Best friends since high school, Mark Mishler and Fred Stettler had shared many momentous events in their lives: protesting the Vietnam War during college, being teargassed and arrested at the 1968 Democratic Convention in Chicago, and—to everyone's surprise, most of all their own—breezing through law school with high honors.

It hadn't taken the two young idealists long to discover that they lacked the temperament to take orders from senior partners, so a quarter century ago they had both defected from a large law firm that handled corporate litigation and started their own shop.

Mark and Fred's little storefront operation had quickly grown into one of the Midwest's premier plaintiffs' firms. They had achieved decisive victories in a number of high-profile cases for such disparate clients as the Ku Klux Klan, which had won the right to hold a rally on the capitol steps, and an Amish community, which had obtained a ruling giving them the right to refuse to attach gaudy red SLOW MOVING VEHICLE signs to their horse-drawn buggies. The firm received client referrals from around the country and had more work than it could handle.

After twenty-five years in business together, the firm's founding partners were still a match made in heaven. While both were excellent trial lawyers, over the years they had each carved out their own special niche, and at age fifty-five they were at the top of their profession and having the time of their lives.

Mark, who was tall and balding, had cultivated a good rapport with the media. As a result, he handled most of the firm's press conferences and news releases. Fred, who was medium height and had an unruly shock of reddish brown hair, was a financial whiz and served as the firm's business manager.

Ann had come to work at Mishler and Stettler ten years earlier, after graduating at the top of her University of Wisconsin law school class, and had never regretted her decision to turn down lucrative offers from some of the Midwest's megafirms. Practicing with Mishler and Stettler had given Ann control over her own destiny.

"How did your meeting with the Robinsons go?" Fred asked.

"Fine," Ann replied. "I took their case. I'm ordering a copy of the transcript from the criminal trial. I want to go over it before I decide how to proceed."

"You might want to ask Ken Devlin to give you a hand," Mark suggested. "He has some prosecutorial experience."

"That's a great idea," Ann said, nodding. "I'd forgotten that Ken used to be a DA in a past life. I'll talk to him about it." She patted Mark on the back as she turned to go. "Well, I've got a lunch date. Catch you two later."

Georgia Weis was Ann's oldest and dearest friend. They had grown up together in a small town thirty miles south of Madison and had been buddies since grade school and roommates in college. Ann graduated with a double major in English and history, while Georgia's degree was in business and finance.

When Ann went to law school, her friend got married and went into the insurance field. Now divorced, Georgia was the head of her own agency and one of the state's top female agents. Georgia and her daughter had recently moved in with her new boyfriend, a stockbroker.

Georgia was already seated at a table by the window when Ann walked into a sleek, modern restaurant a few blocks from her office.

"You haven't been waiting long, have you?" Ann asked as she took off her trench coat and tossed it on one of the extra chairs at the table.

"No, I just got here," Georgia replied, running a hand through her dark chin-length hair. As Ann sat down, Georgia reached into the large leather bag on the floor next to her and pulled out a cell phone, which she set on the table.

Ann raised her eyebrows. "Trying to impress someone?" she asked with just a hint of sarcasm.

"I know it's tacky," Georgia replied, "but I've been asked to provide an insurance quote for the new convention center hotel. It's the biggest project I've ever bid on, and it's driving me bonkers. I've got to have the bid in by tomorrow afternoon, and the underwriters haven't gotten back to me yet. So just in case they decide to come to life over the lunch hour"— she picked up the phone and waved it in the air— "I'll be ready for them. Hope you don't mind."

Ann made a face and tried to look perturbed as

she picked up one of the menus that had been left on the table. "Of course not. I'm just jealous that I don't have any business that's so pressing."

"So what exciting things have you been up to?" Georgia asked after a waiter had taken their orders.

Speaking in hushed tones, because it seemed that every other person in downtown Madison had some connection to a law firm, Ann briefly told her friend about the Robinsons' desire to file a civil suit.

"Should be an interesting case," Georgia said, nibbling on a piece of sourdough bread.

"Should be," Ann agreed.

The waiter brought their food and they ate for a time in silence.

"Other than work, how are things going?" Georgia asked as she slowed in eating her pasta with pesto sauce.

"We have four new students in the adult literacy program," Ann replied, taking another bite of her chicken Caesar salad. "We could really use more volunteers."

"I'm hoping in another life I'll have time to do volunteer work," Georgia said. She put down her fork and looked meaningfully at her friend. "So are you doing anything interesting with your life besides teaching English to recent immigrants?"

Ann frowned. They had had this conversation countless times, and it was not one she relished. "Not really," she replied.

"Ann—" Georgia began.

"Can we please talk about something else?" Ann said, cutting her off.

"No, we can't," Georgia answered firmly. "I am not going to let you waste your life just because you got burned once—"

Ann's face flushed. "I'd say that having your fiancé flee the state with another woman seventeen days before your wedding is a little more serious than 'getting burned,' " she said in a hiss.

"Call it whatever you want," Georgia said. "I agree that Richard is the scum of the earth. He should be staked out in the desert and left to be devoured by red ants, or subjected to the torture of your choice, but don't let him ruin the rest of your life. It's been over ten months—"

"You don't have to remind me how long it's been," Ann said, fighting to keep her voice down. "I'm the one who lived through it, remember? Believe me, the whole sordid series of events is indelibly etched on my mind."

The previous June first, Ann was to have married Richard Evans, her longtime boyfriend and the brilliant head of the university's economics department. Instead, two and a half weeks before the scheduled nuptials, Ann's betrothed had run off to become a department head at Stanford, taking his nubile young assistant with him.

A shamed and humiliated Ann, who'd had no warning of what was about to happen, had been left to cancel not only the ceremony but all the pre- and postwedding events, as well as the European honeymoon. Her Vera Wang wedding gown lay in repose in the closet of her spare bedroom. The specially designed Cartier engagement ring was in a bank lockbox following Ann's repeated attempts to return it and Richard's adamant refusal to take it back.

"We've been over this dozens of times," Georgia said soothingly. "I understand how traumatic it all was, but I really think it's time for you to take the plunge and start meeting some new people."

"No," Ann said vehemently. "I'm not interested."

Georgia reached over and patted her friend on the hand. "I know it must be scary for you, but you've got to start sometime. It's not healthy for you to avoid contact with people. It's normal after a breakup to feel hesitant about dating again, but you just have to get past that. Look at me. I felt pretty low after my divorce, but then I met Bill and now things are great."

"Your marriage broke up by mutual agreement," Ann reminded her friend. "You didn't come home one day to find your husband had moved cross-country with his secretary."

"There are a lot of nice men out there," Georgia persisted. "Why don't you let me introduce you to some of them? You could double-date with Bill and me—"

"No," Ann repeated firmly.

Georgia took her hand away. "How long are you going to keep this up?" she asked somewhat crossly. "I care about you. I don't want to see you turn into a crusty old spinster sitting home every night with your cats."

"What's so bad about that?" Ann sputtered. "At

least when I come home at night I know the cats will still be there waiting for me. That's more than I can say for a lot of men."

As Georgia rolled her expressive dark eyes, the cell phone on the table suddenly squawked to life. "Listen," Ann's friend said as she picked up the phone. "Just promise me you'll keep my offer in mind and let me help you when you feel the time is right."

"Okay," Ann said, nodding.

"Good girl," Georgia said, smiling.

As Georgia took the call, Ann sat back in her chair. While she had agreed to keep an open mind on the subject, she had no intention of getting involved with another man—certainly not for the foreseeable future, and possibly not ever. The hurt she had suffered when Richard dumped her was enough to last for several lifetimes.

CHAPTER 3

"The problem with our society today is that young people have no moral compass." The tall, stocky preacher raised his hands toward heaven as he spoke slowly and decisively in a Southern drawl. "And why is that? It is very simple, my friends. Because we as a people have strayed from the precepts of right and wrong contained in the Holy Bible. We must either return to the one true path as followers of Jesus Christ, or we must face eternal damnation!"

As the audience erupted into a loud chorus of "Amens," Rev. Charles Tremaine paused, took a sip of water from the glass on the podium in front of him, and surveyed his flock.

Nearly two hundred people sat on metal folding chairs in the sparsely furnished former warehouse on Madison's north side that served as Tremaine's church. The audience was largely white, young, and middle-class. Men outnumbered women nearly two to one.

Fifty-five years old, Charles Tremaine was an old-fashioned fundamentalist fire-and-brimstone preacher whose roots were in the hills of Tennessee. Since moving to Wisconsin, he had managed to establish a thriving congregation in a city that was well known for its liberal bent. Tremaine called his group the Lambs of God.

As the "Amens" subsided, the reverend ran a hand through his curly salt-and-pepper hair and continued with his sermon. "There are a great many evils plaguing our society today," he drawled. "Abortion is one of the most serious. Homosexuality is another. In an effort to combat these evils, I am pleased to report that through your generous donations the Lambs of God have been able to sponsor a series of billboards that will draw public attention to these sinful behaviors."

"Amen," the audience chanted.

"I am proud to announce that our first billboard will debut next week on Regent Street," Tremaine went on. "Its text will read: 'Abortion, casual sex, and homosexuality are *not* family values. Please join the crusade to stamp out immorality in our time. Put Jesus first.'"

"Amen!" roared the congregation.

"It is my sincere hope that by putting our faith in the Lord we will be able to bring morality back to our society," Tremaine boomed. "To coincide with the billboards, the Lambs of God will also begin a faith-in-action project next week that will include street ministry and peaceful protests at such places as local abortion clinics. Our first target will be the Planned Parenthood clinic. We pray that by making our message heard, we will help those who are not currently following the one true path to see the light and be delivered. We would welcome your participation in this worthy project." The reverend paused and took another sip of water.

"In order to better plan our activities, it would help us if we could get an idea of how many of you might be able to donate a few hours of your time to this valuable effort. A sign-up sheet is located at the back of the hall. Please consider volunteering on your way out. Now as we close our service, let us join hands, bow our heads, and ask for the Lord's blessing."

The congregation dutifully joined hands.

"Gracious Lord, we humbly beseech you, give us strength to persevere against our enemies. Give us the courage to stand up for what we know is right, even though we may face persecution for our beliefs. Lead us and guide us in your righteous path. In Jesus' name, we pray. Amen."

"*Amen*," the crowd thundered.

After the service, Reverend Tremaine mingled with his flock. Half a dozen young men in their late teens and early twenties crowded around him. The reverend seemed to have a special knack for recruiting young male parishioners.

"I signed up for the street-ministry project," one of the youths said proudly. "I want to help stamp out evil in the community."

"Me, too," said another.

"That's wonderful," the reverend said, clapping both volunteers soundly on the back. "What about the rest of you?" he challenged the others. "Don't you boys have a few hours to devote to the Lord's work?"

One dark-haired youth dressed in torn jeans and a black leather jacket shrugged. "Do you really think street ministry and peaceful protests can accomplish anything?"

"I surely do," the reverend replied. "I think they ca be very useful tools in the fight against Satan."

Another young man in the group snorted.

"What's the matter, son?" the reverend challenged. "Don't you believe that people's minds and hearts can be changed through prayer?"

"Well . . ." The young man hesitated a moment, then said boldly, "In my experience, that's not the most effective way to change somebody's mind."

"And what have you found to be more effective?" the reverend asked.

Several of the young men began to snicker. The speaker balled up his right hand into a fist and slammed it hard into his left palm. "Well, personally, Reverend, I've always found that puttin' the smack down on somebody works a whole lot better than trying to stand around and reason with 'em."

The other youths nodded in agreement.

"So you're saying that violence rather than peaceful protest is the way to win people over to the Lord," Reverend Tremaine said sternly. "Is that your view?"

The young man shifted uncomfortably from one foot to another, then gave a small nod. "I guess so," he said.

Reverend Tremaine glared at the young man for a

FINAL JUSTICE

moment, then broke into a broad grin and clapped him on both shoulders. "Son, in the battle against the forces of evil the Lord needs all manner of soldiers and all sorts of tactics and techniques. And if what you are able to offer the Lord is your swift right arm and your brute strength, then I say amen to that!" The reverend made a fist and slammed it into his other hand. "Put the smack down on 'em for the Lord!"

The other youths in the group whooped and shouted "Amen!"

The reverend put his arms around two of the boys and pointed them toward the card table that held the sign-up sheet. "Now that we've cleared the air on that topic, how would you boys like to reconsider your stance on volunteering for our cause?"

"You bet!" one of the youths said eagerly.

"Count me in," the other agreed. "I'll bet my cousin Joey would like to volunteer, too."

"That's the spirit, boys," the reverend praised. "The Lambs of God welcome all who wish to join us in our crusade." He leaned close and whispered in the lad's ear, "And if your cousin has some experience in hand-to-hand combat, so much the better."

CHAPTER 4

The transcript from the criminal trial against Bill Robinson's attackers arrived on a sunny Monday morning. Ann had briefly paged through the two boxes full of materials, then had had Kari set up a meeting later in the day so she could discuss the case with Ken Devlin, another one of the firm's partners.

"Thanks for agreeing to help me with this," Ann said as she set her legal pad and pen down on the oval walnut table in one of the firm's conference rooms and took a seat in one of the navy upholstered chairs. "I assume you're familiar with the background of the case."

Ken Devlin, who was seated next to Ann, snapped a smart salute. "Your humble servant stands ready to help you in any way I can," he said. "It was a damn shame the outcome of the criminal trial wasn't more positive."

Ken, who was tall, blond, and drop-dead gorgeous, was forty-two years old and had joined Mishler and Stettler twelve years earlier following a five-year stint as a prosecutor in a southwestern Wisconsin county.

He handled primarily personal-injury cases and had been the lead attorney in an automobile-defect case in which the firm had recently collected an eight-million-dollar verdict. Ken's wife was an accountant, and the couple had two teenage girls. Although Ann had heard rumors that the marriage was in trouble and that his wife might even want a divorce, Ken seemed to be a devoted husband and father.

"What do you know about the DA who prosecuted the case?" Ann asked.

"Ted Lawrence?" Ken leaned back in his chair and gave the question some thought. "He's a career politician. He's been in office twenty-five years. And he's been very successful at what he does."

"Is he a good prosecutor?" Ann asked.

Ken nodded. "First-rate. Ted is a real smart guy. He also loves the limelight and performing for a crowd. I've always thought that in an earlier age he would have made a great orator. He reminds me just a bit of William Jennings Bryan. Juries normally love him. It's not like him to lose a big case like this."

"Do you think what happened was just a case of a conservative jury not wanting to believe a gay victim's story?" Ann asked.

Ken shrugged. "That's hard for me to say until I know more about the details of the case."

"Well, I've skimmed through some of the transcript and from what I've seen so far, your buddy Ted Lawrence didn't do a very good job on voir dire."

"Really?" Ken asked with surprise. "How so?"

"At least three potential jurors openly admitted

prejudice against gays, and Ted did very little to follow up on their views. In each instance, he just said, 'Now, Mr. So-and-so, you would be able to put your personal views aside and decide this case based solely on the evidence presented, would you not?' All three answered yes, and all three ended up on the jury. One of them was even elected foreman."

"That does seem a bit lax on old Teddy's part," Ken admitted.

"Lax?" Ann said, raising an eyebrow. "Seems like a piss-poor job to me. I would've been all over those people, asking lots of probing questions, and if I wasn't completely satisfied they could be impartial—which I probably wouldn't have been—I would have struck them." Ann's face hardened. "From what I can tell, that jury contained people who were prejudiced against Bill Robinson, and Ted Lawrence's failure to strike them was an out-and-out error."

"I don't have an answer," Ken said, wadding up a small piece of paper and lobbing it at Ann. "By the way, I saw the notice you posted in the lunchroom saying the literacy center is looking for more volunteers."

Ann nodded. "We're very shorthanded. There's a waiting list for classes, and it's growing all the time. Why? Are you thinking of signing up?"

"Patsy and I talked about it a couple years ago, but when it came down to actually doing it, she lost interest. She's recently become quite active with the battered women's shelter."

"She has?" Ann asked with surprise. "Somehow Patsy has never struck me as the volunteer type."

"She never has been before, but for some reason she's really gung-ho over this group. Some weeks she spends so much time helping them out that the girls and I feel like orphans. Anyway, I was thinking of volunteering at the literacy center myself. No reason why I shouldn't pursue my own interests, and literacy is certainly important."

"We'd love to have you," Ann said enthusiastically. "It's very rewarding, and the other volunteers are all nice."

"I know one who's very nice," Ken said, reaching across the table and taking her hand.

As Ken gave her hand a squeeze, Ann looked up and their eyes met. For a fraction of a second she felt her pulse race just a bit. She flashed Ken a dazzling smile. "If you think I'm nice now, just wait until you see what I'll do for you once you sign up as a literacy volunteer," she said seductively.

"In that case, I'll cancel the rest of my appointments and sign up today."

On the way home from work that day, Ann stopped at Woodman's Supermarket to pick up a few items. She had just gotten milk and eggs and was rapidly pushing her cart toward the frozen-foods section when a voice in the next aisle brought her to an abrupt halt.

"I am pleased to hear you enjoyed my sermon," a man drawled. "The Lambs of God are always looking for new members. I hope you and your family will consider joining us in our crusade against the evils of modern society."

A woman murmured something in response, but Ann was too shocked to hear what was being said. She felt as if she had heard a ghost—no, make that an evil spirit. She took a deep breath to calm herself, but her mind was screaming, *Charles Tremaine is back in town.* As she processed this disturbing fact, Ann's right hand involuntarily went to her forehead, where her bangs concealed a two-inch scar, a vivid reminder of her last contact with Tremaine. From the time they met, she had disliked the man with a passion, and the feeling had obviously been mutual.

Two and a half years ago the reverend and his followers had targeted a Madison abortion clinic and its two physicians with a course of harassment designed to run them out of business. Instead, the doctors had dug in their heels and hired Ann to get the persecutors off their backs. Ann had gone to court and gotten a restraining order prohibiting the Lambs of God from coming within one hundred feet of the clinic, its doctors, or its patients. When some of the Lambs, including Tremaine himself, violated the order, Ann promptly had them arrested and fined.

Ann had been sleeping late one Sunday morning when she'd been awakened by a phone call from a reporter.

"Do you have any comment about Reverend Tremaine's comparing you to the Antichrist?" the obviously rookie newsman asked.

"What did you say?" Ann asked groggily.

"In his sermon this morning the reverend said that all those who support legalized abortion were the devil's handmaidens," the reporter said. "He mentioned you by name."

"Is that right?" Ann asked, wide-awake now. "And how did you happen to hear about this remark?"

"Oh, the reverend called me yesterday and invited me to his nine o'clock service. Said I might find it interesting. So I was wondering if you had anything to say in rebuttal."

"Yes," Ann replied fiercely. "Tell the reverend he can go to hell!" With that she had slammed down the phone.

Three weeks later, Ann had gone to the clinic to meet with her clients when the protest turned into a riot. As Ann tried to push her way through the crowd and make her way up to the building, some of the demonstrators began shouting at her and tried to block her path. The entire crowd began pushing and shoving. Realizing that she might be in danger, Ann tried to retreat, but the unruly mob wouldn't let her pass.

Someone grabbed Ann's arms and pinned them to her side. She tried unsuccessfully to break free, then began to scream. Then, to her horror, she saw several bricks being lobbed in her direction. She tried to duck but one of the missiles found its target. It hit her in the forehead, above her right eye. She slumped to the ground, blood gushing out of the wound and running down her face. After what seemed like an eternity, an ambulance came and Ann was transported to a nearby hospital, where she received twelve stitches and was kept overnight for observation.

Ann's physical injuries healed quickly but the incident left deep emotional scars. For months she suffered from nightmares in which she relived the riot. It had taken all of her courage and determination to force herself to continue working on the case. Every time she drove by the clinic she felt as if she were having a panic attack. She had never told anyone about her psychic trauma, not even Richard or Georgia. She still had a fear of crowds and was wary of being around strangers.

The person who threw the brick was never identified. Although Reverend Tremaine was at the scene at the time the riot broke out, he vehemently denied urging the crowd to resort to violence. Ann thought otherwise, but there was no way to prove it.

The issuance of the restraining order was affirmed on appeal, and soon afterward the reverend had apparently left town. Ann heard he had relocated to Iowa. The attack was the most terrifying incident in Ann's life, and she had sincerely hoped she would never hear the reverend's name again. And now here he was in her grocery store. Did that mean he had moved back to the area? The thought made Ann nauseous.

Her need to replenish her supply of frozen dinners suddenly evaporated. She wheeled her cart around and began to retrace her steps back toward the dairy section. If the reverend exchanged a few more pleasantries with his prospective parishioner, Ann might be able to exit the store without Tremaine's seeing her.

Ann picked up her pace and was nearly running

when she reached the end of the aisle. She turned sharply to the right and promptly collided with another cart. As she opened her mouth to apologize to the hapless customer, her stomach lurched. It was the reverend himself.

He spoke first. "Well, well," he said, his eyes drifting leisurely—and leeringly—up and down Ann's body. "If it isn't Ms. Ann Monroe in the flesh. How very nice to see you again. You are surely looking well." He flashed a lascivious grin.

Ann pulled her cart backward and started to move around him. "I'm sorry I ran into you," she said curtly as she continued on her way.

"Tell me, are you still representing the same godless clients?" Tremaine called after her.

Ann's jaw clenched and she swung back to face her old nemesis. "You bet I am," she said boldly. "Godless clients are my specialty. And what about you? Are you back in the area?"

Tremaine nodded. "My family and I moved back a few months ago. I've been conducting services in the old Bashford warehouse up on Northport Drive. You should come join us sometime. It might do your soul good."

"Thanks for the invitation, but I'm afraid I'm all booked up for the next decade or so. Now if you'll excuse me, I'm late for an appointment." As she started to move on, Tremaine stepped in front of her cart, blocking her way.

"If you ask me, I'd say that our meeting today was downright providential," Tremaine said.

"Really? I could have sworn it was just plain bad

luck on my part. Now would you please get out of my way."

Tremaine laughed and stepped aside. "Good seeing you again, Ms. Monroe. Something tells me we'll be running into each other again real soon."

Ann drew herself up to her full height and met his challenge with one of her own. "If that's true, I just hope that the next time around I'm driving a semi instead of a shopping cart."

Tremaine's jaw dropped and Ann took off toward the checkout lanes before he had a chance to retort.

CHAPTER 5

For the past five years Ann had been a volunteer at a literacy group. Two or three evenings a month she would help adults learn to read and write English. The majority of the center's students were recent immigrants who wanted to improve their language skills in order to better their employment prospects.

The evening after her run-in with Reverend Tremaine was one of Ann's volunteer sessions. Rather than bothering to go home, Ann worked until six o'clock, then grabbed a sandwich and a cup of soup at the Subway restaurant across the street from the office before heading off to a community center not far from downtown.

Ann had spent the last six months teaching English to a young Chinese couple. Chu and Lu Tan had arrived in Madison the previous fall under the sponsorship of Chu's cousin, who owned a local Chinese restaurant. Chu had been a chef in his native land, and he and his wife were working as cooks in the cousin's establishment. They hoped to own and operate their own restaurant someday. In the meantime they were working hard, saving as much money as they could, and trying to hone their language skills.

While Lu was quiet and shy, her husband was outgoing and gregarious. He greeted Ann jovially when she walked into the meeting room in the community center's lower level. "Good evening, Miss Ann!" Chu enunciated perfectly in his heavily accented English. "How are you this evening?"

"I'm fine," Ann said. She crossed the room until she reached the small table where the young couple was sitting, eagerly poring over their books. "How are you and Lu getting along?"

"We are fine," Chu said. "Are we not fine, Lu?"

Chu's wife smiled and nodded shyly.

"What are you studying tonight?" Ann asked, leaning over her students.

"Lu is reading a mystery story," Chu replied. "And I am learning American history."

"What have you learned about American history?" Ann inquired.

"I have learned that George Washington fathered our country," Chu replied proudly.

Ann pursed her lips, trying hard not to laugh. "That's very good," she said, patting Chu on the shoulder. "Give me a minute to hang up my coat and get a cup of coffee, and then we'll work on some verb forms, okay?"

"Excellent! We have been looking forward to an evening of conjugation," Chu said happily.

Ann walked into the community center's small kitchen, where she hung up her coat and poured herself a cup of coffee. As she opened a cupboard and took out a jar of powdered creamer, a tall, dark-haired woman in her forties walked in. "Hi, Ann," the woman said.

"Hi, Marge," Ann replied. Marge Harker, the literacy center's volunteer coordinator, was the head librarian at one of the city's public high schools and had become interested in literacy about ten years earlier, when Madison began experiencing a large influx of minorities. She had almost single-handedly built the adult night program from a single Hispanic family who was tutored once a week to a seven-days-a-week curriculum that served nearly a hundred.

"How are the Tans doing?" Marge asked as she poured herself some coffee.

"Wonderfully," Ann replied. "They're making such enormous strides that it won't be long before they're more proficient at English than I am."

"That's great!" Marge said. "We've got more new students starting next week. We're desperate for additional volunteers. Maybe the Tans will be willing to stay on and help tutor new people once they've graduated from the program."

"I think we should use Chu as our spokesman," Ann said, stirring the creamer into her coffee and then taking a sip. "I've never worked with anyone who's so enthused about learning the language."

"Yeah, I wish my high school students had half the enthusiasm of most of our people here," Marge agreed, sipping her coffee. "Speaking of students, would you happen to be in the market for some new clients?"

Ann looked perplexed. "You have some students who need a lawyer?"

Marge nodded and moved closer to Ann. "I'd be in hot water if the administration knew I was talking to you," she said confidentially, "but two students were suspended today for coming to the aid of a girl who was having a severe allergic reaction to some food."

"What happened?" Ann asked, intrigued.

"I don't know all the details," Marge replied. "But apparently a girl collapsed in the lunchroom, and a brother and sister who suffer from serious allergies themselves rushed over with an inhaler and some other medicine. It probably saved the girl's life, but the principal threw the book at them."

"Why?" Ann asked.

"The school has an absolute antidrug policy," Marge explained. "The principal claims the students' actions violated it."

"That attitude seems ridiculously rigid," Ann said. "Surely there have to be some exceptions for cases like this."

"I agree," Marge said. "But the principal didn't. The boy is going to graduate this spring. He's the class valedictorian, and as part of the punishment the principal is refusing to let him give his speech."

"You're sure these students are in the market for some legal help?"

Marge nodded. "Some friends of theirs were in the library this afternoon complaining bitterly about the injustice of it all. I couldn't help but overhear, and you know me. . . ." She paused a moment and smiled sweetly. "I also couldn't help but offer to find someone to help them out—discreetly, of course. Would you be willing to talk to them?"

Ann smiled. "Of course. What are their names?"

"Taylor and Talia Crabb," Marge answered. "They're great kids, destined for grand things, I'm sure. Their parents are both engineers."

"Have them call me and set up an appointment," Ann said. "I'll see what I can do."

"Thanks a lot," Marge said, patting Ann soundly on the arm. "I really appreciate it. And remember, when you contact the school administration, threatening to sue them for all they're worth, kindly leave yours truly's name out of it."

"No problem," Ann said.

Taylor and Talia Crabb and their mother, Jackie, met with Ann the following afternoon. As Ann ushered them from the firm's reception area down the hall to her office, she observed that Taylor was a tall, brown-haired eighteen-year-old, while his seventeen-year-old sister, a high school junior, was slender and blond. Their mother was auburn-haired and stylishly dressed.

"Have a seat," Ann said as she showed them into her office. "I understand you had a misunderstanding with the principal. "Why don't you tell me what happened."

"Taylor and I were both in the lunchroom," Talia said, "but we were sitting at different tables. I was with two friends and we were done eating and were going to go to the bathroom when all of a sudden a girl at the next table, Marilyn Jegerlehner, started gasping for air and grabbing her throat like she couldn't breathe. At first I thought she was choking, but then one of her friends yelled that she was allergic to some food."

"What happened then?" Ann asked.

"I've had asthma since I was little," Talia said. "So I always carry an inhaler with me. I got out my inhaler and ran over there and helped Marilyn use it."

"Did you actually put the inhaler in her mouth?" Ann asked.

Talia nodded. "I gave her two squirts. It seemed to help for a minute, but then she started getting worse. She started to slide off her chair. I think she was passing out. That's when I turned around and saw Taylor and screamed for him to get over there with his epipen."

"What's an epipen?" Ann asked.

"It's short for epinephrine," Taylor explained. "I'm extremely allergic to a number of things—bee stings, corn, and shellfish, to name a few. If I ate just one shrimp it could kill me. So I carry a dose of epinephrine so that in an emergency I can give myself a shot."

"Have you ever had to do this?" Ann asked.

Taylor nodded. "Oh, yes. About once a year for the past ten years. Anyway, when Talia screamed and I ran over there, I could see that Marilyn was going into anaphylactic shock. I knew there wasn't much time, so I got my epipen out of my pocket and gave her a shot."

"Where did you give her the shot?" Ann asked.

"In the thigh, through her slacks."

"Did it work?"

"Yeah, she started coming around right away."

"That's when Mr. Beckwith showed up," Talia said.

"He's the principal," Mrs. Crabb explained.

"We wanted to stay with Marilyn and make sure she was okay," Talia said. "But Mr. Beckwith hauled us off to his office and read us the riot act."

"I understand you were both suspended from school," Ann said.

"For three days," Taylor replied. "Plus he says I can't give my valedictory address." The young man's face was grim. "I've been working on my speech all year. How can he cheat me out of that?"

"What do Marilyn's parents think about this?" Ann asked.

"They're so grateful that Taylor and Talia saved their daughter's life," Jackie Crabb said. "They've tried talking to Beckwith, but they've gotten nowhere. We're hoping you might have better luck."

"I might," Ann said. "I assume there were a lot of witnesses to this incident. Talia, you mentioned being with some friends. What were their names?"

"Georgianne McDonald, Teresa Miller, and Annah Bull," Talia replied.

"Did anyone else see what happened?"

"Yeah," Taylor replied. "Howard Grossen, Mike Stark, and Barb Gottschalk."

"Were there any faculty members in the lunchroom?"

"Mrs. Stuvengen—Bobbe Stuvengen," Talia said.

"She's a speech teacher. She saw the whole thing. She tried to stick up for us when Beckwith hauled us away, but she didn't get anywhere either."

"We understand the antidrug policy, of course," Jackie Crabb said. "We're very much against drugs. But the policy just can't have been intended to apply in a situation like this."

"I agree," Ann said. "How is Marilyn doing?"

"Fine," Jackie replied. "She was checked out at the emergency room, and the doctor there said that if she'd been brought in, he would have given her exactly the same treatment—and even the same dosage—as Taylor administered."

"Do they know what caused her allergic reaction?" Ann inquired.

"Peanut oil," Jackie said. "She knew she was allergic to peanuts, but she ate a pork dish cooked in peanut oil and almost lost her life."

"Good thing Talia and Taylor were there," Ann said. She jotted a few more notes on a legal pad. "I'll talk to Principal Beckwith as soon as I can and see if we can't resolve this."

"Do you think he'll listen to you?" Taylor asked. "I've got my heart set on giving that speech."

"I'll see what I can do," Ann said. "Hopefully he'll listen to reason."

"It was nice meeting you," Jackie Crabb said. "We appreciate your trying to straighten this mess out for us."

Ann shook hands with the three family members. "Nice meeting you, too. I'll be in touch."

After the Crabbs had left, Ann got out her phone

book to find the number of the high school principal's office. It might be fun to sink her teeth into the unreasonable attitudes that seemed to be running rampant at the Crabbs' school.

Late that afternoon, Ann was making revisions on a court of appeals brief due the following day. She had several hours' more work ahead of her and decided that she needed to stretch her legs a bit. She walked down the hall and found herself in front of Ken Devlin's office. Seeing him inside, Ann stepped in.

"Hello, there," Ken said, looking up from his desk.

"Hi," Ann replied. She took a seat in front of Ken's desk and momentarily closed her eyes.

"You look beat," Ken said. "Why don't you call it a day?"

Ann opened her eyes again. "I can't just yet. I have an appellate brief due tomorrow."

"Ann," Ken scolded. "You push yourself way too hard. You really should take some time off."

"I can take care of myself!" Ann found herself snapping at him. Then she immediately caught herself. "I'm sorry," she apologized. "I didn't mean it to come out like that. It's just that I'm so sick of well-meaning people trying to tell me what I should be doing, how I should be feeling. It's my life, dammit, and I'll muddle through it in my own way."

Ken got up from his chair and came around the desk to stand behind her. "No one means to meddle, but we all care about you," he said, putting his hands on her shoulders and kneading her tense neck muscles. "I'm sorry if my concern sometimes comes across as oversolicitous."

For a moment Ann put her head back and enjoyed the pleasant sensations brought about by Ken's ministrations. It had been a long time since someone had rubbed her neck. Richard used to give her massages when she got tense. As Ken's fingers dug into her shoulders, Ann suddenly found herself having no interest in thinking about Richard. She allowed Ken to continue for another minute, then decided maybe she was starting to enjoy this attention just a bit *too* much.

"Thanks," she said, pulling away from him and standing up. "That really did the trick. I should be able to polish off that brief in no time."

"I'll be around for a while if you need another treatment," Ken said a bit flirtatiously.

"Oh . . ." Ann found herself at a loss for words. "Well, I'll keep that in mind."

Ann walked back to her office, closed the door, and sat down at her desk. *What just happened back there?*

"I am really pathetic," she murmured aloud. "I've gotten to the point where I'm so starved for male attention that I am starting to have carnal thoughts about a married coworker who just happens to be my best friend at the firm." She shook her head in disgust. Maybe Georgia was right. She'd been moping around too long. Maybe it was time to start seeing men. *Single* men.

By the time Ann put the finishing touches on the brief, it was eight o'clock and the office was virtually empty.

FINAL JUSTICE

The parking ramp adjacent to the building was also deserted. As Ann walked toward her car, she heard a loud cracking sound, like a piece of metal hitting the cement floor on the level above her. The sound so startled Ann that she involuntarily jumped and turned her ankle. Cursing at the pain, she covered the last twenty feet to her car as quickly as she could. Once safely inside, she immediately locked the doors.

As Ann backed her car out of her parking space and headed for the exit, she suddenly heard another car's engine roaring to life on the level above her. Almost unconsciously she sped up the pace of her descent. Within seconds she heard the other car squealing around a corner. Ann felt a chill go through her and she, too, increased her speed.

By the time Ann reached the bottom of the parking ramp and pulled her car out onto the quiet street, the other car was right behind her. Glancing in her rearview mirror, she saw a late-model dark sedan with two men inside.

They're after me! Ann thought in panic. *I've got to get away!* She squealed around the corner and accelerated far past the posted speed limit. As she reached the next intersection the light was changing from yellow to red, but Ann stepped down on the gas and tore through. To her horror, the dark car did the same.

Visions of the abortion clinic riot began to run through Ann's head. *They're going to get me!* she thought again. She accelerated some more. A couple blocks ahead was a railroad crossing. As Ann approached she saw the familiar red lights begin to flash and heard the loud clanging sound that signaled the approach of a train. Only vaguely cognizant of the danger of her maneuver, she floored the gas pedal and sailed across the tracks just seconds before the white barrier arms descended. Taking her foot off the gas, she looked in the rearview mirror. The dark car was safely behind the barrier. Ann breathed a sigh of relief. Only then did she realize that her whole body was shaking.

By the time she arrived home ten minutes later, Ann had calmed down considerably and begun to feel more than a little foolish. There was no reason to think the people in the dark car were after her. Madison was full of crazy speed-demon drivers. The abortion clinic riot was ancient history. And even if Reverend Tremaine was back in the area, there was no reason to believe he or anyone else wanted to harm her.

"Get a grip," Ann said aloud as she let herself into the house and locked the door behind her. She was an intelligent and independent woman. She would not let this irrational fear overtake her. She headed for the kitchen to feed her two cats, then turned back to double-check that the door was in fact securely locked.

CHAPTER 6

The following morning as Ann lingered in the firm's break room sipping coffee, Kari rushed in.

"Ann, Denise Riley from Planned Parenthood is on the phone. She says it's urgent."

Ann followed Kari down the hall. Back in her office she picked up the phone. "Denise, it's Ann. What's up?"

"Ann, thank God you're there!" Denise Riley, the director of the local Planned Parenthood office, exclaimed when Ann picked up the phone. "We're under siege here."

Over the past several years, Ann had handled a number of mundane matters for Planned Parenthood, including negotiating their current lease. She had never heard the organization's normally unflappable director sound so upset. "What do you mean, you're under siege?" Ann asked.

"There were about fifty picketers out front when I arrived at ten minutes to eight," Denise replied. "When I asked who they were, they said they were the Lambs of God. The picketers are all carrying placards denouncing premarital sex and claiming we're an abortion clinic. We've never performed abortions here!" she said indignantly.

At the sound of the words *Lambs of God* and *fifty picketers*, Ann's stomach lurched and the blood drained out of her face. "Are they blocking the entrance to your clinic?" she asked.

"They're not exactly blocking the entrance, but they are approaching our patients as they arrive, apparently to try to stop them from keeping their appointments."

"Is Reverend Tremaine there?" Ann asked, "or is he making his followers do all the dirty work?"

"I'm not sure," Denise replied.

"If he's there, you'd know it," Ann said sagely. "He loves to be the center of attention, and he'd be shooting his mouth off. Have you called the police?"

"Not yet. I wanted to talk to you first."

"Well, call the police and tell them to send some officers over immediately," Ann directed. "I'll come right over, too," she added, even though the thought of having to face down another group of picketers terrified her.

"Is there anything lawful I can do in the meantime to break up the demonstration?" Denise asked. "Would I get in trouble if I turned the hose on them?"

"I don't think being doused with cold water is going to faze those people much. Just sit tight. We'll see if we can get the police to urge them to disband."

"Thanks, Ann. You're a lifesaver."

"I doubt that," Ann murmured as she hung up the

phone. On the short drive to the clinic Ann gave herself a pep talk. Everything would be fine. This wouldn't turn out like the abortion clinic protest. This demonstration would remain peaceful. There was no reason to be frightened. But as she approached the clinic and saw the mob of people carrying signs marching in front of the building, she felt as if she might vomit.

As she pulled into the parking lot, Ann could see Denise Riley out on the sidewalk having what looked like a heated discussion with some of the picketers. *Just focus on Denise and ignore everyone else*, Ann told herself. But as soon as she got out of her car, two young men and a young woman who appeared to be in their late teens or early twenties approached her.

"Abstinence is God's method of birth control," one of the young men said. "Premarital sex is a sin."

"The people in there are baby killers," the young woman chimed in, putting a hand on Ann's arm. "You don't want to go in there."

"I most certainly *do* want to go in there," Ann said shrilly, pulling her arm free. "I am the clinic's lawyer. Perhaps you've heard Reverend Tremaine speak of me. I'm Ann Monroe, Beelzebub in the flesh."

The three young people jumped back as if Ann had announced she was a leper. Swallowing hard, she made her way through the crowd of protestors and walked over to Denise Riley.

"Don't you people have anything better to do than harass us?" Denise shouted at the protestors. "Don't any of you work for a living?"

The picketers hissed at her in response.

"Come on," Ann said, taking Denise's arm. "Let's go inside and wait for the police."

"God, they make me so angry!" Denise exclaimed as she and Ann stepped inside the entrance to the clinic. "Why are they doing this?"

"For some of them, this type of activity seems to be a form of entertainment," Ann said, breathing easier now that she was safe inside. "Oh, good, the police are here," she said as a squad car pulled up alongside the building. Two uniformed policemen got out. One of them made his way up to the entrance as the other walked through the crowd, surveying the proceedings. Ann opened the door to admit the new arrival.

"I'm Fred Miller," the officer said. "What's up?"

"I'm Ann Monroe, Planned Parenthood's attorney," Ann said, "and this is Denise Riley, the clinic's director. These people are preventing the clinic from carrying out its business. Is there anything you can do to encourage them to move along or at least stay away from the patients?"

Miller, a tall black man, looked outside and frowned. "Are these those crazy Lambs of God again?" he asked.

"Yes," Ann replied. "Are you familiar with them?"

"I sure am," Miller replied. "I spent more shifts than I care to remember trying to maintain order a couple years back when they were picketing that abortion clinic."

"Then you know that they can turn violent, and they seem to think they're above the law," Ann said.

FINAL JUSTICE

"I sure do agree with you on that, ma'am," Miller said.

The other officer, a red-haired man with a mustache, came inside. "What's the deal here?" he asked.

"This is Ms. Monroe, the attorney for the clinic, and Ms. Riley, the director," Miller replied. "Ladies, this is Officer Jerry Richardson."

"So what's our battle plan here?" Richardson asked his partner.

Miller looked at Ann and Denise. "What would you like us to try to do, keeping in mind that there's no guarantee these people are going to listen to reason?"

"We'd obviously like them to go away," Ann said, "but I guess we'd settle for keeping them a reasonable distance from the clinic's entrance and prohibiting them from talking to the patients."

The two cops nodded in unison.

"We'll give it a try," Richardson said. He and Miller stepped outside. Ann reluctantly followed them. Richardson cupped his hands and shouted to the protestors. "Listen up, people! We understand that you have a right to your opinions, but you are not entitled to intimidate or harass other people in order to try to bring them around to your point of view. If you want to maintain a presence here, you're going to have to follow some ground rules. Rule number one: You must stay at least fifty feet away from the clinic entrances. Rule number two: You must stay an equal distance from persons attempting to enter or leave the clinic. Rule number three—"

"Why do we need all these man-made rules?" a man with a heavy Southern drawl boomed from the edge of the crowd. "Since when aren't the Ten Commandments good enough?"

Like the Red Sea, the crowd parted, and Rev. Charles Tremaine, dressed in a dark suit, regally made his way through the throng of followers and up to where Ann and the policemen were standing.

Tremaine peered at Ann, who was still standing slightly behind the two officers, then said in a silky-smooth voice, "Why Ms. Monroe, how very nice to see you again so soon," Tremaine drawled. "Didn't I tell you that our paths were going to cross again?"

Ann balled her hands into fists. "Yes, but I was hoping that was just wishful thinking on your part," she replied curtly.

"Why, I am truly disappointed with your attitude. I do always enjoy conversing with an attractive lady such as yourself. And I found some of our past discussions so very enjoyable."

"The only thing I would find enjoyable at the moment would be for your followers to get out of here so this clinic can get back to doing its important work," Ann retorted.

"And what work might that be, Ms. Monroe?" Tremaine asked quizzically. "Encouraging promiscuous behavior? It seems to me there are plenty of other people already doin' that."

"This clinic helps prevent unwanted pregnancies and sexually transmitted diseases," Ann replied, feeling a bit less frightened now. "And it provides its services free of charge to those who can't afford to pay."

"This clinic and others like it aid and abet the performing of abortions," Tremaine countered. "Abortion is murder and it is a violation of the Fifth Commandment. That is why I have encouraged my flock to rise up against it."

"No abortions are performed here. And your flock has no right to intimidate clinic patients. Isn't that right, Officer?" Ann asked, turning to Richardson for support.

"That's right, ma'am," the cop replied. Addressing Tremaine he said, "I would appreciate it if you would tell your people that they can't do anything that will impede this establishment from carrying out its business, nor are they entitled to prevent anyone from coming or going."

"I will not tell my parishioners to disband or to alter their current course of action," Tremaine said, sticking his chin in the air.

"If they persist in their harassment, we're going to start making arrests," Richardson cautioned.

"Most of us have been arrested before," Tremaine replied. "You see, Officer, we believe in the Word of God as set forth in the Holy Bible. Are you aware of how many of the early followers of Christ were arrested, imprisoned, even put to death for their beliefs? We consider it a privilege to emulate those early martyrs."

"I don't want any martyrs on my watch," Richardson shot back. "Now I'll give you ten minutes. Either get this group under control and keep them away from the clinic entrance and its patients, or I'm gonna call for some backup and we'll start hauling people away."

Tremaine lifted his arms to the heavens. "Do as you must, Officer," he said.

Richardson grimaced, then pulled Ann aside. "Listen," he said in a low voice. "If you want, I'll be happy to throw the whole lot of 'em into temporary lockup, but you know as well as I do that they'll all make bail and be back out here by noon. Now, I don't want to tell you how to go about your business, but I would suggest that if you could get a judge to sign a temporary restraining order setting forth exactly what type of behavior is prohibited here, it would make life a hell of a lot simpler for us all."

Ann nodded. "I'll go work on it right away. In the meantime, do you mind staying here to make sure things don't get out of hand?"

"No problem," the cop said. He motioned to the black cop. "Fred and me will stay here till you get back."

"Thanks," Ann said. "I appreciate it." She stepped back into the clinic to tell Denise Riley about the game plan, then came back outside and bravely pushed her way through the crowd toward her car.

"Admitting defeat so soon?" Reverend Tremaine taunted as she passed him.

Ann ignored him and kept walking. As she approached her car, she saw something stuck to her back bumper, covering up the Darwin plaque that Fred Stettler had brought back about a year earlier following a trip to Berkeley. A parody on the Christian fish symbol, this fish had four legs, and in the center of its belly was the word *Darwin*. Most of Mishler and Stettler's employees' vehicles sported similar ornaments.

Someone had written, *Evolution is merely a myth. Put your trust in the Lord* on a piece of paper and taped it to her car.

"Oh, honestly!" Ann grumbled. As she stood there crumpling the paper into a tight ball, she saw that one of her rear tires was completely flat. "Dammit!" she sputtered. There would be no way to prove it, but she was willing to bet that one of the protestors had punctured it.

She turned her head and looked back toward the clinic, where Tremaine was waving his arms around, apparently preaching to his followers. Her fear dissipated, replaced with a burning anger. She had gotten the better of Tremaine and his people once and she'd do it again, even if it meant working sixteen-hour days. Filled with new resolve to best the reverend at his latest game, she got in the car, pulled out her cell phone, and called Kari to come and pick her up.

CHAPTER 7

Within a few hours of Kari's picking her up from Planned Parenthood's parking lot, Ann had obtained a temporary restraining order restricting the Lambs' picketing activities at the clinic. She had also filed a bare-bones lawsuit asking that the Lambs be prohibited from conducting any type of demonstration near the clinic and demanding that the group be ordered to pay damages for disruption of the clinic's business.

Later that day, Ann met with the high school principal who had suspended Taylor and Talia Crabb for coming to the aid of the young student who had been suffering a severe allergic reaction.

Roger Beckwith, the high school principal, seemed to have been dodging Ann's calls. It was not until Ann spoke with the district's superintendent and threatened to file a lawsuit against the principal if no one got back to her immediately that Beckwith's secretary called to set up a face-to-face encounter. Ann did not take kindly to people trying to give her the runaround, so she arrived at the school with her hackles up.

The meeting was held in Beckwith's office. "It's a pleasure to meet you, Ms. Monroe," the middle-aged, heavyset principal said as he shook Ann's hand and invited her to take a seat at a round, smoky-colored glass table on one end of his rectangular office. "Your stellar reputation in the community precedes you."

Ann sat down and smoothed out the skirt of her black suit, fighting back the urge to make a face.

Beckwith sat down across from her.

"Mr. Beckwith, since you've had the benefit of several days to think about your handling of this matter, I wondered if perhaps you've had a change of heart," Ann said.

"A change of heart? No, why should I? I handled it by the book."

"I see," Ann said. "Well, then, let me come right to the point." She took a legal pad and a manila folder out of her briefcase. "In my opinion, your treatment of Taylor and Talia Crabb was completely unjustified. Their parents have retained me to see that you and the school district make amends."

"Amends?" Beckwith said, frowning. "What do you mean by amends?"

"Remove all mention of the suspensions from Taylor's and Talia's permanent files and allow Taylor to deliver his valedictory address."

"Impossible," Beckwith said.

"It's not impossible," Ann countered. "It's the only fair thing to do."

"This school has a stringent antidrug policy," Beckwith said vehemently. "Those students violated it."

"They may have violated the letter of the law," Ann agreed, "but they surely didn't violate its spirit when they saved that girl's life. I'm certain that no one intended the policy to prohibit the use of lifesaving drugs in an emergency situation."

"If we start making exceptions to our drug policy, there would be no stopping point," Beckwith said. "The next thing you know we'd have students claiming they were handing out marijuana for medicinal purposes. No, I firmly believe that it is far better to leave Pandora's box closed."

Ann opened the manila folder and pulled out a sheaf of papers. "I have a letter here from Marilyn Jegerlehner's parents saying that in their opinion not only should Taylor and Talia not be punished, they should each be given a medal of honor for saving Marilyn's life. I have similar letters from many of Marilyn's relatives and friends." She set the documents on the table in front of Beckwith.

"I do not run my school based on public opinion," Beckwith said, sticking out his chin.

"No, sir, it appears to me that you run it with a rigidity that flagrantly flaunts common sense," Ann retorted.

"Injecting that girl with drugs was both foolhardy and dangerous," Beckwith said, his voice rising. "How did the Crabbs know that she wasn't allergic to the medication? Giving her that shot could have killed her. Someone had already called the paramedics. The Crabbs should have minded their own business and waited for the professionals to arrive and take over."

FINAL JUSTICE

Ann pulled another document out of her folder and set it down on the table on top of the others. "According to the emergency room doctor who treated her, Marilyn would have died within five minutes if Taylor Crabb had not given her that shot. She did not have the luxury of waiting for the paramedics. She needed immediate help, and the Crabbs provided it."

Beckwith shook his head firmly. "Ms. Monroe, it's easy for you to sit here and make these statements with the benefit of twenty-twenty hindsight. Not only did the Crabbs disobey the school's drug policy, they acted in an irresponsible manner. I simply will not have that type of behavior rewarded."

Ann was getting angrier by the minute but fought to keep her temper in check. "Taylor Crabb has been at the top of his class all four years of high school," she said. "I might be able to talk his parents into not challenging the suspension if you allow him to deliver the valedictory address."

"It's out of the question," Beckwith said.

"Is that your final word on the subject?" Ann asked, looking him squarely in the eye.

"It is."

Ann stuffed her legal pad and the manila folder back into her briefcase, snapped it shut, and then stood up. "In that case, I guess our business is finished."

"Conceding defeat so easily?" Beckwith asked hopefully.

Ann snorted. "Hardly." She turned and headed toward the door of the office.

In an instant Beckwith was also on his feet, beating her to the door. "What do you intend to do now?" he asked, sounding nervous for the first time.

"What does it matter if you truly believe your decision was the right one?"

"I was just curious," the principal sputtered.

Ann smiled sweetly. "You'll be hearing from me." With that enigmatic remark, she opened the door and walked briskly out into the hall.

On the short drive back to the office, Ann's anger escalated. By the time she pulled into the parking ramp adjacent to her building, she was fuming. The first person she saw as she got off the elevator on the fourth floor was Fred Stettler.

"How's it going?" Fred asked jovially.

"Terrible," Ann said in a growl.

"Really?" Fred said, frowning. "Would you care to talk about it? Maybe I can help."

Once inside Fred's office, Ann briefly filled him in on her meeting at the high school. "This seemed like a no-brainer," she sputtered. "I would have bet money that once they were given a little push, the school would back down." She tossed her head defiantly. "Those damn fools obviously don't know who they're dealing with."

"What do you have in mind?" Fred asked.

"The end of the school year isn't far off, so I've got to move fast," she said. "Assuming Taylor and Talia's parents give their okay, I'm going to sue the school district seven ways to Sunday."

Fred laughed. "Good idea, but it'll probably take you a while to draft a complaint. In the meantime, why don't you think about turning up the heat a little."

"How?" Ann asked.

"How about calling on one of our friends in the Fourth Estate?" Fred suggested. "I'd be willing to bet one or two well-placed newspaper articles could go a long way toward jump-starting settlement negotiations."

"Great idea!" Ann exclaimed. "Why didn't I think of that? I'll put Gary Carlson on the case. This should be right up his alley." She rubbed her hands together gleefully. "When Gary is done, that principal won't know what hit him. Thanks for the idea, Fred. This is going to be fun!"

"All work should be fun," Fred said. "That's been the firm's motto since the day we opened our doors." As Ann walked briskly toward the door, Fred chuckled and called after her, "Break a leg, kid. Something tells me that principal will rue the day he messed with you."

"So what've you got for me today, Annie?" Gary Carlson asked jocularly as he put his feet up on her desk.

Ann briefly explained the Crabbs' situation.

"Big bad principal versus Good Samaritan students," Gary said, running a hand through his curly gray hair. "That's got a nice ring to it."

Gary had been a reporter for various Midwestern newspapers for the past thirty years. Early in his career, while handling the local news beat for one of the Madison papers, he had gained a reputation as a tenacious investigator who would stop at nothing to get the full story. On more than one occasion his persistence had garnered him a black eye.

Ann had met Gary soon after she joined Mishler and Stettler. He had been covering the local court scene and sat in on one of the first cases Ann had tried with Fred Stettler. Their client was a Wiccan priestess who claimed that a former employer had fired her because of her religion.

For the seven days it took to try the case, the bespectacled reporter, who always looked as if he had stepped out of an L.L. Bean catalog, had sat in the back of the courtroom rarely taking notes and often seeming to pay little attention to the testimony. But somehow each night he managed to produce an article that captured the very essence of the day's events and frequently contained precise quotes from various witnesses.

"So what do you think of my coverage of the case?" Gary asked Ann one day during a break.

"Your articles are very good," Ann replied. "You don't seem to take many notes. Do you carry a tape recorder?"

Gary had clutched his chest as if he were in pain. "A tape recorder? Surely you jest." Then he tapped his forehead with his right index finger and said, "You've got to have it in here. A tape recorder isn't going to do you a damn bit of good if your brain's only operating at half power. You remember that." He turned to go, then swung around again. "By the way, your client is going to lose."

"What makes you say that?" Ann asked with surprise.

Gary leaned close and said in a stage whisper, "Because she's a witch." He gave a cackling laugh and walked down the hall.

Ann and Fred had lost the case. In speaking to some of the jurors afterward, Ann had learned that whatever her religious beliefs might be, their client was viewed as unsympathetic, a conniver, and just generally not a nice person.

A couple of weeks later Gary had called Ann and asked if she'd like to go to lunch. She had accepted the invitation and asked at which restaurant she should meet him. "It's too nice out to sit in a restaurant," Gary replied. "Meet me at noon at the hot dog stand at the corner of East Main and Martin Luther King, Jr., Boulevard."

While walking around the capitol square eating Chicago-style hot dogs, Ann said, "I guess your assessment about our client was right. Religion aside, the jurors thought she was a witch and deserved to be fired. That was very perceptive of you."

"Perception is my middle name," Gary replied. "For example, I perceive that you are falling madly in love with me. Am I right?"

Ann had stared at him.

"Just kidding!" Gary said, laughing heartily. "Say, are you going to finish your sauerkraut? If not, can I have it?"

Over the years Ann and Gary had developed a very good professional relationship as well as a warm friendship. Three years earlier Ann had put him onto a story that turned into the high point of his career.

A young woman had died under mysterious circumstances, but police ruled the death accidental. Her distraught father wouldn't accept that ruling and insisted that his son-in-law had murdered the girl. Ann had represented the father's sister in a personal-injury action, and when the former client contacted Ann to see if there were any other avenues they could pursue, Ann had suggested they talk to Gary.

The reporter had thrown himself into the investigation with a vengeance, and due in large part to his digging, police reopened the case and the husband was eventually charged with and convicted of murder. The series of articles Gary had written about the case had won him a Pulitzer prize. He had taken a year's sabbatical and turned the story into a full-length book. He was very grateful to Ann for sending the lead his way and was always eager to talk to her about other potential stories.

"Here are the names and phone numbers of the pertinent parties," Ann said, handing him a sheet of paper. "I'm sure they'll all be happy to talk to you—all but Principal Beckwith, that is."

"He'll talk, too, if he knows what's good for him," Gary said, folding the paper up and putting it in his pocket. "So what else is new? How's your love life?"

Ann merely gave him a look that said, "Don't go there."

"That bad, eh?" Gary said. "You've got to get back

out there in circulation. Just because that bastard Roger—"

"It was Richard," Ann interrupted.

"Whoever," Gary went on blithely. "Just because Mr. Economist got carried away with irrational exuberance and headed for sunny California with some floozy doesn't mean you have to spend the rest of your life in permanent mourning."

"Why is everyone so worried about the rest of my life?" Ann demanded. "It hasn't even been a year yet. Shouldn't I be entitled to some time to recuperate?"

"You've had plenty of time for that," Gary said dismissively. "You've got to get back out there and mingle. Why, I would personally be happy to escort you to some of the city's newest hot spots, where you just might meet Mr. Right."

"That's very big of you," Ann said drolly. "And what do you suppose your wife would have to say about that?"

"I'd tell her it was a humanitarian effort. Besides, she knows that with your high moral standards I'd be completely safe. So how about it? I'd be free tonight, for instance."

"I appreciate the offer," Ann said. "Even though I didn't realize that my love life had risen to the level of a public disaster. But I think I'll pass for now."

"Oh, all right. Suit yourself," Gary said in mock anger. He swung his legs off the desk and stood up, then came around the desk and gave Ann a kiss on the cheek. "Hang in there, sweetie," he said in a much softer tone. "There's somebody out there for you. Who knows, Mr. Right may be just around the corner. Now I must away to interview the folks you've identified. If I hurry, I might be able to have something in tomorrow's press."

"Thanks a lot, Gary," Ann said, wondering why the thought that Ken's office was just down the hall suddenly popped into her head.

"Don't mention it," Gary said, heading for the door. "Thank you for the scoop. I think I'm going to have fun with this one. Catch you later."

Ann smiled to herself as she anticipated the opening line of his article. *Priggish principal preys on popular preppies.* Or maybe *Beckwith bites the big one.* However the article started out, Ann was willing to bet that it would send Principal Beckwith running to the store for a supply of antacids.

CHAPTER 8

Two days later, Ann was in Judge Lisa Bies's courtroom asking that the temporary restraining order she had obtained against the Lambs of God be extended.

Judge Bies had been appointed to the bench two years earlier and had distinguished herself as a commonsense jurist who would tolerate no posturing or game playing in her court. Ann was hopeful that the judge would give short shrift to the theatrics Ann anticipated from Rev. Tremaine at the hearing.

"*Planned Parenthood v. The Lambs of God, Rev. Charles Tremaine, et al.,*" the bailiff called the case.

"May I have the appearances, please?" Judge Bies asked.

Ann gave Denise Riley, who was seated beside her at one of the counsel tables, a reassuring nod and stood up, smoothing down the skirt of her black suit. "Ann Monroe for the petitioner," she said, then sat down again.

A tall, thin, middle-aged man seated next to Tremaine at the other counsel table got to his feet. "Thomas Ravenswood for the respondents."

The judge nodded and looked at the file in front of her. "We're here on the petitioner's motion for a temporary injunction that would continue the provisions of an ex parte temporary restraining order that I issued after concluding that action was necessary in order to adequately protect the petitioner's rights pending a hearing on the matter. Ms. Monroe, you have the floor."

Ann again stood up. "Your Honor, in order to more fully explain the reasons why the petitioner is seeking an injunction, I would like to call Denise Riley, the director of the clinic."

After affirming that her testimony would be truthful, Denise took the witness stand and told what she had encountered when she arrived for work Wednesday morning.

"Approximately how many people were picketing?" Ann asked.

"There were forty to fifty. Some were in the parking lot. Others were marching up and down on the sidewalk in front of our front entrance. Many of them were carrying signs. Some said things like, 'Stop the Slaughter of Innocent Babies.' Others said, 'Let God Show You the Way to Abstinence.' Still others had graphic photos of aborted fetuses."

"Did you speak to any of the picketers that morning?"

Denise nodded. "Yes, I did. When I got out of the car I told them we did not perform abortions at our clinic, and I asked them to please leave the premises."

"What was their response?"

FINAL JUSTICE

"One man shouted that I was a baby killer. Several others began praying very loudly."

"Did the picketers have any contact with the patients?"

"Yes. As patients were getting out of their cars, several of the demonstrators came within a couple of feet and tried to persuade the patients not to keep their appointments."

"Did the patients bow to this pressure?"

"Some did, yes."

"Ms. Riley, around noon on Wednesday each of the picketers was served notice that a temporary restraining order had been issued that prohibited them from coming closer than within fifty feet of the clinic entrance or to any patient. What effect, if any, did the issuance of that order have on the demonstration?"

"To some extent it helped defuse the extremely tense atmosphere that had existed for the entire morning. As soon as the order was issued, the two policemen who were at the clinic made sure that its terms were obeyed."

"Are there still picketers outside the clinic?"

"Yes, about thirty-five."

"Did the picketers indicate whether they were part of a group or congregation?"

Denise nodded. "Yes. They said they were the Lambs of God and that it was their purpose in life to help infidels such as myself become enlightened."

"Thank you, Ms. Riley," Ann said. "I have no further questions."

"Mr. Ravenswood," Judge Bies said. "Your turn."

"Thank you, Your Honor." The Lambs' lawyer got to his feet. "Ms. Riley, did any of the picketers physically interfere with your patients' entering the clinic?"

"No," Denise admitted.

"Did any of the picketers prevent any of your patients who wished to do so from walking through the front door of the clinic?"

"No."

"Thank you," Ravenswood said sweetly. "I have no further questions of this witness."

"You may step down, Ms. Riley," the judge instructed. "Ms. Monroe, do you have any additional witnesses?"

"No, Your Honor," Ann replied.

"Mr. Ravenswood?" the judge asked.

"The respondents call Rev. Charles Tremaine to the stand."

"This ought to be quite a performance," Ann whispered to Denise. As the reverend made his way to the witness stand, Ann turned around and surveyed the spectators in the courtroom. She saw Gary Carlson sitting in the back, and, to her surprise, Bill Robinson was seated next to him. Ann gave the two men a quick smile and turned her attention back to the witness, who had just loudly promised to tell the truth.

So help me God.

"Reverend Tremaine, are you the pastor of a congregation called the Lambs of God?" Ravenswood asked.

"I am."

"Did you suggest to your members that they picket the Planned Parenthood clinic?"

"I did," Tremaine answered, nodding emphatically. "You see, for quite some time my flock and I have been concerned about the moral decline of society. After reflection and prayer we decided that one thing we might do to help reverse this trend was to have passive protests outside businesses that we felt embodied immoral philosophies."

"And you felt that Planned Parenthood was one of these?"

"Yes. That organization is well known to encourage rampant promiscuous sexual behavior."

"Was it your goal to shut the clinic down?" Ravenswood asked.

"No, sir," Tremaine replied. "Our goal was merely to encourage free thought and dialogue."

"Did you tell the members of your congregation that they were to stop patients from entering the clinic?"

"No, sir. I told them that they should remember they were doing the Lord's work and that they should treat all persons with respect and dignity, even though they might have views that are abhorrent to our own."

"Thank you, Reverend," Ravenswood said. "I have no further questions."

Ann was on her feet even before Judge Bies looked her way.

"Reverend Tremaine, this isn't the first time the Lambs of God have picketed a health clinic, is it?" Ann asked.

"Objection," Ravenswood said. "What the Lambs did in the past has no bearing on this situation."

"The group's past behavior helps to show their motive, intent, and purpose, with respect to this particular demonstration," Ann said.

"I'll allow it, within reason," Judge Bies said. "Objection overruled. Do you remember the question, Reverend Tremaine?"

"Yes, I remember it," Tremaine replied haughtily, "and the answer is no, this is not our first experience with peaceful demonstration."

"Approximately two and a half years ago you and your followers picketed a Madison abortion clinic almost continually for a period of four months, did you not?"

"That is true."

"And isn't it also true that in spite of the fact that an injunction had been issued requiring you and your followers to stay a reasonable distance away from patients entering the clinic and from the clinic's entrance, that injunction was repeatedly violated?"

"Objection," Ravenswood said again. "This line of inquiry is getting farther afield all the time."

"Overruled," the judge said. "But Ms. Monroe, I'd suggest that you make your point and move on."

Ann nodded. "Isn't it true that your followers were issued over three hundred citations for violating the injunction covering the abortion clinic?" she demanded.

"I don't keep track of numbers," Tremaine hedged.

"Do you recall how many citations were issued to you personally?"

"No."

"Does the number forty-two ring a bell?"

Tremaine didn't respond.

"Isn't it true that you didn't pay a single one of those citations, which levied forfeitures totaling forty-three hundred dollars?"

"The Lord does not expect his people to pay money to the devil."

"The devil didn't issue those citations," Ann said hotly. "The City of Madison issued them, and you haven't paid a single one. If you don't want to be governed by the laws of this state, then I suggest you move elsewhere."

"Objection!" Ravenswood spouted.

"Withdrawn," Ann said politely. "I have no further questions, Your Honor."

"Mr. Ravenswood, do you have any other witnesses?" the judge asked.

"No, Your Honor."

"All right," the judge said. "I am prepared to make my ruling." She referred to her notes. "In order to issue an injunction I must find that it is necessary to preserve the status quo; that the petitioner has no adequate remedy at law; that the petitioner will suffer irreparable injury if the injunction is not issued; and that the petitioner has a reasonable probability of success on the merits of its claim. Having considered the witness testimony and the arguments of counsel, I conclude that all of these conditions have been met. I am therefore issuing a temporary injunction under the same terms and conditions as the ex parte temporary restraining order that was issued two days ago."

The judge paused a moment, then said, "I would, however, caution both sides not to rely too heavily on past history. Ms. Monroe, the mere fact that members of this group may have violated an injunction in the past does not mean they will do so in this instance. Mr. Ravenswood, the flip side of that concept is that your clients are expected to abide by the terms of my order. If they choose not to do so, it will be at their peril." She slammed her gavel down on the bench. "Next case."

As Ann and Denise walked out of the courtroom, Gary and Bill gave them a thumbs-up sign.

The women were barely out in the hall when Ann heard a booming voice behind her. "You may have won this round, Ms. Monroe," Tremaine said slickly as he and Ravenswood walked by. "But don't start feeling too complacent yet. The Lambs and I have a lot of fight left in us yet."

"So do I," Ann boldly called after him.

"Something tells me we haven't seen the last of him," Denise commented.

"Oh, you can count on that," Ann said.

Gary and Bill came out in the hall as the reverend and his lawyer got on the elevator.

"Good job," Gary said, giving Ann a hug.

"Yeah, you were great," Bill said enthusiastically.

"I was surprised to see you here," Ann said to her young client. "Were you checking out my courtroom technique?"

"No, I just wanted to see the leader of that religious group in the flesh," Bill said. "Since I hear he's the one responsible for putting up billboards around town bashing gays, I wanted to get a good look at him."

"What did you think?" Ann asked.

"He looks like a big tub of lard with a mouth to match," Bill said.

Gary laughed. "Good description. I don't suppose I can use that in my article."

"Come on, everybody," Ann said. "I'll buy you all a cup of coffee and a doughnut. Battling the forces of evil always gives me an appetite."

CHAPTER 9

The next day Ann drove to Mount Pleasant to interview Chuck Ryder, another gay university student who, according to Bill Robinson, had also been harassed by Jenkins and English.

"Yes, I know of at least one other person who was hassled by English and Jenkins," Bill had confirmed. "His name is Chuck Ryder."

"Is he still attending UW, Mount Pleasant?" Ann inquired.

"As far as I know, he is," Bill replied. "I think he's a senior."

"Do you know if the district attorney interviewed Chuck?"

"I imagine he did," Bill answered. "I gave him Chuck's name and phone number."

"Is Chuck a friend of yours?" Ann asked.

"No, I've never met him," Bill said. "He called me while I was still in the hospital. He said English and Jenkins had given him and his partner a hard time, too, and that about a month before I was assaulted they tried to jump him, but he got away from them."

"Did Chuck report the attempted assault?" Ann asked.

"No," Bill replied. "He said at the time he didn't want to get involved in the legal system. He apologized to me for not reporting it. He said he felt awful and that he'd always wonder if I would have been assaulted if he had had the guts to come forward."

"When you met with the DA and his staff to prepare for the trial, was any mention ever made of calling Chuck as a witness?"

Bill paused a moment, remembering. "Gee, I can't remember for sure, but I don't think so." He hesitated, then asked, "From what you've seen so far, do you think I might be able to win a civil case?"

"It's a little early to tell, but I think so," Ann replied.

"Good," Bill said with obvious relief.

"I'll be in touch again soon," Ann promised.

Mount Pleasant was an hour's drive northwest of Madison. It was a sunny spring afternoon, and Ann enjoyed the leisurely drive through some of Wisconsin's prime farming country. Ann had enjoyed spending her formative years in a predominantly rural area. Everyone knew their neighbors. No one locked their doors. Violent crime was virtually nonexistent. It was a sheltered and somewhat idyllic society and one that probably no longer existed, she thought ruefully. Most farms were now big businesses, and no area was immune from crime.

The city of Mount Pleasant, the Jasper County seat, was an attractive community of eight thousand, which was roughly the same number of students enrolled at its University of Wisconsin branch campus. The college consisted of twenty or so redbrick buildings that dotted a hilly area on the north side of town.

After her conversation with Bill Robinson, Ann had called ahead and made arrangements to meet Chuck Ryder at his apartment at three o'clock. She found the address without difficulty. It was a large, attractively painted Victorian home about a block from campus. Chuck and his partner occupied an upper flat.

Ann rang the doorbell, then stood on the wraparound porch and waited for Chuck to appear. A moment later a slender, dark-haired young man wearing jeans and a green sweatshirt came running down the stairs.

"Chuck?" Ann asked.

"Hi," the young man said, offering his hand. "You must be Ann."

They shook hands.

"Come on upstairs," Chuck said.

Moments later Ann and Chuck were seated across from each other in mismatched, somewhat shabby recliners.

"Sorry about the furnishings," Chuck apologized. "And the mess in here. I'm afraid neither Larry nor I is a very good housekeeper."

"That's all right," Ann said, smiling. "Neither am I. There are too many more fun things to do than clean house." She reached into her briefcase and took out a legal pad and a pen. "Thanks so much for agreeing to see me. Bill Robinson told me how kind you were to call him when he was in the hospital. That really meant a lot to him."

Chuck smiled ruefully. "It would have done him a lot more good if I'd reported my little run-in with those two creeps."

"No one can blame you for not wanting to get involved," Ann said. "How were you to know that they'd go after someone else?"

"I should have known," Chuck replied bitterly. "They looked like the type who were itching to cause trouble for somebody."

"Where and when did you first encounter them?"

"I'd seen them around campus a number of times," Chuck said.

"Even though they were still in high school?" Ann asked.

Chuck nodded. "The high school isn't that far from campus. And one of them—Jenkins, I think; he's the bigger one—had a souped-up truck with a loud muffler. He liked to drive it around town and make noise. I guess he thought that was macho."

"Did either of them ever speak to you?" Ann asked.

"One night while my partner and I were walking home from the library, Jenkins and English squealed by in their truck and one or both of them hollered at us out the window."

"What did they say?" Ann asked gently.

"Something like, 'You queers shouldn't be allowed out in public.'"

"How long after this did they try to physically assault you?"

"About a week."

"What happened?"

"It was about seven-thirty at night. It was just getting dark. I'd been at the gym and was walking home alone. All of a sudden they jumped out at me."

"Both of them?" Ann asked.

Chuck nodded. "They must've been hiding behind a garage or something. I didn't notice anything and all of a sudden there they were."

"Where was this?"

"About two blocks from here."

"You're certain it was Jenkins and English?"

"I'm positive. It was the same guys I'd seen riding around in the truck. I didn't know what their names were until they were arrested for assaulting Bill, but once I saw their pictures in the paper, I knew it was the same two punks."

"What happened when they jumped out at you?"

"They scared the shit out of me," Chuck admitted. "They both lunged at me and one of them hollered, 'Hey, faggot!' At that point I knew they weren't in the mood to make small talk, so I took off."

"You were able to get away from them?"

"Yeah. Fortunately I've been running competitively since I was a kid. The old adrenaline must've really kicked in, because I don't think I ever moved so fast in my life. I sprinted away from them like a rabbit. The two of them might be strong, but they're not in the greatest shape, so there was no way they were going to catch me. I was out of sight before they knew what hit 'em."

"You were lucky to be able to escape," Ann said.

"No kidding," Chuck said. "When I got back up here I must've looked like death warmed over, because Larry took one look at me and said, 'What happened to you? You look like you've seen a ghost.' I told him I'd just had a narrow miss with the devil. At that point he thought I'd been drinking or something. Then I told him what had happened, and he wanted me to call the police."

"Why didn't you?" Ann asked.

Chuck sighed. "I don't know. I guess because I didn't want to get mired down in some legal morass. No offense to your profession or anything," he said, "but I've heard too many horror stories about witnesses or victims who try to do the right thing and then end up putting their own lives on trial. I'm very comfortable with my lifestyle, but that doesn't mean I want it to end up in some news story, sounding all twisted and ugly. I was in my last year of school here. I wanted to concentrate on graduating and getting a job. I figured I didn't need any complications in my life."

Chuck paused for a moment, then went on. "Deep down I guess I knew I should report it, but I rationalized it by telling myself that nothing had happened, no crime had been committed. Believe me, I have regretted that decision every single day since I heard Bill was attacked. That's why I called Bill in the hospital and told him I'd help him in any way I could. I guess he must have passed my name on to the DA."

"Did anyone from the district attorney's office ever interview you?" Ann asked.

"Yeah, the DA himself called me and we talked on the phone."

"Ted Lawrence?"

Chuck nodded.

"Do you recall when that was?"

Chuck drummed the fingers of his right hand on his knee, trying to remember. "I think it was probably a couple weeks after Bill was assaulted."

"What did he say when he called you?"

"That he'd gotten my name from Bill Robinson and he wanted to hear what had happened to me."

"Did Lawrence indicate that he might want to call you as a witness at the trial?"

"I think he said he might be in touch," Chuck replied.

"Did he ever get back to you?"

"No."

"You never heard another word from him?" Ann asked, surprised.

Chuck shook his head. "No. Why? Do you think he should have called me as a witness?"

"I was just wondering," Ann said, but privately she was finding Lawrence's apparent decision not even to attempt to present Chuck's testimony at trial more and more inexplicable.

"Would you have testified if you'd been asked?" Ann inquired.

"In a heartbeat," Chuck answered without hesitation. "I would have loved to do something to help Bill out."

"Maybe you still can," Ann said. She briefly explained the possibility of filing a civil suit against Bill's attackers.

"Just say the word and I'll make myself available," Chuck said.

"Have you heard of anyone else who was harassed by Jenkins or English?"

"No, but it wouldn't surprise me if there were others," Chuck replied.

"Thanks a lot for your time," Ann said, getting up from her chair. "This has been really helpful."

"It was my pleasure," Chuck answered.

As she walked to her car, Ann mulled over what she had learned. Jenkins and English had tried to attack another gay man shortly before their attack on Bill Robinson. The DA prosecuting the criminal case, a man with twenty-five years' experience, had spoken to the target of the earlier attempt but had not even tried to get that testimony before the jury.

Why?

Was it a tactical decision? An oversight? Or something more sinister? It was possible the answer to that question could explain the jury's verdict.

Ann got in her car and was starting to head out of town when she passed the Copper Kettle Restaurant. Since this was the place where Jenkins and English had first encountered Bill Robinson, there was a chance someone who worked there might be able to shed some light on the young men's past behavior. She turned right at the corner and parked on a quiet side street, then walked back to the restaurant.

The Copper Kettle was a no-frills, slightly shabby establishment that served large helpings of food at reasonable prices. A sign hanging over the front door indicated that the building's maximum occupancy was seventy-five.

It was late afternoon, too early for the dinner crowd, and only a handful of tables were occupied. There were three waitresses on duty. Ann approached the tall, thin, middle-aged woman who was stationed behind the cash register, explained who she was, and asked if the woman knew Jenkins or English.

"Sure, I know 'em," the woman replied. "They're rude and they've got filthy mouths, Jenkins especially."

"Do they come in here often?" Ann asked.

"Not anymore. They used to stop in after school, but Jenkins got in a fight with another kid a few months back and the owner told him he was no longer welcome."

"When you say they have filthy mouths, at whom would they direct their bad language?"

"Whoever happened to be around," the waitress replied. "Other kids their age, old people, it didn't seem to make much difference."

"Do you know who Bill Robinson is?" Ann asked.

"I recognize the name as being that gay kid who got beat up," the waitress answered. "But I don't know him."

"You never saw him come in here?"

The waitress shrugged. "A lot of kids that age come in here. I generally don't know one from the other, unless they cause trouble like Jenkins."

FINAL JUSTICE

"Would either of the other waitresses know Jenkins or English?" Ann asked.

The waitress shook her head. "You can ask 'em but I doubt it. They're both new. Just started in the last couple months."

"Thanks for your time," Ann said.

"No problem. Come back sometime when you're hungry. We always carry at least six kinds of homemade pie."

"I'll keep that in mind," Ann replied.

She walked back to her car, engrossed in her thoughts about the case. Other than corroborating Chuck Ryder's story, the trip to Mount Pleasant had been a bust. If she couldn't find any other victims of Jenkins's and English's wrath, she'd just have to focus on the purely legal aspects of the suit.

As Ann rounded the corner and approached her car, she began to mentally run through the various causes of action she might include in the complaint. There was battery, of course, and intentional infliction of emotional distress. And the kids' parents would deserve their own unique set of claims.

Ann was about fifty feet from her car when she began to dig through her purse looking for her keys. "They're here somewhere," she grumbled to herself. If she didn't haul so much junk around with her it would be easier to locate the important items. As she shoved her right hand down toward the bottom of the purse, she was paying no attention to her surroundings. So when someone behind her roughly grabbed her left arm and spun her around, she was

85

too startled to do anything but make a pitiful gasping sound.

Ann found herself in the clutches of a tall, stocky young man with dark hair who looked to be in his late teens or early twenties. Next to him stood a shorter but equally hefty blond kid.

In spite of her terror, Ann managed to find her voice. "Let go of me!" she shouted, trying hard to pull away from her captor.

The dark-haired kid only gripped her arm tighter. "We hear you've been asking questions about Sam Jenkins and Brad English," he said menacingly. "If you know what's good for you, you'll knock it off."

"Why should I?" Ann demanded, her teeth chattering from fright.

"That jury said they were innocent, and that's the end of it. Don't go stirring up trouble."

Ann's heart was pounding so hard that she was afraid she was having a heart attack. *They're going to kill me,* she thought wildly. *This is the end.*

"Are you listening to me?" the young man said in a growl, digging his fingers deeper into her biceps. "If you're smart, you'll get out of this town and never come back. And if I were you, I'd think long and hard about trying to help people like that fag Robinson or you might just end up in the same shape as him."

As terrified as Ann was, this comment enraged her, and somehow she managed to get a bit of leverage with her right arm and club the young man in the head with her purse. At the same time she screamed at the top of her lungs and stomped on the kid's foot. His face contorted with anger and it appeared that he was on the verge of punching Ann when a car rounded the corner half a block away. In an instant the bully released Ann and he and his companion sprinted across the street into an alley.

Ann was so badly shaken by the incident that she slumped to the ground. The passing car paid her no heed, probably thinking she was an inebriated college student. After a minute she managed to get to her feet and unsteadily made her way to the car. Once she was safely locked inside, she sped back toward Madison as though the seven Furies were in hot pursuit.

She was fifteen miles away from Mount Pleasant when it occurred to her that perhaps she should have reported what happened to the police. She had a cell phone with her. It wasn't too late. After considering the idea for a couple of minutes, she decided against it.

The main reason for her decision was that she knew the police would want her to come to the station to discuss the incident in person, and she most assuredly did not want to return to Mount Pleasant—not now and possibly not ever. Besides, she hadn't actually been harmed, there had been no witnesses, and the cursory description she could provide of the two kids probably matched a couple thousand college students, so the odds of the police apprehending anyone were remote.

It was after six o'clock when Ann pulled into her driveway. She felt totally drained and was very much looking forward to having a glass or two of wine and then maybe taking a hot bath.

She retrieved her mail out of the box and walked back to the house. Out of the corner of her eye she saw a piece of paper on the step outside her front door. Thinking that it was a piece of trash that must have blown there, she walked over and picked it up. It was a letter-size sheet of paper, folded in thirds. On the front in bold black print were the words, THE TRUE FACTS ABOUT THE GAY COMMUNITY.

Frowning, Ann opened the little pamphlet and skimmed its contents. *Homosexuals engage in acts that are both beastly and filthy. Those of us who are truly interested in promoting family values must stop this perversion. We must persuade our legislators to once again criminalize all homosexual acts.*

Even though she was quite sure of its source, Ann turned the flyer over. The small print at the bottom read, *For more information on how you can help stop the abomination of homosexuality, please contact the Lambs of God, Rev. Charles Tremaine, Pastor.* Underneath that was the handwritten comment, *Ann, Hope you find this interesting. Best regards, C. Tremaine.*

Ann's feelings of fear and exhaustion vanished in an instant, replaced with a burning anger. She said aloud, "All right, Reverend Tremaine. If you want a battle, you've got one. And if you think you can scare me off with bricks or thugs or anything else, well, then, you've got another think coming."

CHAPTER 10

As soon as Ann got to the office the next morning, she called Bill Robinson. Ann knew that the Lambs relished publicity, and she felt it was only fair to warn Bill that the group might very well target his lawsuit as an example of modern morals gone awry. As Ann had expected, her warning did nothing to lessen her client's determination to see his attackers held accountable for what they had done.

"I'm not afraid of a bunch of pompous windbags," he said. "What harm can they do to me?"

"They can try to drag your name through the mud. They can try to set you up as an example of what they feel is wrong with society." Ann paused a moment. "They might even target you for physical violence." After giving the matter a lot of thought, she had decided not to mention her encounter with the two young punks in Mount Pleasant. It was probably just an isolated incident, so why get everybody up in arms over it?

"I've been through worse, remember?" Bill responded. "I say, full speed ahead."

"Good for you," Ann said. "I should be ready to file the complaint in a few days. I'll let you know for sure which day it'll be so you can prepare yourself for the new onslaught of press coverage."

"I'll be ready," Bill assured her.

Ann spent the next two days finishing the draft of the complaint.

Around noon on the second day, Ken Devlin walked into Ann's office. "How's it going?" he asked pleasantly.

Ann looked up at him and smiled. "Slowly," she said.

She looked at her copy of the complaint. "I was wondering if you think I should try to talk to the jurors who served on the criminal case to find out why they voted the way they did. We've all been speculating about what went wrong at the trial. Why not ask the people who could tell us?"

"Sure," Ken said. "It's worth a try. You realize, of course, that there's no guarantee any of them will talk to you. A lot of jurors are very hesitant about going on the record about what happened during deliberations, and if they refuse to cooperate, there's nothing you can do."

"What do you mean, they won't talk to me?" Ann said, pretending to be hurt. "I'm friendly and low-key, although persuasive. Why wouldn't they talk to me?"

"I beg your pardon," Ken said, winking at her. "What I meant to say was, I'm sure they'll all pour out their hearts to you."

He got up and came around the table to sit next to Ann. "I'm sorry I haven't been able to give you a hand with the complaint, but the past few days have been an absolute nightmare." He rubbed his hands over his eyes.

Ann had heard that the settlement Ken had negotiated in one of his cases had threatened to collapse when one of the defendant insurance companies reneged on its agreed-upon payment. Ken had been forced to haul the recalcitrant company into court to get the judge to enforce the settlement agreement.

"Is the settlement back on track now?" Ann asked.

Ken nodded. "Yeah. I got that settled yesterday."

Ken's voice sounded rather strained, so Ann asked, "Is something else wrong?"

Ken took a deep breath, then exhaled. "Patsy filed for divorce yesterday," he said quietly. "She moved out of the house last night."

"Oh, no!" Ann exclaimed. She immediately leaned over and gave Ken a hug. "I'm so sorry. That must have been awful for you. What are you doing at work? You should take some time off."

Ken returned Ann's hug. "Where should I be, off buying a hair shirt?" he quipped. "This has been coming for a long time, although I'll admit it was still a shock to actually be served with the papers."

"How are the girls taking it? Are they with Patsy?"

Ken shook his head. "They're staying with me, and they're handling it really well. They've known for years that we weren't getting along. I think in some ways it was probably a relief. At least they won't have to put up with our constant bickering."

"Where did Patsy go?"

Ken snorted. "She is currently residing with one of her partners, with whom she admits she's been having an affair for the past year. I suspect it's been going on longer than that, but I guess it doesn't make much difference now."

"Which partner?" Ann asked.

"Bruce Lindholm."

Ann made a face. "I know Bruce Lindholm. He's a pompous ass."

"Exactly," Ken said. "I hope they'll be very happy together. Listen," he said, putting his hand on Ann's shoulder. "I'd like to wait a week or so before I make this grist for the office rumor mill."

"I won't breathe a word," Ann promised. "I am really sorry, and if there's anything I can do to help, just let me know. God knows you certainly came through for me last year when Richard sprouted wings and flew west."

"Maybe you and I should form a self-help group for the recently rejected," Ken said lightly. "I appreciate your concern, but I think the girls and I will be fine. And now that my settlement is firmed up, I'd be happy to look over the Robinson complaint—that is, assuming you'd like me to."

"That'd be great," Ann said. "I can certainly use all the help I can get. I'd like to go over it one more time. Are you going to be around for a while?"

Ken shook his head. "Julie has swim practice. I've got to run home and change and then head over to the school to pick her up."

"Well, then, I'll have Kari rerun the complaint first thing in the morning, so if you've got a chance to look at it tomorrow—"

"Tomorrow it is," Ken said. He got up from his chair and walked over to the conference room door. "Maybe we could discuss it over lunch."

"That'd be great," Ann said, nodding.

As she watched him exit the room and head down the hall, Ann turned back to the draft of the complaint but found it impossible to concentrate. All she could think about was Ken.

She truly was sorry that his marriage was on the rocks. Even if the union had been unraveling for quite some time, it was still painful when it actually broke apart. Ken was a great guy and his daughters were wonderful girls. Ann hoped the divorce wouldn't prove to be too traumatic for any of them.

Ann picked up her pen and aimlessly drew circles on her legal pad. She guessed no relationship was immune from deteriorating. She'd always thought Ken and Patsy were a happy couple. Of course, she'd thought she and Richard were happy, too. She drew a smiley face and then added hair and glasses. It must be that misery loved company, because this was virtually the first time that thinking about Richard's departure hadn't caused a sick feeling to develop in her stomach. And now Ken was in the same boat.

They were kindred spirits. Both deserted. Both abandoned. Ann stopped doodling. Both *unattached*. Feeling just a tad guilty, she smiled, then turned her attention back to the Robinson complaint.

* * *

"You seem kind of distracted tonight," Georgia said. "Is something wrong?"

Ann leaned back against the cushions of one of the pair of overstuffed couches in her living room. "Not really," she answered without much conviction.

It was early in the evening. Georgia's daughter was with her father, and Ann and her friend had ordered in pizza and were now relaxing with a glass of wine.

"Come on, what gives?" Georgia asked, putting her feet up on a needlepoint footstool as she sat on the matching couch across from Ann.

Ann hesitated a moment. All evening she had been dying to tell her friend about the breakup of Ken's marriage, but up until now she had managed to restrain herself. She took a sip of wine and leaned forward. "If I tell you something, you've got to promise to keep it secret."

"I love secrets," Georgia said, leaning forward eagerly. "Spit it out."

"Do you promise not to tell?"

"Cross my heart and hope to die. Now hurry up. I haven't got all night. I have to pick up Stacey at nine."

"Okay," Ann said, taking a deep breath. "Ken Devlin's wife left him. She's been having an affair with one of her partners and she took off and left Ken and the kids."

"Wow!" Georgia exclaimed. "That's pretty scandalous behavior for an accountant. They'll probably revoke her CPA status." Ann's friend took a sip of her wine. "Actually that news doesn't surprise me all that much. I saw Ken and his wife together about a month ago, and it didn't look like they were hitting it off."

"You saw Ken and Patsy? Where?"

"At Marshall Field's. Didn't I tell you?" Seeing the cross look on Ann's face, Georgia went on. "Well, I intended to tell you. I guess I forgot. Anyway, I was downstairs in Linens looking for a shower gift and they must have been there for the same purpose."

"Did you talk to them?"

"No. They were a couple aisles away, but I thought I recognized Ken's voice, so I looked up, and sure enough, it was them. Normally I would have gone over to say hi but they were obviously in the middle of a fight."

In spite of herself, Ann was curious. "What were they fighting about?"

"I don't know, but it was clear they couldn't agree on anything. Ken said they didn't have time to look for a gift because they had to pick up one of the girls. Patsy said that if Ken hadn't been late meeting her they'd have plenty of time to shop. Finally Ken told her to take all the time she wanted because he was leaving. He stormed off and went up the escalator. She followed him about thirty seconds later."

Georgia refilled her wineglass. "So now they're splitsville. Well, that clears the way for you to make a move on Ken, doesn't it?"

"Don't be ridiculous!" Ann exclaimed.

"What's so ridiculous about it? You'd be a match

made in heaven. Two lawyers." Georgia paused and made a face. "Think of all the fun you could have discussing the rules of evidence."

"I'm really not sure I'm ready for that," Ann demurred.

"You've got to take the plunge sometime," Georgia said. "It might as well be with someone you genuinely like. After all, what have you got to lose?"

CHAPTER 11

"Ms. Monroe, when do you expect the Robinson case to be set for trial?" the eager reporter asked.

Ann suppressed a laugh. "Well, since the case was just filed today, I don't expect a trial date to be set for at least six months." That answer didn't slow the reporter down a bit. "What type of damages are you seeking?"

It had not taken long for word of Bill Robinson's civil suit to get out. Ann sent one of the firm's messengers to the Jasper County Courthouse to file the summons and complaint around noon. The messenger then gave authenticated copies of the documents to a local process server, who would see that a copy was personally delivered to each of the defendants. Almost before the messenger arrived back in Madison, Mishler and Stettler's phone lines were jammed as reporters attempted to reach Ann for comment about the case.

Anticipating the media's interest in the lawsuit, Ann had Mark Mishler help her draft a press release explaining that Bill Robinson was suing Samuel Jenkins and Brad English for the torts of battery and negligent infliction of emotional distress. Jenkins's and English's parents were being sued under the parental responsibility statute and for negligent supervision of their sons.

"Jenkins and English were acquitted of all charges," the reporter went on. "Isn't it double jeopardy to sue them again for the same acts?"

"An acquittal on the criminal charges does not foreclose a civil suit based on the same conduct," Ann patiently explained. "In a criminal case, the state as plaintiff prosecutes a wrongdoer to vindicate the public's rights, while in a civil case the victim of the wrong brings the action on his own behalf."

While Ann fielded phone calls from reporters, Kari was kept busy faxing copies of the complaint to various media outlets. In appreciation for the nice job he had done in bringing the Crabbs' grievance against the high school to light, Ann had given Gary Carlson a scoop by furnishing him with a copy of the complaint and sitting down with him for an hour-long interview the morning the suit was filed. She hoped that the next day's newspaper would have an article about the case that was sympathetic to Bill's point of view.

Ann had warned the Robinsons that they could also expect a flood of calls from reporters. Her prediction was borne out by a call she received from Laurie Robinson around four o'clock that afternoon.

"It's been a circus here for the past two hours," a harried-sounding Laurie reported when Kari interrupted another of Ann's calls to put her through.

"Tom is in Detroit until tomorrow, so I've been dealing with all the attention on my own. Most of the press people I spoke to were polite enough, but after talking to about twenty people in a row I started to get a little weary, so I turned the answering machine off and drove over to a friend's. I'm going to spend the night here. I don't think I'd get any rest at home."

"Are they bothering Bill, too?" Ann asked, concerned about how her young client might be affected by the attention.

"I think he's making himself scarce for the time being," Laurie replied. "I talked to him yesterday and he said he planned to spend a couple days with a friend off campus. I tried to call his dorm room just a few minutes ago and didn't get an answer, so I assume he followed through on his plan."

"Remember," Ann said, "if anyone gives you a hard time, refer them to me. I'll do everything I can to make the litigation experience as painless as possible for all of you."

"Thanks," Laurie said. "We appreciate all you're doing for us, and we have our fingers crossed that this time around the case will have a better ending."

Ann had no more than hung up from talking to Laurie than another spate of media calls came in. She patiently explained the nature of the Robinsons' claims to each caller and expressed optimism that the Jasper County jury chosen to hear the civil suit would view the evidence differently than the criminal case jury had done.

It was close to five o'clock when Ken Devlin

stepped into Ann's office. "How are you holding up?" he asked.

"Fine," she replied. As she looked up at him, the conversation she'd had with Georgia came rushing back, and in spite of her best efforts to remain nonchalant, Ann felt her face redden.

"You've gotten lots of calls about the case?" Ken asked.

Ann nodded.

"Sorry I couldn't check in with you earlier," Ken said, coming around Ann's desk and taking a seat in one of her client chairs, "but I've been tied up in depositions all day. How are you doing trying to contact the jurors from the criminal trial?"

"Lousy," Ann replied, making a face. "So far I haven't found anybody who's willing to talk to me."

"I warned you that might happen," Ken said. "A lot of jurors, particularly those who serve on high-profile cases, just want to put the whole experience behind them once the trial is over. What was the composition of the jury?"

"Six women and six men," Ann replied. "And one female alternate."

"How many have you contacted so far?"

"I've reached three personally, and none of them would talk. I've left messages for the others and I intend to keep trying to get hold of them."

"Who was the foreman?"

Ann referred to some notes on her desk. "A man named Claude Furseth. He's one of the people who hasn't called back." Ann leaned back in her chair. "I can't put my finger on it, but I just have the feeling that there was something fishy about that trial."

"You mean because Ted Lawrence didn't offer 'other acts' evidence?" Ken asked.

"No, I think it goes beyond that," Ann said. "Although I'm not sure just what it is."

Kari stepped into the office. "Excuse me, Ann, but there's a reporter here from one of the local TV stations who'd like to do a brief interview with you."

Ann made a face and ran her hands through her hair. "Oh, great. I probably look like a wet rag."

"You look wonderful," Ken said encouragingly.

"Thank you," Ann said. She turned back to Kari, who was waiting at the door expectantly. "All right. Give me a couple minutes to run to the rest room and try to make myself presentable. Which reporter is it?"

"Linda O'Dell with Channel Fifteen," Kari replied.

"I'll leave you to your ablutions," Ken said, getting up from his chair.

Ann felt that the interview with the television reporter went quite well. The reporter said the segment would probably air on the ten o'clock news. Ann took a few more calls about the case, then finished up some odds and ends before calling it a day around six-thirty. She went home, had a light dinner, and puttered around the house for a while. She switched on the television at ten and about three minutes into the newscast saw a shot of the reporter standing in front of Mishler and Stettler's office building.

"Many of our viewers will recall the criminal trial that took place in Jasper County circuit court in early March," the reporter said. "Two young defendants, Samuel Jenkins and Brad English, were acquitted of all charges as a result of their assault on Bill Robinson, an openly gay man who was attending the University of Wisconsin, Mount Pleasant. Today Robinson filed a civil suit against Jenkins, English, their parents, and their insurance companies. Robinson's attorney had this comment about the case."

Ann grimaced slightly as the scene shifted to a shot of her standing by the door to one of the firm's conference rooms. "Even though the jury in the criminal trial apparently did not conclude beyond a reasonable doubt that the defendants committed a hate crime, the attack on Bill Robinson was heinous and it was motivated out of hatred and prejudice because Bill Robinson is gay. Under the burden of proof that applies in civil cases, we believe that a jury will find the defendants liable for causing Bill Robinson severe physical and mental anguish."

I look like I haven't slept in a week, Ann thought critically. There were bags under her eyes, and her suit was wrinkled. She was so busy scrutinizing her appearance that she failed to focus on the fact that the segment about the case was not yet over until she heard a familiar name.

"Area minister Charles Tremaine had this comment about the Robinson case," the reporter went on.

Upon hearing Tremaine's name, Ann snapped to attention. As she peered at her television screen, there he was, big as life, his face dark with five o'clock shadow. "The jury in Jasper County did the right thing in exonerating those two boys of all charges," Tremaine drawled. "Those jurors obviously believed that those boys' actions were provoked by the tawdry behavior of that homosexual. There is clearly something wrong with our legal system when the homosexual is now able to put those two fine young men through the agony and expense of a second trial after they've already been declared innocent in a court of law."

As Ann gritted her teeth, Tremaine smiled sweetly at the camera and continued. "I was shocked when I heard about this lawsuit. However, once I learned the name of the attorney representing the homosexual, everything became clearer. I have had previous dealings with Ms. Ann Monroe and I have seen firsthand the depths to which she will sink in order to obtain new clients and garner publicity for herself."

Ann's mouth fell open as she heard Tremaine say her name. Then he cast his eyes toward the heavens. "In the spirit of the Easter season which has just recently passed, I would ask the members of my congregation and the entire community to pray for the homosexual involved in this case, to ask almighty God to heal the sickness which infests his body and soul."

The corners of Tremaine's mouth dropped slightly as he added, "As for Ms. Monroe, I will add a special prayer that she may be delivered from the personal demons that obviously plague her."

The television screen shifted back to the reporter.

"For NBC Fifteen news, this is Linda O'Dell reporting."

For a long moment after the scene had shifted to the next story, Ann sat motionless, trying to fight back the twin feelings of fear and revulsion that came from knowing Tremaine and his followers had now decided to target Bill Robinson's case and her personally. But then her anger overcame her fear. Making a low, guttural sound, she hurled the TV remote control at the wall. It hit with enough force to dislodge the batteries and send them rolling around on the floor.

"Damn him!" Ann said aloud, pacing back and forth in her living room. What gave that pompous ass the right to go on television and disparage her and her client?

Her fatigue and fear forgotten, Ann reached into her briefcase and pulled out the portion of the Robinson file she had brought home. As she read through the complaint for the hundredth time, she jotted notes to herself on a possible strategy for handling the discovery phase of the case. If Reverend Tremaine was going to be scrutinizing her every move, she'd better be doubly prepared.

CHAPTER 12

As soon as the lawsuit was filed, Ann began receiving nasty letters chastising her for taking Bill Robinson's case. Because she had handled many controversial cases, she had gotten her share of hate mail before and generally didn't let it bother her. But about ten days after filing the lawsuit she received a letter that she found truly disturbing.

It was anonymous, of course, and came in a plain envelope postmarked Madison. The letter was printed in dark ink and appeared to have been written with a heavy hand, because in a couple of places the pen strokes had almost torn a hole in the paper. The text was short and to the point:

> *We warned you not to get mixed up with that fag Bill Robinson. You should have listened to us. Back off while you still can or you're going to be sorry.*

Ann's throat constricted and she felt all clammy when reading it. She was almost certain that the letter had been written by the punks who had accosted her in Mount Pleasant. Rather than tossing it straight into the wastebasket, as she did with most hate mail, she reread it a couple of times, then opened her top desk drawer and tucked the note inside. She sincerely hoped she would never hear from the author again, but in case she did, she knew it might be a good idea to have a record of the correspondence.

Ann was still sitting at her desk, mulling over the venomous feelings that must motivate people who sent such letters, when she heard a knock at the door.

"Sorry to barge in on you if you're busy," Kari said, "but everyone's here for the Jenkins deposition. They're waiting for you in conference room two."

"Thanks," Ann said, pushing back her chair and getting to her feet. She closed the desk drawer where she had stashed the nasty letter and headed down the hall.

Although Ann doubted that she would learn anything particularly useful from taking the depositions of Bill Robinson's attackers, it was still important to get the youths' stories on the record so they could be impeached if they changed their versions of events at trial.

Samuel Jenkins was the young man who, according to Bill Robinson, had been the more vicious of his two assailants. Sitting across from him in one of Mishler and Stettler's conference rooms, Ann thought Jenkins looked like a typical high school jock: tall and stocky, with an unruly mass of dark brown hair. Acne spots dotted his chin and forehead. He was dressed in khaki pants and a tan-and-red-checked shirt. In fact, Ann thought, he looked very much like the two young ruffians who had confronted her in Mount Pleasant. She couldn't help but wonder if they were friends of Jenkins's.

"Would you please state your name and address for the record," Ann directed the witness.

"Samuel Jenkins, Route One, Mount Pleasant, Wisconsin," came the sullen answer. The young man seemed ill at ease, bouncing his right leg rhythmically up and down.

The Jenkins family had retained Patrick Jagoe to defend them. Ann had dealt with Jagoe, an attorney in his early forties who was a partner at a large Madison firm, on quite a number of other cases and had always found him to be reasonable. She hoped that quality would be an asset in this difficult case.

"How old are you, Mr. Jenkins?" Ann asked pleasantly.

"I turned eighteen on December third."

"Do you attend school?"

"Yeah, I'm a senior at Mount Pleasant High School."

"You'll be graduating in June?"

"Yeah."

"Are you a good student?"

Jenkins shrugged. "I get by."

"Are you planning to go on to college?"

Another shrug. "I thought I'd work for a while. I figure I can always go back to school later."

"I'd like to turn your attention to the events of September nineteenth," Ann said. "Do you recall what day of the week that was?"

"It was a Thursday."

"Please describe for me what you did that day."

"I drove to school about quarter to eight."

"What type of vehicle do you drive?"

"A white Ford pickup."

"What time did you leave school?"

"About three-fifteen."

"Where did you go after that?"

"Me and Brad English needed to collect some soil samples for an agriculture class, so we decided to drive out of town and pick them up."

"What's the name of the teacher of the agriculture class?"

"George Stewart."

"When did you need the samples?"

"The next day."

"What type of soil samples were you supposed to collect?"

"We had a whole list. Silt loam, clay, glacial till, and some others."

"Where did you go to get these samples?"

"We went a few different places, but we started out a few miles out of town."

"Which direction from Mount Pleasant?"

"North."

"You drove your truck and Brad English rode along with you?"

"Yeah."

"Did you have equipment along to collect the samples?"

"We had some Ziploc bags and a garden shovel."

"Where was your first stop?"

"The first stop was to get clay at Dave Mulder's farm, about a mile out of town."

"What kind of soil were you looking for after that?"

"We thought we might be able to get two or three samples in one stop," Jenkins explained.

"Which ones?"

"Ah . . ." Jenkins hesitated for a moment. "Silt loam, glacial till, and woody peat."

"Where did you go to find those soil types?"

"A couple more miles north on Stark Road."

"Did you collect the three samples in that stop?"

"We got the silt loam and the glacial till."

"What about the peat?"

"That's what we were looking for when . . ." His voice trailed off. "When it happened."

"The attack on Bill Robinson," Ann prompted.

"He attacked us," Jenkins corrected her indignantly.

Sure he did, Ann thought. *And pigs can fly.* "Can you tell us what happened?"

Jenkins took a deep breath; then the words came out in a rush. "Me and Brad were walking through the woods looking for a peat sample. We couldn't find any, and we thought maybe we didn't know what to look for. Brad said he'd go back to the truck and get the book that showed a picture of peat. When he hadn't come back in about five minutes, I went to look for him. That's when I saw them." He stopped and stared at the floor.

"Who did you see?" Ann prompted.

"Brad and Robinson."

"Where were they?"

"Near the shoulder of the road. Robinson had Brad down on the ground and was punching him in the face."

"What did you do then?"

"I ran over and tried to pull Robinson off Brad."

"Did you succeed?"

"Yes."

"Then what happened?"

"Robinson hit me in the mouth," Jenkins said indignantly. "He broke two of my teeth."

"What happened next?"

"I had to defend myself. I hit him back."

"Where did you hit him?"

Jenkins hesitated. "I don't remember. I think maybe in the stomach."

"Was Bill Robinson still standing after that blow?"

"I think so."

"Did you hit him again?"

"Yeah, because he kept coming at me. He was acting crazy. He had a wild look in his eyes and he kept punching away at me really hard."

Ann thought this speech sounded rehearsed and contrived. "Did Bill Robinson say anything while this was happening?" she asked.

"No."

"Did either you or Brad English say anything?"

"No."

"Did you try to push Bill Robinson away so you and Brad could leave?"

"No."

"Did you try to get to your truck?"

"No."

"How many times did you hit Bill Robinson?"

"I don't remember."

"Did Brad Jenkins hit Bill Robinson after you arrived on the scene?"

"I'm not sure. He might have, but by that time Brad was hurt. He was holding his shoulder and whimpering."

"Did Bill Robinson ever ask you to stop hitting him?"

"No."

"How long did this whole episode go on?"

"I don't know."

"Several minutes?"

"I suppose so."

"And during that entire time, no one uttered so much as one word?"

"That's right."

Ann paused for a long moment to give everyone in the room time to absorb the absurdity of this claim before continuing her questioning. "Did you make disparaging remarks about Bill Robinson's sexual orientation at any time during this incident?"

"No."

"Are you sure of that?"

"Positive," Jenkins said at once.

"At what point did you stop hitting Bill Robinson?"

"When he finally stopped trying to hit Brad and me."

"And what condition was Bill Robinson in at that point?"

"I'm not sure what you mean," Jenkins hedged.

"Was Bill Robinson lying on the ground?"

"Yes."

"Was he still conscious?"

Another hesitation. "I'm not sure. I think so."

"Was he bleeding?"

"I don't know. I really didn't notice. Brad and me were hurt, too."

"Did you try to render Bill Robinson assistance for his injuries?"

"No," Jenkins said hotly. "I told you, we were hurt, too."

"So you and Brad English left Bill Robinson lying there and went back to your truck?"

"Yes," Jenkins said, his face reddening.

"Where was your truck parked?" Ann asked.

"Nearby," Jenkins answered vaguely.

"How far from the site where the altercation occurred was the truck parked?"

"It was around the corner, on a side road, maybe an eighth of a mile away."

"Was the truck visible from where the altercation took place?"

After another silence, Jenkins admitted, "No."

Ann paused a moment. "Was it just a coincidence that your truck was parked so that as Bill Robinson rode by on his bike he would probably not have suspected anyone was in the area?"

"Objection," Patrick Jagoe said. "Argumentative."

"Withdrawn," Ann said. She leaned back in her chair and looked the witness right in the eye. She expected him to look away, but he did not. They stared at each other for a long moment during which Ann could have sworn Jenkins's expression turned from mild irritation to rage.

"No further questions," Ann said, turning away from the witness in disgust. There was no question in her mind that this young man was capable of great violence. The question was whether she would be able to prove that his attack on Bill Robinson had been both premeditated and completely unprovoked. She sincerely hoped the answer was yes.

If Samuel Jenkins looked like a jock, Brad English seemed to be the picture of an all-American, clean-cut kid. Ann took English's deposition the day after Jenkins gave his testimony. As the court reporter set up her equipment, Ann sat back in her chair and casually gave the new witness the once-over.

Like Jenkins, English was above average in height, although his build was slimmer than his compatriot's. He was neatly dressed in dark slacks and a cream-colored shirt and conservative tie. He looked as though he would have little difficulty fitting in on a prep-school campus. It was hard to believe he'd had a hand in Bill Robinson's beating.

The English family was represented by Pat Cox, a young attorney from a midsize Milwaukee firm. Although Ann had not met Pat before, she had had prior dealings with the firm and found them to be straight shooters. In a case that featured both difficult-proof problems and highly controversial subject matter, Ann was grateful that both of the opposing counsel seemed to be fairly congenial people.

In her preliminary questioning, Ann ascertained that English had turned eighteen in February. He was a B student who, like Jenkins, was in his final semester at Mount Pleasant High School. He was planning to go to college and major in landscape architecture, after which he would perhaps join his father's landscaping firm. Ann cringed a bit when she heard that English had been accepted at the university in Madison. She sincerely hoped he and Bill Robinson would never again cross paths.

English's memory of seeing Bill Robinson at the Copper Kettle was vague. "He could have been in there. It's a pretty popular place in the late afternoon."

"You have no specific recollection one way or the other about seeing him?" Ann asked.

"That's correct."

"Do you recall ever having a discussion with Samuel Jenkins about Bill Robinson's sexual preferences?"

"I don't recall."

"Do you recall ever making derogatory remarks in public about anyone's sexual preferences or sexual orientation?"

"I don't recall."

In almost all respects, English corroborated Jenkins's version of events leading up to the attack. He and Jenkins were just looking for soil samples. They weren't stalking Bill Robinson. Jenkins had parked his truck on a side road because they thought they might be able to find some soil samples on that road. When they didn't, they decided to walk around and look for some instead of moving the truck.

English also claimed he went back to the truck to get the pamphlet that showed pictures of the various soil samples while Jenkins stayed in the woods.

"What happened then?" Ann asked.

"I had the pamphlet in my hand and I was on the road, walking back toward the woods, when a guy rode up on a bike and stopped in front of me," English replied.

"The guy on the bike was Bill Robinson?"

English nodded. "Yes. I didn't know his name then, though."

"When you saw him, did he look familiar? Did he look like someone you'd seen before?"

"I don't know. Like I told you, I can't say for sure if I ever saw him before that day."

"What happened after he stopped his bike?"

"He got off the bike and started walking toward me."

"Did he say anything as he walked toward you?"

English shook his head. "Not at first. He just came toward me."

"Did you say anything?"

"Yeah, I said, 'What do you want?' or something like that."

"Did he reply?"

"Not really. He just kept walking, and then, all of a sudden, he let out a horrible yell and jumped on me."

"Without any provocation on your part, this stranger got off his bike, walked over to you, yelled, and then jumped on you?" Ann said, trying to keep the sarcasm out of her voice.

"That's right."

"What happened then?"

"He knocked me down and then he started punching me really hard."

"Did you hit him back? Try to resist?"

"I tried. I think I did manage to hit him a few times, but he was awfully quick and he punched really hard. Then he got up on his knees so he'd have better leverage and he grabbed my left arm and twisted it over my head. It felt like my arm had been pulled out of its socket."

"Did either of you say anything while all this was going on?"

"I was yelling, 'Stop it!' but he wasn't paying any attention."

"Did he say anything?"

"Not anything you could understand. He was making some funny grunting noises and his eyes looked all wild, like he was nuts or on drugs or something."

"What happened then?"

"Sam came out of the woods looking for me, and when he saw what was happening he ran over and jumped on the guy and tried to pull him off."

"And then?"

"The guy started punching Sam and I got up. I wasn't real fast because my shoulder hurt so bad, but I did finally get on my feet."

"How long did Sam and Bill Robinson continue fighting?"

"I don't know. It seemed like a long time, but I suppose it was only a couple minutes."

"And when it ended, Bill Robinson was lying on the ground, unconscious?"

"I didn't think he was unconscious," Brad said, somewhat defensively.

"Well, isn't it true that when the fighting stopped, Bill Robinson was on the ground and was not moving?"

"I guess so," English admitted.

"What did you and Sam Jenkins do then?"

"We left."

"You left Bill Robinson there on the ground, not knowing his condition, not knowing if he needed medical attention?"

"We were hurt, too," English said, raising his voice for the first time. "We needed to get medical attention ourselves."

"Did it ever occur to you to send help for Bill Robinson when you got back to town?"

English hesitated a moment, then shook his head. "We thought he was probably on drugs and after he slept it off for a while he'd be okay."

"Were you surprised when you learned that Bill Robinson suffered a lacerated liver as a result of the beating you and Sam Jenkins gave him?"

"Yeah, sure," English said, shifting uneasily in his chair. "I didn't think he was really hurt."

"I have no further questions at this time," Ann said, dropping her pen on the table in disgust. "But I reserve the right to reconvene this deposition at a later date if the need arises."

CHAPTER 13

Jesse Greer leaned forward in his chair and pointed his finger at the computer screen. "Can you make this picture look a little clearer? Her face looks a little fuzzy."

The young red-haired man seated next to Greer deftly clicked his mouse a number of times, bringing the picture into better focus. "How's that?"

Greer stared at the screen intently for a moment, then broke into a broad grin. "That's terrific, Mark," he said, clapping the other man on the back. "You are a fucking computer genius. Ann Monroe should look so good in the flesh as she does on our Web site."

"She looks like quite a fox to me," Mark agreed. "What about the other broad?" he asked, clicking to another screen. "Do you want me to enhance her picture a little bit, too?"

Greer glanced at a photo of Denise Riley and waved his hand dismissively. "Nah. Don't bother. That old cow looks good enough the way she is. Go back to Monroe's page and show me the text."

Mark complied and Greer nodded approvingly.

"All the important data seems to be there. Office address and phone number. Home address and phone. Have you got the same info listed on the Riley bitch?"

Mark nodded.

"That's good." Greer cocked his head. "I wonder if there's some way we could make this a little more dramatic."

"What do you mean?" Mark asked.

"I'm not sure. Could you try making the background a little lighter and the text bolder?"

Mark complied. "How's that?"

"Better," Greer said. "But it's still missing something. Can you think of a way we could highlight the pictures so people hitting on the site will understand right away that these two bitches are pure evil?"

Mark considered the possible options for a moment. "What if we put a big black circle around each picture and then superimposed the 'no' symbol on top of that?"

"What the hell is the 'no' symbol?"

"Think of the signs you see all over the place that indicate 'no smoking.' They show a cigarette with a big slash mark through it. That slash mark is the 'no' symbol."

"All right!" Greer said. "Try that."

Within minutes Mark had added a heavy black slash mark over the photos of Ann and Denise. "What do you think of that?"

"Greer frowned. "It's not bad, but I guess I was thinking of something even more dramatic."

Mark again considered the problem, then said, "How about bull's-eyes?"

"Excellent!" Greer exclaimed. "You are the man!" He and Mark exchanged high-fives. Greer stared at the screen and nodded enthusiastically. "Bull's-eyes will send just exactly the right message about those two godless bitches."

CHAPTER 14

Shortly before noon on the day after the Jenkins and English depositions, Ann was doing some research on one of her other cases when she got a call from a very disgruntled Denise Riley.

"I've been arrested," Denise announced without preamble.

"Arrested!" Ann exclaimed. "For what?"

"For battery," Denise replied.

"What happened?" Ann asked.

"I got to the clinic about a half hour early this morning," Denise explained. "The police hadn't arrived yet but there were already ten picketers there. Two of them, a man and a woman, came up to my car when I pulled into the parking lot. I think they were going to try to keep me from getting out. I rolled down the window and told them to move—politely, of course," she added drolly. "When they didn't move I told them they were violating the terms of the injunction. They called me a baby killer and various other choice names."

"What happened then?" Ann asked.

Denise sighed. "I told them once more to back off, a little louder this time. When they still didn't move, I rolled up the window, shut off the engine, and rather abruptly gave the door a big shove—and inadvertently hit the young woman in the knee."

Ann grimaced, envisioning the scene. "Was she hurt?"

"From the way she carried on you would have thought I'd amputated her leg. She sort of collapsed on the ground, grabbed her knee, and started moaning loudly. I'm sure she was faking. Anyway, a policeman arrived right after that. The woman's male companion yelled for the cop to come over, claiming I'd attacked the poor girl."

Denise sighed. "I explained I was just trying to get out of my car and that the two demonstrators should be ticketed for getting too close to me. The officer listened to us snipe at each other for a while, and I guess he finally got disgusted, because he arrested all three of us—the two of them for violating the injunction and me for battery."

"I can probably get the charge against you dropped," Ann said. "What was the officer's name?"

"Dan Brecht. I think he's a rookie. He looked very young. I really can't blame him too much. He probably didn't know what to do and thought this would be a good compromise. My pride is more wounded than anything."

"Don't worry," Ann said. "I'll take care of it. I do have a suggestion, though," she said tactfully.

"Go ahead," Denise instructed.

"From now on it might be a good idea if you kept

your cell phone with you at all times," Ann said, "and if something like this happens again, call the police and sit tight till they arrive instead of trying to handle it yourself."

"You're right, of course," Denise said. "I should have known better. It's just that I'm getting so damn frustrated with this protest. How long do you think those people are likely to keep it up?"

"It's hard to say," Ann admitted. "They picketed the abortion clinic for months. They might very well be prepared to do the same here."

"Don't any of them have to work for a living?" Denise grumbled.

"I think they take turns manning the barricades," Ann said. "And I've heard that sometimes they even import reinforcements from other states to enable them to maintain a continuous presence at a particular site. I hope you're not getting discouraged yet, because you could be in for a long siege."

"Oh, they're not going to get the better of me," Denise promised. "I'll fight them till my last breath. I just don't understand what motivates them. We're a valuable health resource for low-income women. Why would anyone make us out to be such ogres?"

"I don't know," Ann replied. "As I told you before, it's possible that Reverend Tremaine targeted your clinic at least in part because you're my client."

"How can someone with so much hatred inside him dare to call himself a minister?" Denise wondered. "I thought religion was supposed to encourage tolerance, not divisiveness."

"I don't think Charles Tremaine has one ounce of

tolerance for anyone the least bit different from himself," Ann said.

"Well, maybe we'll just have to teach him some," Denise suggested. "Thanks for letting me blow off some steam, Ann. And I'm sorry I lost my cool with the demonstrators this morning. I promise I'll try to keep my temper under control from now on, and I hope my actions didn't screw up the injunction in any way."

"Don't worry about it," Ann said kindly. "Just concentrate on keeping the clinic running smoothly and let the police and me handle the rest."

"Will do," Denise said.

The following morning Ann received a call from a very haughty Thomas Ravenswood.

"Ms. Monroe," the lawyer for the Lambs of God said with a sniff. "Are you aware of the vicious assault that occurred in the Planned Parenthood parking lot yesterday?"

"No," Ann replied, playing dumb. "What happened? Did Charlie Tremaine wig out and sock somebody in the mouth?"

"No, Denise Riley assaulted one of the protesters with her car door," Ravenswood retorted. "I'm calling to put you on notice that we intend to sue your client for every cent it has."

"Since it's a nonprofit organization, that won't be much. What's the injured party's name?"

"Samantha Pablo," Ravenswood answered. "She is twenty years old and an honors student at an up-

FINAL JUSTICE

standing Christian college. It looks as though she has suffered permanent injury to her knee."

"So her claim would be for pain and suffering and permanent inability to genuflect?"

"Really, Ms. Monroe, I do not appreciate your callous attitude toward religion. Have you no conscience?"

"I have a perfectly good conscience," Ann replied in a louder tone. "And nothing would make it or me feel better than if Reverend Tremaine and his followers disappeared from the face of the earth."

"This impertinence is uncalled for," Ravenswood said in a snarl. "I'll be filing the complaint on behalf of Ms. Pablo shortly."

"Can't wait to see it," Ann said. "I always enjoy reading good fiction."

Upon hearing that comment, Ravenswood slammed the phone down without any further comment.

"This is not one of my better weeks," Ann muttered to herself as she tried to turn back to the research she'd been doing when Ravenswood called. Denise Riley had been arrested. The clinic was going to be sued. The protesters showed no sign of weakening in their resolve. And Ann had made absolutely no headway in the Robinson case. What else could possibly go wrong?

The answer to that rhetorical question came only two hours later, when she got a phone call from Taylor Crabb.

As soon as she heard her young client's voice, Ann felt an immediate twinge of guilt. "I'm afraid I haven't gotten very far with your case," she apologized. "I've told the school district's lawyer that I want to take some depositions, but he hasn't gotten back to me. I promise I'll follow up on it first thing on Monday."

"I'm not calling about our case," Taylor said.

"You're not?" Ann said, surprised.

"No, I'm calling to let you know that I just stumbled across a Web site that I think you should know about."

"What kind of Web site?" Ann asked warily.

"It's sponsored by that Lambs of God group, and it targets you and the Planned Parenthood director."

Ann swallowed hard. "What do you mean, 'targets' us?"

"It starts out with a bunch of blather about all the things wrong with today's society," Taylor explained. "Lack of family values, decline of morality, et cetera. Then it lists a number of organizations that are supposedly contributing to the problem. One of them is Planned Parenthood. If you click on an icon there, pictures of you and the director pop up, along with your names and home and work addresses."

"Oh, my God!" Ann exclaimed, her heart pounding in her chest. "What's the URL of this site?"

Taylor told her. "I came across it purely by accident. Talia and I have been keeping a scrapbook of all the publicity that's been generated by our case, and I search the Web every day or two to see what's out there. One of the ways I search is by your name. That's how I found this. It must have just been posted in the last couple days, because it wasn't there when I looked earlier in the week."

"Thanks a lot, Taylor," Ann said. "I really appreciate it. And I promise I will light a fire under the school district about your case on Monday."

As soon as she hung up the phone, Ann accessed the Web site. *Are you tired of the decline of family values?* the Lambs' home page asked. *If you are, join with us in sending a message to those groups that have aided in society's moral decline.* The list of groups that followed included the abortion clinic where the Lambs had previously picketed, the Freedom from Religion Foundation, also one of Ann's clients, and Planned Parenthood.

Clicking on the Planned Parenthood icon, Ann gasped in horror as she stared at photos of herself and Denise Riley. Their faces were encased in bull's-eyes. Under each photo was a brief curriculum vitae. Hers read, "Ann Louise Monroe; Occupation: Attorney. Employer: Mishler and Stettler, 10 North Pinckney Street, Madison, Wisconsin. Home Address: . . ."

Similar information was provided about Denise Riley. *We're going to die!* Ann thought wildly. *They're going to kill us.*

Calm down, she told herself, taking a couple of deep breaths. She'd be no help to herself or Denise if she got hysterical. She needed to think like a lawyer, not like a victim. What legal courses of action were available to stop this indignity?

Her brain was so addled that she couldn't think straight. *Ken*, she thought. Ken would know what to do. She got up out of her chair and raced down the hall.

It was now after five o'clock, and since it was Friday night most people had already left. Seeing a light in Ken's office, Ann brightened. Maybe he was still there. She stepped inside, but the office was empty. Her spirits dropped. She really needed to talk to someone, and it was Ken whom she most wanted to talk to.

Ann walked over to his desk and looked at his daily planner. The notation for the afternoon read, *Rehabilitation expert deposition in Brunner at Foley and Lardner 2:00 P.M.* Ann knew Ken normally stopped back at the office after depositions or court appearances to check for messages. She sat down in his chair and wrote out a brief note explaining what she had just discovered and giving the URL of the Web site.

I'll be home all night, she wrote. *Please call me.* She set the message on his chair, where he'd be sure to find it, then went back to her office. There was no point in hanging around. She would go home, call Denise Riley, and wait for Ken to call. She quickly shut off her computer, gathered her coat and briefcase, and headed for the parking ramp.

CHAPTER 15

During the short drive home, Ann's efforts to remain calm failed and her feelings of dread increased. She pulled her car into the garage, shut the door behind her, and rushed into the house without even bothering to get the mail out of the box. She poured a glass of wine and drained half of it in one long swallow before phoning Denise Riley to inform her about the Web site. Unlike Ann's, Denise's first reaction was one of anger rather than fear.

"Those bastards!" Denise exclaimed. "Why would they do such a horrible thing? I'm sorry now that I didn't break that damn girl's leg."

"Be extra vigilant about safety," Ann urged, leaning against the kitchen counter as she spoke on the phone. "And tell everyone else connected with the clinic to do the same. This may be nothing, but we have to realize that there are zealots out there, and this could push one of them over the edge." Memories of the abortion clinic riot came rushing back, making her feel nauseous.

"I'm not afraid of those people," Denise said

boldly. "To acknowledge that they frighten me would be admitting they have some power over me, and they don't. They deserve nothing but contempt."

"I agree, but please be careful anyway," Ann repeated. One of her cats jumped up on the counter, and she deftly lifted him off with one hand. "Some of Tremaine's followers might be even nuttier than we think."

"Thanks for the warning," Denise said, "but don't worry. Nothing's going to happen. I think the Lambs are just that—all bluster and no bite."

"I hope you're right," Ann said fervently. "Sorry to have been the bearer of bad tidings. I hope this doesn't ruin your weekend."

"No chance of that," Denise said cheerfully. "My daughter and I are leaving for Chicago early tomorrow morning to do some serious shopping."

"Good for you," Ann said, wishing she possessed half her client's courage. "I'll talk to you next week."

"Okay. And thanks again for all you're doing for us, Ann. I really appreciate it."

After Ann disconnected from the call to Denise, she finished her glass of wine and poured another. She felt as though the walls were closing in on her. She had to talk to someone or she was going to crack up. She snatched up the phone again and dialed Georgia's number.

After five rings, her friend's answering machine picked up. "Hi, it's me," Ann said into the phone when she got the signal to record a message. "Call me the minute you get home. I don't care how late it is. It's urgent. Talk to you later. Bye."

Ann replaced the receiver and rubbed her hands over her cheeks. Her skin felt cold and clammy. She tried momentarily closing her eyes but she couldn't shake the image of her photo encased in a bull's-eye.

"Oh, God," Ann said aloud. She was starting to feel worse, if that was possible. She really needed to talk to someone. She recalled that Georgia's boyfriend belonged to one of the city's exclusive country clubs. Maybe they were having dinner there. If so, Ann might be able to track them down. Now if she could just remember which club it was.

Bishop's Bay? No, that didn't sound right. Maple Bluff? No. Blackhawk? That seemed to ring a bell. Georgia and Bill lived on the west side. It would make sense that Bill would belong to Blackhawk Country Club. Ann would call there and have them paged. She got out her phone book to look up the number. As she turned to the business pages, the doorbell rang.

"Oh, no!" Ann said under her breath. One of the Lambs had come for her already. She looked around her in desperation. Should she hide? Should she call 911? The doorbell pealed again. Cold with fear, she set the phone book down on the counter and tiptoed to the front door. As the bell rang a third time, she peeked through the peephole to see what sort of monster lay in wait.

She gasped. It was Ken. She opened the door, he stepped inside, and she fell into his arms.

"I was so worried," Ken said, hugging her tightly. "That Web site is despicable. We've got to do something about it right away. Did you talk to Denise?"

Ann nodded.

"What was her reaction?"

"Quite nonchalant," Ann said, taking a slight step back but still maintaining physical contact with him.

Ken looked into her eyes. "And how are you doing?"

"I'm not as brave as Denise, I'm afraid." Ann's chin began to tremble. *Oh, no,* she thought. *I don't want to make a fool out of myself by crying in front of him.*

She blinked hard, trying to think of something to say, but before she could form any words, Ken suddenly pulled her into his arms and kissed her passionately.

Ann's emotions switched from fear to surprise to exultation in a matter of seconds. She put her arms around Ken's neck and pressed herself against him, feeling him hard against her. His hands caressed her back, then moved up to her breasts. Ann moaned and ran her fingers through his hair.

They stood in Ann's living room for several minutes, pawing each other like randy teenagers, before Ken broke their clinch. Taking Ann's hand gently in his own, he moved toward the stairway, at the top of which was Ann's bedroom. She didn't hesitate for a moment. She merely reveled in the moment and let him lead her up the stairs.

The light in the hallway provided enough illumination that there was no need to turn on a light in the

FINAL JUSTICE

bedroom. As Ken again took her in his arms, Ann found herself wondering vaguely whether he had ever been in her bedroom before. All of Mishler and Stettler's attorneys did a fair amount of socializing with each other, so Ken, Patsy, and the girls had been to her house on any number of occasions, and he probably had been in the room at some point, if only to deposit coats on the bed before returning downstairs to the party.

Then Ann recalled that the last time she had been with a man in this room was with Richard—the night before he had abruptly left town. She had often despaired of ever again being with any man. And in spite of the amount of time she'd spent recently thinking about Ken, this moment seemed more fantasy than reality.

Ken pulled off her suit jacket and tossed it on a chair, then unbuttoned her blouse. He kissed her again and the rest of their clothing seemed to melt away as if by magic. The next thing Ann knew, Ken was sliding into bed and pulling her in next to him.

Ken caressed Ann's breasts with his hands, then leaned down and flicked his tongue over her nipples. He suckled one, then the other, lightly at first and then a bit more intensely until Ann was moaning with pleasure. As Ken's mouth continued lavishing attention on her breasts, he reached down and began stroking her lightly with one finger. By the time he slid the finger inside her, Ann was aching with desire.

"Now!" she said urgently, pulling him on top of her.

Ken happily obliged and in a moment he was inside her.

Ann wrapped her legs around him, ran her fingers up and down his back, murmured his name. She had almost forgotten the sheer carnal pleasure of the sexual act. Now she was reminded how glorious it could be, especially with a lover as skilled and ardent as Ken.

Ann had always thought Richard was pretty good in bed, but he couldn't hold a candle to Ken. She had never had a more sensual bed partner. Several times he brought both of them to the brink of orgasm but then slowed down just long enough so that neither's climax was imminent. Then when he again increased his movements the sensations were even stronger. Finally neither of them could hold back any longer and they came simultaneously and vocally, calling out each other's names.

Few words were spoken. It wasn't until they lay spent in each other's arms that Ken traced his index finger down Ann's nose and asked, "Do you have any idea how long I've been wanting to do that?"

Ann looked at him in astonishment. "No. How long?"

"Probably since before you got engaged to Richard."

"Are you serious? Why didn't you say something?"

Ken laughed. "What was I supposed to say? I didn't exactly have any standing. After all, you were marrying Mr. Right and I was already married. But I have to tell you, one of the first thoughts that went through my mind the day Patsy walked out was, 'Maybe now I'll have a chance with Ann.' "

"You're kidding!"

"Not at all. I just wasn't sure if there was any chance my feelings might be reciprocated."

"Oh, they were reciprocated, all right," Ann assured him.

"I didn't quite know how to approach you," Ken admitted. "I valued your friendship so much and I didn't want to jeopardize it by making a stupid pass at you. But this afternoon when I got back to the office and saw your note and looked at that damn Web site, I just flipped." He leaned close and kissed her.

"Thank God for that," Ann said, running her hand over the light growth of hair on his chest. "I'd been thinking about the possibility of you and me together ever since your split with Patsy, but it never occurred to me that you might be having similar feelings."

"Well, what do you know?" Ken said, shaking his head in amazement. "I guess we were both on the same wavelength all along but didn't know it. Think of all the time we wasted." He leaned over and kissed her again. Just then the phone rang.

"You'd better get it," Ken said. "It might be about the Web site. I called the police before I left the office and filled them in on it. Maybe they have some suggestions on what to do."

Ann nodded and, leaning over him, picked up the phone next to the bed. "Hello?" she said rather dreamily.

"I called the second I got your message," a distraught Georgia said. "What's wrong?"

Ann fought back the impulse to laugh. "Nothing's wrong," she told her friend. "False alarm."

"What do you mean, nothing's wrong?" Georgia demanded. "You sounded positively manic when you called before."

"I was overreacting to something. Just forget it."

"I will not forget it!" Georgia said. "Do you want me to come over?"

"No!" Ann sat up in bed, pushing Ken away from her. "Don't come over!"

Ken pursed his lips, trying hard not to laugh.

"Look," Georgia said in a calmer tone. "It's perfectly normal for you to be feeling anxious today. I kept intending to call you but I had an absolute day from hell. I was worried about you, though. I kept wondering how you were holding up."

"How I was holding up?" Ann repeated, wondering if there was some way her friend could have found out about the Lambs' Web site. "What do you mean? Why wouldn't I be holding up?"

"You *have* lost your mind!" Georgia exclaimed. "Don't you know what day this is? It was one year ago today that Richard took off on you."

Ann's mouth fell open, and there was a stunned silence. With all the turmoil in her life of late she had completely forgotten that this was the one-year anniversary of her being dumped.

"Hello?" Georgia called. "Are you still there?"

"I'm still here," Ann said. "And I haven't lost my mind, and I'm no crazier today than I ever was." She paused a moment to clear her throat. "I'm sorry I sounded goofy when I called you earlier. I was just having a very bad moment and thankfully it has passed. The significance of today's date doesn't particularly bother me. In fact, I think I'm coping pretty well, all things considered." She reached over and tickled Ken's chest. "So you go back to whatever it was you were doing, because I have everything under control here."

"Well . . ." Georgia hesitated. "If you're sure you're okay."

"I'm positive," Ann assured her. "I appreciate your concern, and I'll call you soon."

"All right," Georgia said. "Take care of yourself. You still sound a little nuts to me."

Ann hung up the phone. "That was Georgia," she explained to Ken. "I kind of freaked out over the Web site and needed to talk to someone, so I called her earlier and left a cry for help. She was going to race right over and rescue me but I talked her out of it."

Ken leaned over and took her in his arms again. "You should have told her you were in good hands," he said.

Ann chuckled. "I should have. She would have died. No, I take that back. Actually she would have congratulated me. She's been worried that I've turned into a hermit. She's been after me for months to start seeing men."

"She can stop worrying now," Ken said, gazing approvingly at her body. "You are both seeing a man and being seen by him."

They kissed some more. After a time Ken turned more serious. "I'm still very concerned about that Web site. It's nothing to joke about. Those people could mean business."

"I know that," Ann replied, shivering a bit. She snuggled closer to Ken.

"I want you to be really careful. I'm going to do everything I can to get yours and Denise's pictures off that site. And first thing tomorrow I'm going to start going through the transcript from the criminal trial to see if we can't figure out what went wrong."

"Normally this is where I'd say that I'm a big girl and I can take care of myself, but you know what? I would love to have you look out for me."

"I was hoping you'd say that." Ken moved so that he was again on top of her, and she pulled him down, eager to forget about everything except the pleasures of the moment.

A bit later he said, "When you were talking to Georgia, you said something about not being any crazier than usual in spite of what day it was. What's so significant about today's date?"

"Well . . ." Ann hesitated a moment, then said, "It was one year ago today that Richard left me."

"Oh." Ken said. "Happy anniversary. If I'd known, I would've baked a cake."

Ann laughed and snuggled up to him, secure in the knowledge that she would remember *this* evening for a long time to come.

CHAPTER 16

It was after eleven o'clock when Ken reluctantly said his good-byes to Ann.

"Patsy took the girls to a bridal shower in Milwaukee," Ken explained as he finished dressing. "They said they probably wouldn't be back until midnight, but I'd like to be home before they arrive."

"I understand." Ann had slipped into a white cotton nightgown.

"Be sure to keep all your doors and windows locked," Ken said sternly as they walked downstairs. "The threat posed by that Web site is no laughing matter. If anything weird happens, call the police right away and stay put until they get here."

"I'll be fine," Ann assured him.

Ken leaned down and kissed her. "Thank you for an absolutely incredible evening."

"You're very welcome," Ann said. "If you play your cards right, I might invite you back for an encore. Now go," she said, giving him a little shove. "I'd hate to have the girls beat you home."

As she watched Ken's black Lincoln Navigator pull

out of the driveway, Ann thought back on all that had happened in the last few hours. When she got up that morning she'd certainly had no inkling of what the day held in store. She went back upstairs and, thoroughly exhausted by the day's—and night's—activities, quickly fell asleep.

Ann awoke abruptly at four-thirty, her heart pounding. What had roused her from her slumber? Could she have heard something outside? Shivering slightly, she sat up and in the dim moonlight could see both cats napping peacefully at various spots on the bed. If there had been a noise, the animals surely would have stirred.

It was probably a case of sensory overload, Ann thought to herself as she lay back down and tried to get comfortable again. Too many things happening at the same time. It was no wonder she was jumpy.

Try as she might, Ann was never able to fall back to sleep. At six-thirty, in frustration, she reached for the phone and dialed Georgia's number. After four rings, her friend's sleepy voice came on the line. "Hello?"

"It's me. We need to talk right away," Ann said urgently. "Can you meet me at the farmer's market?"

"What time is it?" Georgia asked groggily.

"Six-thirty," Ann replied. "Can you meet me in an hour?"

"You want me to get up at six-thirty on a Saturday?" Georgia asked, sounding more alert now. "You *are* nuts."

"Meet me at the foot of the State Street steps in an

hour, and I'll explain everything. I promise it'll be worth your while."

"It'd better be or I'm hauling you directly to the loony bin," Georgia groused.

Seventy minutes later the women were sipping coffee and nibbling on pastry as they mingled with the early-morning shoppers making their way around the capitol square, where, each Saturday from May through October, area growers offered various food items, fresh produce, and bedding plants for sale.

"Oh, my God!" Georgia exclaimed after Ann had filled her in on the previous evening's events. "You mean you were actually in bed with him when I called? No wonder you sounded strange. I've got to hand it to you: You sure do know how to take your mind off the one-year anniversary of Richard's leaving town."

"Do you think this was a mistake?" Ann asked anxiously.

"You have great sex with an attractive, intelligent, legally separated man and you ask if it was a mistake?" Georgia finished the last bite of her pastry and licked the frosting off her fingers. "Earth to Ann. Read my lips: It was not a mistake. It was the answer to my prayers. And it should have been the answer to yours, too."

"Maybe it was a dumb move," Ann said, ignoring what her friend had just said. She took a sip of coffee. "It's probably just a rebound relationship for him."

"Stop being such a pessimist," Georgia scolded. "The guy is obviously crazy about you, and he's concerned for your safety as well. That's so sweet."

"It is sweet," Ann agreed. "But what if his kids hate me? What if he reconciles with Patsy?"

"What if the world is overtaken by Martians?" Georgia teased. "Don't worry. Everything is going to work out okay."

"I hope so," Ann said, tossing her empty coffee cup into a trash container. "I don't mean to be difficult. I'm just tired and overwrought. I don't know if I should jump for joy or break down and cry."

"Don't do either of those things," Georgia said, patting her friend on the arm. "Just take it one day at a time for a while. Who knows, this might turn out to be the best thing that ever happened to you. And if it doesn't work out, well, at least you tried."

"I suppose you're right," Ann said a bit hesitantly.

"Of course I'm right," Georgia said, looking back over her shoulder to where they had bought their snacks. "Now that we have that situation under control, let's go back and get another pastry. Talking about sex always gives me an appetite."

CHAPTER 17

The nasty reality of the Lambs' Web site hit home for Ann as soon as she arrived at work on Monday.

"Any important messages?" she asked Kari as she breezed by her secretary's desk on the way toward her office.

"I wouldn't call them important," Kari replied, "but oh, my, yes, there certainly are a lot of messages."

Ann stopped and frowned. "What do you mean?"

"You had over a dozen voice mail messages," Kari said. "All in response to that Internet posting."

Ann's face fell. "You're kidding! What did they say?"

"I put them all on your desk. You can see for yourself."

Ann walked into her office. After dropping her briefcase on her chair, she picked up the messages and thumbed through them. "They really said these things?" she asked, coming back out to Kari's desk.

Kari nodded. "I'm afraid so."

Ann swallowed hard and read some of the messages aloud. " 'I hope you rot in hell, you worthless bitch.' 'May God condemn your soul for all eternity.' 'While I do not believe in abortion, it's a shame your mother didn't abort you. The world would have been better off without another baby murderer in it.' "

"That's my personal favorite," Kari commented.

Ann tossed the message slips down on her secretary's desk. "None of them left their names?"

"No, but what would you have done if they had?" Kari asked, rolling her eyes. "Called them up and invited them over for brunch?"

"I suppose not," Ann agreed. "Did you save the actual voice mail messages?"

"Sorry, but I already erased them all."

"Shit!" Ann exclaimed. "I would've liked to listen to them myself."

"What for?" Kari asked.

"To hear these people's tone, I guess. To judge if they sounded serious or not."

"They sounded serious, all right," Kari replied. "Believe me, I did you a big favor by erasing them. The words look bad enough in print. They sounded really vitriolic when spoken."

Ann sighed. "I'd better call Denise Riley and see if she got a dose of the same medicine."

"What's the matter with those people?" Kari asked. "I thought they were supposed to be so religious."

"Don't forget, the Inquisition was spawned by religious people, too," Ann said.

It was midmorning before Ann saw Ken. He had called her on Sunday during a break in his younger daughter's swim meet just to chat for a few moments and to find out if any of Tremaine's followers had been in contact. When she'd replied that all was quiet, Ken had been greatly relieved.

"I've been so worried about you," he had said, his obvious concern coming through loud and clear over the phone line.

"I think most of the Lambs are pacifists at heart," Ann had said.

"Most of them probably are," Ken agreed, "but it only takes one nut willing to be a martyr. I've been thinking about you constantly since the moment I left your house. I wish I could come over and hold you right now."

"Your girls need you today," Ann said. "I'm doing okay."

"Well, I promise that my first order of business on Monday is going to be to get an order requiring the Lambs to remove all mention of you and Denise from that Web site," Ken had said firmly.

When she first saw Ken standing in her doorway on Monday morning, Ann's face lit up. "Hi," she said. "How was your weekend?"

"Fine," Ken said, stepping inside the office and closing the door behind him. "How was yours?"

"Luckily, it was rather quiet," Ann replied. "It gave me a chance to rest up from all the activity on Friday."

Ken put his arms around her. "Yeah, I needed some extra rest, too," he said. "I guess I must be a little out of practice."

"Out of practice?" Ann laughed. "I thought you

must have come directly from a Kama Sutra convention."

"In addition to being very beautiful, you are very good for my ego," he said, kissing her. Then he said, "I hear you got some rotten messages."

Ann nodded and showed him the message slips Kari had transcribed. "Maybe this will be the beginning and the end of it," she said hopefully, sitting down in her chair.

"I doubt that," Ken said. He sat down in one of the chairs in front of Ann's desk and rifled quickly through the message slips. "Pretty classy. These people certainly have a way with words, don't they?"

Ann shrugged. "I guess when you feel strongly about something, proper grammar isn't all that important. I called Planned Parenthood this morning. Denise Riley wasn't in yet, but the receptionist confirmed that they'd received an equal number of messages with similar content."

Ken nodded. "I've already filed a motion seeking a temporary injunction stopping the Web site."

"Thank you," Ann said.

"You're welcome. Now, on a slightly different note, I am happy to report that after putting you off with all sorts of lame excuses last night I finally sat down with the transcript of the Robinson criminal trial."

"That's great. Did anything jump out at you?"

"As a matter of fact, it did. I agree with you completely that Ted Lawrence did a piss-poor job of jury selection," Ken replied.

Ann nodded eagerly. "I was hoping you'd say that."

"In a case as controversial as Bill Robinson's, jury selection is crucial," Ken went on. "And from what I see, Ted barely touched the surface of the gay-prejudice issue. As you pointed out, several people who ended up on the jury expressed doubt that they could believe a gay man was the victim of an unprovoked assault. Ted made only the most halfhearted attempt to rehabilitate them and didn't ask the judge to strike any of them for cause. It's quite inexplicable for an experienced prosecutor to have done such a poor job. Have you made any headway talking to any of the people who served on the jury?"

Ann shook her head. "No, they all keep brushing me off or just plain refuse to talk. So you think it's worth trying to pursue that angle?" she asked eagerly.

"Definitely," Ken replied. "I just can't figure out what was wrong with Ted. The Ted Lawrence I knew could do a better job of voir dire in his sleep than what is reflected in that transcript."

Ann leaned across the desk and took Ken's hand. "I think we might be onto something here."

As Ken squeezed her hand, Ann thought for a moment, then said, "I know you made the suggestion early on and I resisted, but now I'm thinking that this might be a good time for me to have a little chat with good old Ted Lawrence."

The discussion with Ken left Ann feeling reenergized about the Robinson case. As soon as he left her office, she picked up the phone and called the Jasper County Courthouse.

Ann was accustomed to dealing with large bureaucracies and expected that she would have to leave her name and phone number with some underling and then sit back and wait for the district attorney to return her call. To her surprise, within twenty seconds of Ann's identifying herself to the pleasant-sounding woman who answered the phone, Lawrence came on the line.

"Ms. Monroe, this is Ted Lawrence. What can I do for you?" The prosecutor's voice sounded low and affable.

"I'm representing Bill Robinson in a civil suit against the two young men who attacked him last fall," Ann replied.

"So I've heard," Lawrence said. His tone of voice seemed to have changed somewhat. Ann couldn't quite tell if she detected amusement or wariness.

"I've been reading the transcript from the criminal trial," Ann went on. "I was hoping that if I could figure out why the jury chose not to believe Bill's story, it might give me some ideas on how to best present my case."

"And has the transcript helped you in that regard?" Lawrence asked.

"Unfortunately it hasn't," Ann said, making sure she sounded chagrined. "That's why I'm calling. I was wondering if you'd be willing to meet with me to discuss the case in a little more depth."

There was a pause. "I guess I'm at a bit of a loss," Lawrence finally said. "Since there are few similarit-

FINAL JUSTICE

ies between criminal and civil cases, I'm not sure what would be gained by our meeting."

"I'm hoping that getting your take on the whole trial might help me get some things straight in my mind," Ann plunged on, injecting a tone of helplessness into her voice. "To tell you the truth, I feel as though I'm in a bit over my head with this one. It would mean so much if I could talk to you, just for a few minutes."

"Well . . ." Lawrence hesitated a moment, but then his ego took over. "I suppose I could spare a few minutes for a colleague in need."

"Oh, thank you so much," Ann gushed.

"When did you have in mind?"

"Anytime that's convenient for you," Ann said. "It just so happens that the deposition I had scheduled for this afternoon was just canceled. I know it's short notice, but—"

Lawrence rose to the bait. "I could see you around three o'clock today. Would that suit you?"

"That would suit me just fine," Ann replied.

"All right. I'll look forward to seeing you then."

"Thank you. I can't tell you how much I appreciate this."

"The pleasure is all mine, Ms. Monroe," Lawrence said jovially. "See you soon."

Ann dropped the phone back into its cradle. "I'm not so sure that our meeting is going to be all that pleasurable for you, Ted," she said aloud. "But I hope it will help me figure out what the hell really happened at that trial."

* * *

Because her last visit to Mount Pleasant had ended in the confrontation with the two young men, Ann was on her guard during the entire drive. She constantly checked her rearview mirror to make sure she was not being followed. Once she reached the city limits, she scanned parked cars and scrutinized pedestrians to see if she could spot anyone who looked menacing. In the courthouse parking lot she virtually ran from the car up the steps of the building. Not until she was actually inside did her heart stop pounding and her breathing return to normal.

In the past dozen years Ann had seen Ted Lawrence on television numerous times, so she was aware that he was a big man. Although it was often said that TV cameras made people look larger than they actually were, in the flesh the gray-haired Jasper County district attorney looked even more commanding than he did on the small screen.

Lawrence stood about six-foot-three and must have weighed well over 250 pounds. His handshake was so firm that Ann felt as if her right hand had been caught in a vise. Although he was no longer the raging lion he'd been in his youth, there was no doubt that Ted Lawrence was still a force to be reckoned with.

"Please have a seat, Ms. Monroe," Lawrence said after the pleasantries of their introduction.

Ann sat down in one of the chairs in front of Lawrence's desk and briefly glanced around her. The office furnishings were pretty much standard government-issue: a wooden desk too old to be stylish and too new to be considered an antique; several metal file cabinets; a host of bookshelves. On the wall behind Lawrence's desk hung a sign that said, AGE AND TREACHERY WILL ALWAYS OVERCOME YOUTH AND SKILL. Now that Lawrence was approaching sixty, Ann wondered if that had become his personal credo.

"Thank you again for seeing me," Ann said. She gestured at his desk, which was piled high with papers. "I can imagine how busy you are, so I'll try not to take up too much of your time."

Lawrence leaned back in his black leather chair and surveyed his visitor with a detached expression. "I am always pleased to help out a young colleague," he said in his measured, low voice. "I know it's hard to imagine such a thing, but I used to be young myself." He paused a moment, then winked at Ann and added, "However, I was never as attractive as you."

Ann forced herself to smile and ignore the blatant sexism in his remark. "I was wondering if you could give me your gut reaction as to why the jury didn't believe Bill Robinson's story. From talking to him and from reading the trial transcript, he sounds so sincere."

Lawrence drummed his fingers over his chin. "How can you ever really tell what might have influenced a jury's thinking? You've handled some jury trials, haven't you?" he asked pleasantly.

"A few." Ann tried hard not to react to Lawrence's condescending manner. She had tried dozens of cases to juries. She was quite sure Lawrence was well aware of her background and her reputation, which meant each of them was blowing smoke at the other. *Let the best posturer win*, Ann thought.

"Then you understand how unpredictable jurors can be," Lawrence went on. "Yes, Bill was very sincere. He was a damn good witness, and I believed every word he said. Why didn't the jury believe him?" He threw up his hands in a gesture of helplessness. "I don't think we'll ever know the answer to that question."

"Did the jury appear to be sympathetic as your case was going in?" Ann asked.

"I'd say so. At least I didn't notice any of them glaring at me or nodding off, both of which have happened on occasion in other cases." Lawrence gave a little chuckle.

"How did Jenkins and English come across as witnesses? I've taken both their depositions, and their story just seems to have holes bigger than Mount Saint Helens."

"They weren't the world's greatest witnesses, but they are fairly clean-cut young men and, more important, they're local kids."

"You mean the fact that Bill Robinson didn't grow up here in Jasper County might have influenced the jury?"

"Anything is possible."

"Am I correct that neither Jenkins nor English had any prior criminal record?" Ann asked.

"That's right."

"Neither one had any prior charges whatsoever?"

"No."

"Was there any evidence that they might have tried to harass any other gay people before they attacked Bill?"

"I take it you're referring to Charles Ryder," Lawrence said without batting an eye.

Ann nodded. "Why didn't you call Chuck as a witness?"

"Because unlike our two young defendants, Mr. Ryder *does* have a criminal record," Lawrence answered smugly.

"He does?" Ann asked, genuinely surprised. "What were the charges?"

"Disorderly conduct, lewd and lascivious behavior, and solicitation of prostitution, to name a few. In terms of impeachability, Mr. Ryder was a lawyer's nightmare."

"Did you consider making a motion *in limine* asking the judge to exclude details about his past record, or perhaps reading a prepared statement to the jury explaining it?"

"Of course I considered those things," Lawrence replied indignantly. "I have been the district attorney here for a quarter century. I consider all options in every one of my cases. After giving the matter due consideration, however, I decided to forgo Mr. Ryder's testimony. Jasper County is a rather conservative place. I didn't want to turn the trial into a symposium on gay rights."

"But the whole issue of Bill Robinson's being gay was central to the case, wasn't it?" Ann asked. "After all, you were trying to prove that what Jenkins and English did amounted to a hate crime. The jury had already heard evidence about Bill's sexual orientation. What difference could it have possibly made for the jury to also hear that the defendants previously tried to assault another gay man?"

"In view of Mr. Ryder's less-than-squeaky-clean record, I felt it could prejudice the jury against Bill."

"From what I can tell by reading the transcript, the jury selection process seems to have moved along fairly quickly."

Lawrence shrugged. "I don't really recall."

"Do you have any recollection why you struck the jurors you did?"

Lawrence scratched his head. "I think one woman was a shirttail relation to one of the defendants. I believe one man said he'd known the English family for years and he knew Brad English was a good kid who wouldn't have done anything bad. Other than those two, I don't specifically remember what I thought about any of the others. You have to realize that I've tried quite a few cases since this one."

"I understand," Ann said, trying to sound sympathetic. "Did you talk to any of the jurors after the verdict came in to find out why they acquitted both defendants on all charges?"

Lawrence shook his head. "No. I rarely talk to jurors after a trial is over."

"Why not?" Ann asked with surprise. "I almost always do. It helps me understand what I did right and what I could improve on another time."

"I've never seen much point in it," Lawrence explained. "If they vote to convict, I'm happy. If they vote to acquit, double jeopardy bars me from retrying the defendant. Either way, that particular case is over and done and I move on to the next one. Why bother talking to anyone about a dead issue?"

"I guess I'd just be curious to find out if their view of the evidence coincided with mine."

"You know what they say about curiosity, Ms. Monroe," Lawrence said snidely. "It killed the cat."

"All I know is that Jenkins and English almost killed Bill Robinson," Ann said, glaring at him. "And if I had tried the criminal case, I would have wanted to know why the jury let them go unpunished."

"But you weren't trying that case, now, were you?" Lawrence asked, his eyes dark. "That case is over and done with, and even though you or I may not like the result, there's not a damn thing we can do about it."

"There may not be anything I can do to change the outcome of the criminal case," Ann agreed, her dislike for the big man growing by the minute, "but I am determined to learn everything I can about it to avoid having a repeat of the same lousy result in the civil suit."

"I wish you a lot of luck, Ms. Monroe," Lawrence said. "I'm afraid you're going to need it."

"So overall you were happy with the jury you got?" Ann asked.

"Yes."

"You don't feel they acquitted strictly because of prejudice against gays?"

"Of course not," Lawrence said in a huff.

"But didn't several of the people who served on the jury express doubt that they could be fair to a gay person?" Ann pressed on.

"I really don't recall," Lawrence answered.

"For instance, Claude Furseth, who ended up serving as the jury foreman, expressed downright disdain for gays, did he not?"

"I don't recall," Lawrence said again, beginning to sound a bit like a recalcitrant witness himself.

"I believe his exact words were, 'I don't understand what makes those people tick.'"

"I wouldn't call that disdain. That was merely an opinion. Frankly, Ms. Monroe, I don't remember any of this," Lawrence said, standing up as a signal that the meeting was at an end. "But if a prospective juror said something like that, I'm sure I asked appropriate follow-up questions to see if he could be rehabilitated."

"Oh, you asked some follow-up questions," Ann agreed. "Although in my opinion they were very perfunctory."

"I hate to rush you," Lawrence said, quickly crossing the room and opening the door for her. "But I'm afraid I'm due in court."

Ann slowly got up from her chair and took her time walking over to the door, stretching out Lawrence's obvious unease. "Thanks for your time," she said sweetly. "It's been very enlightening."

As Ann moved toward the door, Lawrence suddenly stepped in front of it, blocking her exit.

"I was trying cases while you were still in diapers," he said in a growl. "I handled the Robinson case in an appropriate and professional manner, just as I handle all my cases. I do not take kindly to

Monday-morning quarterbacks questioning my judgment."

"I wasn't questioning your judgment," Ann said, trying hard not to show that she was intimidated by Lawrence's threatening behavior. "I was merely trying to get a better understanding of what happened at the trial."

"You said you've read the transcript. Well, my work speaks for itself. I will not have my abilities or my ethics disparaged. Is that clear?" Lawrence took a step toward Ann and glared down at her.

Although her first reaction was to retreat, Ann quickly moved forward and pushed right past the big man. "I, too, have another appointment," she said, yanking the door open. "Good day." She raced down the hall before Lawrence had a chance to say another word.

Ann rushed back to the car, got in, and immediately locked the doors behind her. Her questions about the composition of the jury had certainly touched a nerve. She had a feeling that she and Ken were on the right track, and as she pulled the car out of the parking lot and headed out of town she had an even stronger feeling that there was some sort of evil force at work in Mount Pleasant. She sincerely hoped she would not need to make a return trip there anytime soon.

CHAPTER 18

Judge Bies heard Ken's motion to order the Lambs to remove any references to Ann and Denise Riley from their Web site the next morning.

The judge had refused Ken's request to issue an ex parte temporary restraining order prior to the hearing, saying there had not been an adequate showing that immediate action was required. The judge had, however, squeezed the hearing into her busy schedule.

Thomas Ravenswood and his client both seemed to be in good humor as Ken, Ann, and Denise walked into the courtroom. "Good morning, ladies," Ravenswood said cheerfully when he saw them arrive. Inclining his head toward Ken, Ravenswood added, "I see you've brought some reinforcements with you today."

Ann gritted her teeth and walked up to the counsel table with no comment, while Denise Riley glared openly at the Lambs' attorney.

As they were taking their seats, Ann heard Tremaine say to his lawyer in a stage whisper, "I guess the little ladies must have decided that if they want to run with the big dogs they'd better have some testosterone on their side, right, Tom?"

Ravenswood laughed heartily at his client's joke.

Ann leaned over to Ken and said in a low voice, "I swear I'm going to kill them both before this case is over."

Judge Bies called the case and the attorneys made their appearances for the record. Nodding to Ken, the judge said, "Mr. Devlin, please proceed."

"Thank you, Your Honor," Ken said, getting to his feet. "As you are aware, there is currently a lawsuit pending between Planned Parenthood and a local religious group calling itself the Lambs of God. The court previously issued a temporary injunction regulating the Lambs' picketing activities outside the Planned Parenthood clinic." He turned slightly to glance at Ravenswood and Tremaine, then continued.

"The motion before the court today involves highly disturbing material that was posted on a Web site controlled by the Lambs. Sometime last week, photographs of Denise Riley, Planned Parenthood's director, and Ann Monroe, the clinic's attorney, were placed on this Web site. As the court will note from the materials attached to our motion, superimposed over the photos of both Ms. Monroe and Ms. Riley are bull's-eyes, creating the impression that the Lambs are targeting Ms. Monroe and Ms. Riley for harassment and/or violence. The Web site also lists a great deal of personal information about Ms. Riley and Ms. Monroe, including their home addresses and telephone numbers and the makes and license plate numbers of their automobiles. This information would certainly help a person wishing to harm Ms. Monroe or Ms. Riley to find them."

Ken paused a moment and looked at the judge. She appeared to be listening to his remarks with interest.

"Since this material has been posted on the Lambs' Web site, both Ms. Riley and Ms. Monroe have already been subjected to harassment. They have each received numerous phone calls and anonymous letters, all of which were profane in content and some of which contained threats of violence. The posting of personal information about Ms. Monroe and Ms. Riley, in conjunction with displaying their photos in the form of bull's-eyes, serves no legitimate purpose. Instead, it merely invites continued harassment and perhaps violence against Ms. Riley and Ms. Monroe. I would now like to call Ms. Riley to the stand."

After Denise was sworn in, Ken asked her to explain the impact of the Web site posting. "Since the weekend I have received an average of ten to fifteen phone messages a day," she said.

"At the clinic or at your home?" Ken asked.

"Both, although there have been more at the clinic."

"What is the content of these messages?"

"The majority of callers accuse me of being a baby killer or a murderer. Some of them call me other names and some use profanity. For example, when I got to the clinic this morning one of the callers had referred to me as a 'fucking bitch.'"

"Ms. Riley, are the Lambs of God still picketing the clinic on a regular basis?"

"Yes, there are at least thirty of them there every day the entire time we are open for business."

"Since the personal material about you was posted on the Web site, have you noticed any difference in the way you are treated by the picketers?"

"I certainly have," Denise responded. "Several of them have become much more vocal and antagonistic toward me."

"Can you give us an example of what you mean?" Ken asked.

"When these particular picketers see me drive into the clinic's parking lot, they walk over toward my car and make vulgar and threatening remarks."

"What type of threatening remarks?"

"Yesterday one of them said that since I obviously don't value the life of the unborn, maybe my life wasn't worth anything either."

"And you took that comment as a threat?"

"I certainly did," Denise replied.

"Have you received any mail as a result of the Web site posting?"

"Yes, I have received manila envelopes containing photos of aborted fetuses, both at the clinic and at home. Each of those mailings contained a notation referring to me either as a murderer, a worthless bitch, or a godless Communist."

"Thank you, Ms. Riley," Ken said. "I have no further questions."

Ravenswood got to his feet. "Ms. Riley, you indicated that you have received a number of phone messages in the last week."

"That's correct."

"Were these messages all received during hours the clinic was not open and during times you were not at your home?"

"Yes."

"So you have never actually spoken to any of the callers?"

"No," Denise replied. "Apparently they are too gutless to speak to me personally, so they get their kicks leaving messages."

"I move that the last remark be stricken as nonresponsive," Ravenswood said to the judge.

"Sustained," Judge Bies said.

"You have not received any actual threats, now, have you, Ms. Riley?" Ravenswood asked.

"I'd say that being told my life was worthless was a threat," Denise shot back.

"That might be your interpretation, Ms. Riley," Ravenswood replied with a snarl, "but isn't it true that no one has made an overt threat to you?"

"No, but—"

"Thank you, Ms. Riley," Ravenswood cut her off. "No further questions."

Ken then called Ann as a witness to corroborate Denise's experiences. "I, too, have been receiving about ten phone messages a day, both at the office and at home," Ann explained. "And I have also received mailings similar to the ones Ms. Riley described."

"Has this activity caused you any distress?" Ken asked.

"Very much so," Ann answered truthfully. "I am Planned Parenthood's lawyer. I am their advocate. It is quite frightening to think that people apparently believe that I personally participate in abortions—which, I would like to point out, have never been performed at the clinic."

Ravenswood was even more condescending toward Ann than he'd been toward Denise. "Ms. Monroe, as a lawyer, you are the public face for your client, are you not?"

"I suppose you could say that," Ann agreed.

"So why should you be so upset when people who disagree with your client contact you and say so?"

"I wouldn't be at all upset if those people would have the courtesy—and the courage—to contact me directly," Ann said. "But their hiding behind phone calls and letters makes me very nervous. I can't help but wonder if the next step is going to be for them to hide behind a tree and jump out and harm me in some way."

"Do you really believe that you are in physical danger?" Ravenswood virtually sneered at her.

"I do," Ann said, nodding emphatically. "I was injured a couple of years ago when protestors, some of whom were affiliated with the Lambs of God, were picketing a local abortion clinic. I truly believe that so long as my picture and Ms. Riley's are out there on that Web site like some sort of hunted prey, Denise Riley and I are in very real danger of becoming prey to someone with a lust for attention or martyrdom."

"No further questions," Ravenswood said in a snarl.

Judge Bies addressed Ken. "Do you have any further witnesses?"

"No, Your Honor," Ken said.

The judge nodded. "Then Mr. Ravenswood, why don't you tell us why your client should not be ordered to remove the materials that have been referred to from their Web site."

"It is our position that any and all materials posted on the Web site are constitutionally protected free speech," Ravenswood said. "To further explain our position, I would like to call Rev. Charles Tremaine to the stand."

As usual, the reverend loudly averred to tell the whole truth and nothing but.

"Reverend Tremaine, are you familiar with the Web site that has been referred to by Mr. Devlin and the two earlier witnesses?" Ravenswood asked.

"Yes, sir, I am," Tremaine answered, smiling broadly.

What was he so damn cheerful about? Ann wondered.

"Did you have any role in posting the information about Ms. Monroe and Ms. Riley on the site?"

Tremaine chuckled. "No, I did not. I don't personally know much about computers." He stopped and winked at the judge. "I prefer good old-fashioned personal contact. You know, the telephone, face-to-face meetings with people. However, we do have a computer in my home. My wife and stepson use it. So when I heard about the information that had been posted regarding Ms. Riley and Ms. Monroe, I had Jesse—that's my stepson—help me take a gander at it. And frankly I don't see what all the fuss is about."

"Did you tell any member of your congregation to

post the materials that we've been discussing on the Web site?"

"No, I did not. I was not aware they were there until you sent me a copy of the plaintiff's motion."

"Reverend Tremaine, do you believe that the information posted on the Web site constitutes a threat to Ms. Monroe and Ms. Riley in any way?"

"Certainly not," Tremaine answered indignantly. "The Lambs of God is a religious organization. We do not threaten anyone, least of all attractive women."

"Reverend, in your opinion, what is the purpose of mentioning Ms. Riley and Ms. Monroe on the Web site?"

"Well . . ." Tremaine thought a moment. "I guess I would have to say that mentioning those two fine women helps to promote open and free discussion of viewpoints on various issues."

"What issues are you referring to?" Ravenswood prompted.

"In particular, the issues of abortion and homosexuality," Tremaine said. "Planned Parenthood and its lawyer condone those things. The Lambs of God do not."

"And as far as you know, no one connected with the Lambs of God has any intention of harming Ms. Riley or Ms. Monroe?"

"Absolutely not," Tremaine said.

"Thank you, Reverend," Ravenswood said. "No further questions."

Ken sprang to his feet, ready to do battle. "Reverend, what is the purpose of having Ms. Monroe's and

Ms. Riley's pictures displayed in the form of bull's-eyes?"

Tremaine shrugged. "I can't say for sure. I guess maybe it was meant as a thought-provoking gesture."

"And would you say that leaving a dozen rude or obscene messages a day on each woman's voice mail service is also a thought-provoking gesture?"

Tremaine shrugged. "I imagine so."

"Reverend, who is responsible for posting materials to the Lambs' Web site?"

"I don't know."

"Can you find out?" Ken asked.

"I'm not sure," Tremaine hedged.

"Do you mean to tell me that the pastor of the congregation is unable to find out the Webmaster's name?"

"Well, I suppose I might be able to find out who it is."

Ken turned to the judge. "Your Honor, I would request that Reverend Tremaine furnish the court and myself with the name and address of the Webmaster by five P.M. tomorrow."

Judge Bies nodded. "Mr. Ravenswood, please see that your client complies with that request."

"Yes, Your Honor," Ravenswood said.

Ken turned back to Tremaine.

"Reverend, you don't like Ms. Monroe, do you?"

Tremaine raised one eyebrow. "Whatever gave you that idea, sir?"

"Isn't it true that approximately two and a half years ago Ms. Monroe represented a local abortion clinic at which the Lambs picketed for a period of several months?"

"Yes."

"And isn't it true that Ms. Monroe was struck in the head with a brick during a demonstration at the clinic?"

The reverend stuck out his chin. "Yes, but I had nothing to do with that, and I resent your implying that I did."

"Isn't it also true that during the course of that demonstration relations between you and Ms. Monroe became so strained that you denounced her from your pulpit?"

"That was just a little joke," Tremaine said.

"Just like you consider encouraging your followers to harm Ms. Monroe and Ms. Riley to be 'a little joke'?" Ken demanded.

"I never encouraged anyone to harm them," Tremaine sputtered.

"Then why not tell your Webmaster, assuming you can find out who he or she might be, to remove any references to Ms. Monroe and Ms. Riley from the Web site?"

"This is a free country, Mr. Devlin," Tremaine shot back. "Ms. Monroe and Ms. Riley have their strongly held beliefs and the Lambs of God have theirs, and we have a God-given right to express them as we see fit."

"Even if that includes inciting violence?" Ken asked.

"Sometimes the Lord demands vengeance against wrongdoers," Tremaine virtually shouted.

"No further questions," Ken said.

The judge nodded. "Reverend, you may step down. Mr. Devlin, any closing thoughts?"

Ken cleared his throat. "The personal information about Ms. Monroe and Ms. Riley posted on the Web site goes far beyond the scope of protected free speech. I would direct the court's attention to the case of *Planned Parenthood v. American Coalition of Life Activists*, in which the United States district court for the District of Oregon found that similar Web postings did not fall under the banner of protected free speech, constituted a real threat against the persons targeted, and warranted the issuance of a permanent injunction. We respectfully ask the court to issue a similar injunction here. Thank you." He sat down.

"Mr. Ravenswood," Judge Bies called out.

The Lambs' lawyer stood up. "The Oregon case that Mr. Devlin referred to has no bearing here. Some of the materials posted on the Web sites in that matter contained blatant threats to assault or kill people. The Lambs' Web site contains no such material. The references to Ms. Monroe and Ms. Riley are strictly informative, and in no way can they be construed as threatening to Ms. Monroe or Ms. Riley. We respectfully request that the motion for an injunction be denied." He sat down.

Judge Bies was busy scrawling notes on a legal pad. After a moment she looked up. "This is a complex case involving competing interests and values. While I understand that both parties are interested in a rapid resolution to the ongoing dispute, I'm afraid I am not prepared to rule today. Consequently, the court will take the matter under advisement and will issue a decision as expeditiously as possible. In the meantime, I decline to interfere with the material posted on the Web site." She rapped her gavel on the bench. "Bailiff, call the next case."

Ravenswood and his client clearly viewed the judge's refusal to render an immediate decision as a complete victory. They both shot haughty looks in their adversaries' direction as they left the courtroom.

Denise was particularly dejected as she walked down the steps with Ann and Ken. "Dammit!" she exclaimed. "Are those people going to be an albatross around my neck for all eternity?"

Ann put her hand on Denise's arm. "I hope it won't be quite that long. We didn't lose," she said. "Judge Bies clearly wants to do the right thing. There's nothing wrong with her taking some additional time to sort this all out. I think she'll agree with our position in the end."

"I second Ann's comment," Ken put in.

Denise looked skeptical. "If you say so, but from where I'm sitting it looks like so far the Lambs have the upper hand."

"The battle's not over by a long shot," Ann said, wishing she felt half as optimistic as she sounded. "Just hang in there."

"Oh, I will," Denise assured her. "I might gripe to you, but I swear I'll never show any weakness to those people, no matter what they might do to me."

"That's the spirit," Ken said encouragingly as they reached the front door of the courthouse. "Now, why don't you let your lawyers buy you a cup of coffee."

"You're on, Counselor," Denise said, taking Ken's arm. "My mother taught me never to turn down a good-looking man's offer of food or drink."

CHAPTER 19

After having coffee and seeing Denise to her car, Ann and Ken walked back to the office. "Are you going to be home tomorrow night?" Ken asked.

Ann's pulse leaped. "Yes, I am," she replied eagerly. "Why? Are you free?"

Ken nodded. "The entire night. Patsy is taking the girls to see her sister in Ripon after work. They're staying overnight and driving back the next day. How would you like some company?"

"I'd love it," Ann said. Then she added lightly, "I was beginning to wonder if I was just a one-night stand."

Ken jabbed her lightly in the side with his elbow. "I'm absolutely crazy about you, Counselor. I've spent the whole week thinking of nothing but you: when I'd be able to see you again; what I could do to get your picture off that damn Web site; how I'd live with myself if something happened to you in the meantime. And I'm tired of passing you in the office and not being able to let on how I feel. I want to tell the world about us—and the sooner the better. Do you have any objection to that?"

"Objection? How about having some banners made up to help spread the news?"

"I was thinking of hiring a skywriter myself," Ken said, taking her arm, "but banners would be fine, too."

Ken went to his office to prepare for some depositions he would be taking that afternoon. When Ann reached her office and looked at her messages, she saw that Chuck Ryder had returned her call. Ann immediately phoned the young man back. He answered on the second ring.

After explaining that she had recently spoken to the Jasper County district attorney, Ann said, "I hate to have to ask you this, but Lawrence said the reason he didn't call you as a witness at the Jenkins and English trial was that you have a criminal record. Is that true?"

"Yes," Chuck answered without hesitation.

"Can you tell me about it?"

"Sure. Three years ago, when I was a freshman, I was invited to go to Milwaukee for the weekend. I hadn't met Larry yet. I was eighteen and into playing the field—quite heavily, if you catch my drift. To make a long story short, three other guys and I ended up in a seedy club where pretty much anything was available for a price. I felt like a kid in a candy store, and I got a little carried away. Unfortunately, as I was in the midst of a rather intimate encounter with some guy in a back room, the cops raided the place."

"Ugh." Ann grimaced. She felt sorry for Chuck

and at the same time disappointed that Lawrence's story had proven to be true. "What happened then?"

Chuck sighed. "They let me off with probation in return for pleading no contest to all the charges and promising not to get into any more trouble for three years. That time was up three months ago. Believe me, that incident was a major lesson in growing up. I'll never, ever do anything so stupid again."

"When you talked to the DA about the close call you had with Jenkins and English, did he ask if you had a record?"

"Hmmmm . . ." Chuck thought a moment. "To tell you the truth, I don't think the subject came up. I would've told him the truth if he'd asked. Was that really a legitimate reason for him not to use me as a witness?"

"I don't know," Ann admitted. "Lawrence claimed that because of the nature of your prior record, having you testify might confuse the jury or lead them to believe that you made up your story just to pursue some gay-pride agenda."

"That's crazy!" Chuck exclaimed.

"I think so, too," Ann agreed. "If it had been my case, I would have at least asked the judge to allow me to read the jury a statement regarding the circumstances of your convictions."

"I feel awful!" Chuck exclaimed. "Ever since last fall I've been blaming myself for not going to the police. Now it sounds like I failed Bill twice. If I'd gone to the police, Jenkins and English might not have attacked him and there wouldn't have been a criminal trial. And if I hadn't acted like a dog in heat that weekend in Milwaukee, I might have been able to testify at the trial and those two creeps might have been convicted. Everything could've been different if I'd had my act together," he said bitterly.

"Don't be too hard on yourself," Ann counseled. "You tried to help by coming forward after you heard about Bill's assault. You would have been willing to testify. It's not your fault no one asked you."

"Poor Bill," Chuck murmured. "How's the civil case going?"

"Slowly," Ann admitted. "I've got a couple of ideas in the works but so far I haven't made a lot of progress. How are things with you? Are you finished with classes?"

"Yeah. Graduation is Sunday, and then the first of the month Larry and I are moving to Chicago. I'm going to be working for an ad agency as a graphic designer, and Larry took a job with an accounting firm."

"Good for you," Ann praised him. "I love Chicago. I think you'll like it there."

"I hope so. We're both looking forward to getting to a bigger metropolitan area. The professors here at Mount Pleasant were good and the small classes were nice, but there are just a lot more opportunities in a large metropolitan area, plus I think socially we'll just fit in better there."

"Good luck," Ann said. "And thanks again for all your help."

"I wish I could have done more," Chuck said ruefully. He recited his new address and phone number.

"You call me if there's anything I can do for Bill. I'm hoping I might be able to redeem myself yet."

"You already have," Ann said. "But I appreciate the offer, and never fear—if I think of any way you can help us, you'll be hearing from me."

After talking to Chuck, Ann realized it was lunchtime. She grabbed a bite to eat, then threw herself into the task of trying to contact the people who had served as jurors in the Jenkins and English criminal trial. Once again, her efforts yielded a big goose egg.

Jurors' phone numbers had been changed to unlisted. Phones either rang and went unanswered or were picked up by answering machines. Ann was stymied. Speaking to Ted Lawrence had greatly increased her suspicion that the DA had not given his best efforts to questioning the prospective jurors. So what was going on with those jurors? Had they all been abducted by an alien spaceship or something? Why couldn't she get even one of them to talk to her?

After five or ten minutes spent agonizing over how to proceed, an idea occurred to Ann and she picked up the phone and hit one of her speed-dial numbers.

"Gary Carlson," her old friend answered brightly.

"Gary, it's Ann."

"Annie, what's up? Don't tell me you've taken on yet another case in which the opposing side is being championed by that charismatic but morally flawed minister?"

"No. I was calling to ask another favor."

"A favor?" Gary drew the syllables of the word

out. "What will I get in return if I agree to do this favor?"

"An exclusive story?" Ann suggested.

"Nah. Exclusives are a dime a dozen."

"Lunch at the restaurant of your choice?"

"You can do better than that," Gary said in mock indignation.

"*Dinner* at the restaurant of your choice?"

"You're getting warmer," Gary egged her on.

"If you think I'm going to offer a night in a hotel, you can forget it," Ann teased. "I don't need the favor that badly, and besides, at your age you'd probably have a heart attack."

"You are so cruel," Gary said, pretending to be hurt. "All right. You tell me what the favor is. If I'm able to help you out, we'll negotiate an appropriate reward later."

"You're on," Ann said. She briefly explained about the jurors' uniform reluctance to speak to her. "I was wondering if you might have some idea how to break the ice with one or two of them."

"You're saying you can't get even one of them to talk?" Gary mulled the situation over. "That is odd, isn't it? Are they hiding something or are they afraid of someone?" Ann could hear him drumming a pen up and down on his desktop. "I find the question highly intriguing. I accept your challenge to find out more about this."

"Thanks," Ann said gratefully. "I'm at a dead end, but I know if anybody can get to the bottom of it, you can."

"I'll start nosing around right away," Gary promised. "Now getting back to the reward: When you say a night in a hotel is out, does that also exclude those places that rent rooms by the hour?"

"Gary!" Ann scolded.

"All right. I was just checking," he said, laughing. "I'll get right on it and let you know what I find out."

CHAPTER 20

The following morning, Ann met with two of the school district's attorneys in one last attempt to resolve Taylor and Talia Crabb's case. With only ten days remaining until the end of the school year, Ann hoped that the district was now willing to stop its stonewalling and settle the matter in time for Taylor to speak at his graduation.

In advance of the meeting she had sent the district a detailed letter outlining the substantial damages she would seek if the matter went to trial. Apparently seeing the figures in black and white had prompted the district to raise the white flag.

The meeting was held at the opposing law firm, which was located on the opposite side of the capitol square from Mishler and Stettler. "After several lengthy meetings, I think we've convinced the powers that be at the high school that it would be in everyone's best interest to try to settle," Dave Stegner, one of the district's lawyers, said. "So, in that spirit, I'll put it to you straight: What will it take for this thing to go away?"

"Expunge all mention of the incident from the kids' records, allow Taylor to deliver the valedictory address at graduation, plus a public apology in the local press," Ann replied.

"We can probably sell them on the first two conditions," Lil Hawthorne, the other school district lawyer, spoke up. "But I'm afraid the apology is going to be a sticking point. The school authorities are adamant that what they did was appropriate."

"No apology, no settlement," Ann said firmly. "What the school did was definitely not okay, and that fact needs to be acknowledged."

Hawthorne and Stegner exchanged cryptic glances; then Stegner leaned back in his chair and gave Ann a wry smile. "Do you really believe it was all right for one student to inject another with a potentially deadly drug?"

"Taylor saved Marilyn's life by giving her that injection," Ann replied.

"But what if Marilyn had been allergic to the drug and died as a result of what Taylor Crabb did?" Stegner pressed on.

"She would have died if Taylor had done nothing," Ann said. "She's alive because of his actions. It is pointless to sit here and debate what might have been." She shifted in her chair. "So what do you say? Can we come to terms over the Crabbs' claim or not? If not, I've got a lot of work to do back at my office."

Stegner and Hawthorne exchanged another glance; then Stegner said, "Let me go call the superintendent and see what he says. I'll be back in a few minutes." He got up and left the room.

While Stegner was gone, Ann and Lil Hawthorne made small talk. "Are you still working with that literacy group?" Lil asked.

"Yes, a few times a month," Ann replied. "I wish I had more time to devote to it."

"I was thinking of volunteering," Lil said.

"You should," Ann encouraged her. "They'd love to have you. And it's really rewarding. The students are so eager to learn." She scrawled Marge Harker's name and phone number on a piece of paper and handed it to Lil. "Here's the coordinator's name and number. Give her a call. She'll be thrilled to have another warm body come on board."

Lil looked at the piece of paper. "I just might do that," she said. "I've been thinking about it for months but, like all good deeds, it's easier to keep putting it off than to act."

"Talk to Marge," Ann said. "She'll make a believer out of you within five minutes."

Stegner walked back into the room. "It looks like we've got ourselves a deal," he said. "As we predicted, the administration is not happy about having to make a public apology, but when I told them they could be looking at a hefty damage award if this thing went much farther, they reluctantly agreed to fall on their sword."

"I appreciate your going to bat for us," Ann praised him. "It will mean a lot to the Crabbs' parents for Taylor to be able to speak at graduation."

"I'm glad we were able to work it out to everyone's satisfaction," Stegner said. "Now, why don't the three of us put our heads together and draft an apology that will satisfy the Crabbs and the administration."

Ann returned to her office in an upbeat mood, happy that she had finally been able to successfully bring one case to a close. She called Taylor and Talia's mother and relayed the news.

"Thank you so much," Mrs. Crabb said. "Taylor has been quite depressed thinking he wouldn't be able to give his speech. He's going to be just thrilled with this result. We all are."

"I'm glad I could help," Ann said. She put down the phone and shuffled through the stack of mail that Kari had placed on her desk. An envelope with a hand-printed address caught her attention. She slit it open with her letter opener, pulled out the single sheet of paper inside, and unfolded it. The note was written in red crayon:

Not only did you not drop that pervert as a client, now you're representing baby killers, too. You will pay for your sins. Beware. The time for your repentence is at hand.

Ann's hands were shaking so badly that she nearly dropped the paper. The writer had to be one of the punks from Mount Pleasant. She dug through her desk drawer and found the earlier letter she'd received. She held them side by side. The style of printing was the same. Why hadn't she gone to the police immediately after being accosted? Now those thugs were stalking her.

Still holding both notes, she got up and walked quickly down the hall to Ken's office.

"I got the name of the Lambs' Webmaster," Ken said cheerfully. "I've already sent Ravenswood a notice saying that I'll be taking the guy's deposition on Monday." Seeing the distressed look on Ann's face, he asked, "What's wrong?"

Ann showed him the two notes and explained about the incident in Mount Pleasant.

"Oh, Ann! Why didn't you tell me this before?" Ken asked. He got up and came around his desk and put his arms around her.

"It's probably nothing," Ann said, trying to sound brave. "But I'm starting to get spooked."

"It'll be okay. I won't let anything happen to you. Leave the notes with me. I'm going to send copies of them to Judge Bies to supplement my motion to shut down the Web site. This is proof positive that someone is threatening you."

Ann went back to her office but wasn't able to accomplish much the rest of the day. The one bright spot on the horizon was her evening with Ken.

Ken picked up Chinese takeout on the way to Ann's house. At seven o'clock Ann and Ken were sitting in her kitchen, finishing their orange beef and Hunan chicken. The conversation over dinner had been relaxed, even though it focused inevitably on the Lambs' Web site and the threatening notes.

"I started making a list of questions to ask the Lambs' Webmaster at his deposition," Ann said, taking a sip of white wine. "How did he come up with the idea to post photos of Denise and me on the site? Did anyone tell him to do it or was it solely his own idea? What was it supposed to accomplish?"

"Why don't you let me worry about framing the questions for the deposition," Ken said.

"I just want to feel like I'm being helpful," Ann replied.

"If you want to be helpful, why don't you come over here?" Ken held out his arms, and Ann slid off of her chair and onto his lap. She leaned back against him and he lightly touched her breasts. "Now isn't this better than talking about work?"

"Much better," Ann murmured. "Say, we haven't had our fortune cookies." She leaned forward and handed one of the plastic-wrapped cookies to Ken.

They each removed their cookie from its wrapping, snapped the crisp morsel in two, and extracted the small piece of paper.

"What does yours say?" Ken asked after looking at his. "Something provocative, I hope."

"'You are very wealthy even though you do not know it,'" Ann read. "Quite profound. Now your turn."

"'Now is the time to try something new,'" Ken recited. "What do you suppose that could mean?" he asked, resuming his ministrations to her breasts.

"We're supposed to try something new?" Ann repeated. "I think we pretty much exhausted my entire repertoire of amorous adventures the last time you were here."

"Really?" Ken asked in mock amazement. "You poor deprived thing. I guess that's what you get for dating an economist. But you know what? You're in luck, because I just happen to have a couple of pretty cool moves that I'd be happy to teach you. Would you like me to help you clean this stuff up first?"

Ann jumped to her feet. "Clean up first? Hell, no. How about if I race you upstairs?"

"I thought you'd never ask," Ken said.

Half an hour later, Ann stretched out her legs and said, "If I'm going to continue seeing you, I think I'm going to have to start working out more. Where on earth do you get staying power like that? Are you taking hormones or pep pills or something?"

"You know, I don't think I've ever been quite like this with anyone else," Ken said. "But you turn me on so much that I just don't want the experience to end."

"You're like the Energizer bunny. Instead of coming instantly like most guys, you just keep going and going and going."

Ken laughed. "I'll take that as a compliment. Would you like me to rub your legs or back or anything else?"

Ann smiled and languidly ran her hand over his stomach. "Why don't we just cool down for a few minutes and then see what develops."

CHAPTER 21

"Bring the gas can over here," Jesse Greer whispered. Shining his flashlight beam at a plastic container filled with old newspapers, he directed, "Splash a lot of it on these papers."

Ben Kowalski hesitated. "Are you sure this is a good idea?" he whispered back.

Greer wheeled around to face the youth. "What do you mean by that candy-ass remark? You seemed to be a willing enough participant when we set the fire at the Planned Parenthood clinic."

"Yeah, but this is different," Ben whispered back, looking around nervously. "This is somebody's house. What if there are people sleeping inside?"

"This isn't 'somebody's house,'" Greer retorted. "This is the house of a known homosexual. A sodomizer. The lowest form of life on the face of the planet. Why should we give a fuck if someone like that lives or dies?"

"I never signed on to hurt anybody," Ben said, starting to back away.

Greer instantly lashed out and punched the younger man in the stomach. Ben doubled over in pain.

"I thought I made it clear to you earlier that I was in charge of this operation," Greer said into Ben's face in a hiss. "Is there something wrong with your hearing or your brain that caused you not to get the message?"

Ben groaned in response.

Greer grabbed a handful of Ben's hair and pulled him upright. "I'm speaking to you, boy," he said in a growl. "Do you or do you not understand that I am in charge here?"

Ben choked out a response with great difficulty. "I understand."

"Good." Greer let go of Ben's hair. "Now do as I say and pour gas onto those newspapers." He swung around and shone his flashlight on the new minivan parked in the other half of the garage. "And then for good measure, pour some under that van, too. We want to make sure our visit here was worthwhile."

Ben swallowed hard, then picked up the gas can and slowly walked over to the newspaper recycling bin. Before he could pour out any of the gasoline, Greer reached out and put a hand on his arm. "One more thing, kid."

Ben clenched his jaw and tried not to show his fear.

"If you ever breathe a word of what we did tonight to another living soul, you are a fucking dead man," Greer said. "Do I make myself clear?"

Ben nervously bobbed his head up and down. "Yes, Jesse," he said in a squeak.

"Good." Greer grinned at his young protégé. "Now spread that gas around and then let's boogie. It's late and I need my beauty sleep."

CHAPTER 22

By two in the morning Ann and Ken's marathon lovemaking session had finally wound down and they were both dozing when the phone rang.

"If that's Georgia, let me talk to her this time," Ken said as Ann sleepily rolled over him and reached for the phone. "Maybe we should give her a schedule of when we're going to be together so she'll know when not to call."

"Shhh!" Ann said as she picked up the receiver and said hello.

"Ann? It's Laurie Robinson." The woman sounded very distraught.

"Laurie, what's wrong?" Ann asked at once.

There was a pause as Laurie caught her breath. "Someone set our garage on fire," Laurie replied.

"Oh, no!" Ann exclaimed. "Was anyone hurt? When did it happen?"

"No one was hurt, but Tom's new minivan was destroyed and the whole house has heavy smoke damage. We'd gone to a party in Milwaukee and taken my car. When we came back and pulled into the driveway about an hour ago, we could see smoke coming from under the garage door. We called the fire department right away and got two fire extinguishers out of the house and tried to put it out, but it had already gotten a pretty good hold."

"Do the authorities know what caused it?"

"They're still out there looking around, and they said a team from the state crime lab will come tomorrow morning. The fire chief said it looks like someone broke in the door leading from the backyard and then started a fire in the bin where we keep old newspapers. I know we're lucky that it wasn't worse, but when I think what could have happened if they'd done it while we were asleep . . ." The woman's voice trailed off.

"Oh, Laurie, I'm so sorry," Ann said. "Is Bill home?"

"No, he and Terry are planning to stay on campus most of the summer, thank God. I almost hate to tell him about it. I know how upset he'll be. He'll probably blame himself."

"We don't know for sure that the fire is in any way connected to Bill's lawsuit," Ann said, although in her own mind there was little doubt. "Let's try to reserve judgment on that until we hear what the state crime lab people have to say."

"You're right, of course," Laurie said. "It's just that after all that's happened to our family in the past seven months, I sometimes wonder how much more we can stand."

"Would you like me to come over?" Ann asked.

"Thanks for offering, but there's really no need for

that," Laurie said. "I'm sorry to bother you at this hour, but I just wanted you to know what happened."

"I'm glad you called," Ann said. "You keep me posted, and I want you and Tom and Bill to all be very careful. This incident goes to show that you can't take your safety for granted."

"Thanks, Ann," Laurie said. "I'll be in touch again soon."

"What happened?" Ken asked as Ann slowly hung up the phone.

She filled him in on the call.

"Those poor people," Ken said. "They're just not catching any breaks, are they?"

Less than five minutes later, as Ann and Ken were still discussing the Robinsons' plight, the phone rang again.

"Now what?" Ann wondered aloud as she picked it up.

"Ann, it's Denise Riley," a breathless voice announced. "The clinic is on fire. Four fire trucks are trying to put it out."

"I'll be right there," Ann said, dropping the phone. She slapped Ken on the leg and jumped out of bed. "Come on. We have to get down to the Planned Parenthood clinic right away."

"What happened?" Ken asked.

"It looks like the Lambs of God were tired of waiting around for Denise and her staff to end up in eternal hellfire," she said grimly, "so they apparently decided to try to speed things up a bit."

* * *

FINAL JUSTICE

Thanks to an observant passerby who saw smoke coming from the clinic and immediately used his cell phone to dial 911, and to the fast response of local firefighters, damage to Planned Parenthood's building was limited to a rear storage area and one examining room.

"We'll be open for business on Monday as usual," Denise Riley announced triumphantly to the media as the firefighters finished their work in the early hours of Saturday morning. "Whoever was responsible for this vicious and cowardly act did not succeed in shutting us down. Our resolve to carry out our mission to provide quality reproductive care to the men and women of this community remains undeterred."

At Denise's request, Ann and Ken participated in her discussion with the police who responded to the scene. Those officers had been in contact with their colleagues who had responded to the fire at the Robinsons' home, and there was little doubt that the same person or persons had set both blazes.

"We're aware of the picketing that's occurred at the clinic recently," Det. Andy Lowell said, "as well as the Lambs' public statements condemning homosexuality. Have any of the picketers threatened violence against you or the clinic?"

"Yes, they have," Denise replied. "I think the clinic's attorneys can fill you in on the details better than I can."

Ken explained how photos of Denise and Ann, encased in bull's-eyes, had recently appeared on the Lambs' Web site. "I can get you a copy of my motion asking to have the references to Denise and Ann removed, as well as a copy of the transcript from the motion hearing, if it would be helpful," Ken offered.

"Why don't you do that," Detective Lowell said. "It might give us some leads. Does this Reverend Tremaine strike you as a violent person?"

"Do you mean do we think he personally started the fires?" Ann asked.

The detective nodded.

"As much as I'd like to say yes, the truth is I doubt it," Ann admitted. "Torching buildings strikes me as a younger person's pastime, and Tremaine is getting a little long in the tooth. But I fully believe he is capable of inciting his followers to commit violence."

"Can you name any other member of the Lambs who you think deserves some scrutiny?"

Ann shook her head. "Tremaine is the only one I know by name. The rest of them keep a lower profile."

"Well, I'll start by questioning the head honcho and work my way down," Lowell said.

Denise put a hand on the detective's arm. "You will catch the people responsible for doing this, won't you?"

The detective patted Denise's hand. "There are no guarantees in my job, ma'am, but I promise I'll do everything I can to find the lowlife who did this."

Detective Lowell interviewed Tremaine at his home early the next morning. The reverend was clearly not happy to receive this unexpected visitor.

"How dare you accuse me of setting fires!" Trem-

FINAL JUSTICE

aine shouted indignantly. "I am a man of God, not a common criminal."

"I haven't accused you of anything," the detective replied wearily.

"Yes, you have," Tremaine retorted. "For the past fifteen minutes you have stood there and asked me impertinent questions which leave no doubt that you consider me a suspect in those crimes. Do not deny it, sir. I can tell by your tone of voice that you have already adjudged me guilty."

"You are not a suspect, Reverend—at least not at this time. If you were a suspect I would have read you your Miranda rights, and if I had done that and if you had evaded all of my questions the way you've been doing for the past fifteen minutes, by this time I would have arrested you for obstruction of justice, handcuffed you, and hauled you off to the station house."

Tremaine's mouth dropped open at the detective's impertinence.

"But since you are not a suspect," Detective Lowell continued, "we can skip all those formalities. What I would appreciate from you, however, is a straight answer to a few inquiries. If you'll give me that, I'll be on my way and you can get back to working on tomorrow's sermon or whatever else it was you were doing before I so rudely interrupted you. How does that plan sound to you?"

"What do you wish to know?" Tremaine asked, sticking out his chin.

"Where were you between eleven o'clock last night and two o'clock this morning?"

"In my bed, asleep."

"Can anyone corroborate that fact?"

"My wife, Thelma."

"Might I be able to speak to her?" Lowell asked.

"She is not home at present. She is visiting an elderly parishioner at a nursing home."

"When do you expect her back?"

"This afternoon."

"Do you have any idea who might have set the fires at Planned Parenthood or at the Robinson home?"

"Certainly not."

"Did any of your parishioners ever indicate to you that they might be contemplating something like that?"

"Of course not!" Tremaine exclaimed, his face flushed with anger. "The Lambs of God are Christian people who would never resort to violent acts. They make their point through peaceful demonstration and healthy dialogue, not violence."

"But isn't it true that the Lambs as a group, and you personally, have publicly spoken out against both Planned Parenthood's operation and the lawsuit filed by the Robinsons' son, who happens to be gay?"

"That is merely an example of the healthy dialogue I just mentioned."

"So if you had heard that one of your parishioners was contemplating doing something like setting those fires, you would have tried to stop them?"

"Of course I would. I condemn the cowardly acts that resulted in damage to the clinic and the Robinsons' home. I will pray for an end to such violence.

FINAL JUSTICE

However, I will also continue to speak out against the moral decay that exists in our society, and I think Ms. Ann Monroe and her law firm should be ashamed of themselves for trying to put the blame for those crimes on members of the Lord's flock."

The detective could barely contain his disgust at the reverend's antics. "Thank you for your time, sir," he said. "That will be all for now. I may have some more questions for you later, and I will want to speak to your wife at some point."

"My family and I will put ourselves at your disposal," the reverend proclaimed magnanimously.

CHAPTER 23

On Monday, Ken took the deposition of the Lambs' Webmaster. Mark Portsikova was a tall, slender man in his late twenties with red hair and wire-rimmed glasses. Ken had invited Denise Riley to sit in for this deposition, and Denise accepted the invitation immediately.

"I suppose my time could be better spent trying to clean up the damage from the fire," the clinic's director said, "but I figure the mess will still be there when I get back. I don't want to pass up the opportunity to sit across the table from one of these people and let him see that his actions are impacting a real live human being."

In response to Ken's questioning, Portsikova explained that he worked as a computer programmer for a midsize accounting firm. He had been a member of the Lambs of God for three years and had served as its Webmaster for the past eighteen months.

"Were you responsible for posting the photos of Ms. Monroe and Ms. Riley to the Web site?"

"Yes."

FINAL JUSTICE

"When did you do that?"

"About ten days ago."

"At whose request was that done?" Ken asked.

"It was entirely my own idea," Portsikova replied.

"When did you think of it?"

Portsikova shrugged. "I don't remember exactly. Sometime in the last month, I guess."

"Did you consult with anyone else before posting the photos to the Web site?"

The young man shook his head. "I don't believe so."

"What was your intention in posting the photos?"

"To call attention to the plight of the preborn," Portsikova answered at once.

"You've lost me," Ken said. "What is the connection between the preborn and photos of Ms. Riley and Ms. Monroe encased in bull's-eyes?"

"The Lambs of God are strongly prolife," Portsikova answered. "Ms. Riley and Ms. Monroe are abortion advocates. I thought that posting their photos on the Lambs' Web site would help call attention to the suffering of the preborn."

Ann and Denise both glared at the witness. He did not appear to notice.

"Are you aware, sir, that the Planned Parenthood clinic in this city does not perform abortions?" Ken asked.

"That doesn't matter," Portsikova shot back. "It is a tenet of Planned Parenthood's philosophy that abortion is acceptable. And Ms. Monroe is well known as being a supporter of those who murder innocent babies."

"Why didn't you just post the photos in their unaltered state?" Ken asked, ignoring the witness's editorial comments. "What was the point in encasing each of the pictures in a bull's-eye?"

"I guess I thought it'd be more dramatic that way."

"It didn't occur to you that by putting Ms. Riley's and Ms. Monroe's pictures in bull's-eyes that you were indicating they should be a target for other members of the Lambs?"

"No."

"Did you at any time have a discussion with Reverend Tremaine about posting the women's photos?"

"No."

"Have you spoken to Reverend Tremaine since the photos were posted?"

"I spoke to him after Sunday services," Portsikova answered sweetly. "I complimented him on his sermon, which focused on respecting all forms of life."

"Did you have any discussion with Reverend Tremaine about the recent postings to the Web site?"

"No."

"Have you ever had a discussion with the reverend about the Web site's content?"

"No."

Ken shifted in his chair. "Mr. Portsikova, do you have any knowledge about the origin of the fire that was set at the Planned Parenthood clinic on Saturday night?"

"Objection!" Ravenswood boomed. "What is the

FINAL JUSTICE

relevance of this? This witness is not under investigation for causing the fire."

"Well, perhaps he—or some other members of his group—should be," Ken retorted.

"I move that remark be stricken!" Ravenswood said, getting red in the face. "I caution you, Mr. Devlin, either stop these slanderous remarks at once or I will declare this proceeding at an end!"

"Your objection to my last question is duly noted," Ken said. "I direct the witness to answer it pending a ruling from Judge Bies on its relevance."

"Fine," Ravenswood snapped.

"Mr. Portsikova, let me ask you again. Do you have any knowledge about the origin of the fire at Planned Parenthood?"

"No," the witness answered sullenly.

"Have you ever had a discussion with anyone about causing damage to the Planned Parenthood premises?"

"No."

"Do you have any knowledge about the origin of a fire that occurred at the home of Tom and Laurie Robinson on Saturday night?"

"Objection!" Ravenswood fairly yelled. "This proceeding is turning into more of a fishing expedition every minute. What does this other fire have to do with the lawsuit currently pending between Planned Parenthood and the Lambs of God?"

"That's precisely what I'm trying to determine," Ken said. He handed the witness the two threatening notes Ann had received. "Have you ever seen these notes before?"

"No."

"Do you have any idea who might have written them?"

"No."

Ken shifted in his chair. "Mr. Portsikova, do you believe homosexuality is a sin?"

"I object to this entire line of questioning," Ravenswood huffed. "The witness may answer subject to that objection."

"Yes, I do believe it's a sin," Portsikova replied. "The Bible clearly says so."

"And Reverend Tremaine says so, too, doesn't he?" Ken asked.

"All true Christians share this belief."

"Do you know who Bill Robinson is?" Ken asked.

"Yes. He is the young homosexual man who wrongly accused two other men of beating him up."

"Have you ever had a discussion with any other members of the Lambs of God about Bill Robinson?"

"Yes," the witness answered without hesitation.

"What was the nature of that discussion?"

"It was pretty much the consensus of the congregation that the homosexual got what was coming to him."

"You mean the Lambs of God think Bill Robinson deserved being nearly beaten to death?"

"He provoked the attack, no doubt as a result of his uncontrollable animal urges," Portsikova responded.

"So he got what he deserved and the two young men who beat him deserved to be acquitted of all charges. Is that what you believe?"

"Something like that."

"What if Bill Robinson had been killed, either in the attack or in the fire that someone set at his parents' home last Saturday night? Is it your opinion that he would have deserved that, too?"

"He is an adult who is responsible for his own actions. If he sins, he should be struck down. The hundreds of poor preborn souls who are snuffed out of existence every day as a result of abortionists' actions are without sin, yet they suffer."

"So in your mind there is a connection between a gay man like Bill Robinson and people who support abortions?" Ken demanded.

"Yes, sir. They are all sinners."

"And as sinners they all deserve to be struck down?"

"Yes."

Ken threw his pen down on the table. "I have no further questions." He quickly got up and left the conference room.

After the deposition, Ken and Ann met in her office to rehash the witness's testimony. When they had finished, Ken said, "The fact that an educated young man could hold such hateful beliefs is truly frightening. There is no doubt in my mind that the Lambs, individually and as a group, are very dangerous, and it doesn't sound like they have any intention of backing off from their vendetta against you and your clients. I really wish you'd give some serious thought to moving somewhere else temporarily."

Ann shook her head. "We had this discussion over

the weekend. I told you I feel safer in my own house than in some strange place. Besides, where am I supposed to go at a moment's notice?"

"You could move in with me," Ken answered at once. "The girls know that we're dating."

"Knowing that we're dating is one thing. Moving in with you is quite another."

"You could go to a hotel. They just opened one of those extended-stay places on the far west side."

"No," Ann said firmly. "I am not moving."

"Well, then, I think you should get yourself some protection," Ken insisted.

Ann frowned. "You mean a gun? You know I hate guns."

"No, not a gun, round-the-clock security."

"A bodyguard?" She tried not to laugh. "I'm a lawyer, not a Mafia princess."

"Oh, all right," Ken said, getting exasperated. "Then will you at least consider installing a home security system? It's not foolproof but it's better than nothing."

"Okay," Ann agreed. "You win. I'll have someone come out and give me an estimate."

"I'll make some calls for you," Ken said, happy that she was finally listening to reason. "I'll see if I can't get someone to check it out today."

At six o'clock that evening a representative of the Adelphi Home Security Company was filling Ann in on all the features offered by their various security systems.

"Here's the one I'd recommend for this size house

and this location," the sales rep said. He pulled a leaflet out of his briefcase and opened it up. "These are your main components," he said, pointing at a photo. "You'll have a monitor inside your house. It's connected through your phone lines to our monitoring station, which is staffed twenty-four hours a day. If the system detects a break-in or a fire, our people will dispatch local police or fire authorities." He flipped to another page.

"We'll install sensors on your windows and doors and we'll install motion detectors on the front and back of the house." Flipping to another page, he said, "This is your keypad. That will be installed on the front door. You will program that with your own special code, and if someone tries to enter without entering the code or if they fail to enter the correct code after three attempts, our people will again dispatch local authorities immediately."

Ann sighed. "So you're saying if I forget the code or I'm clumsy and don't punch the numbers correctly, the police are going to race over and surround my house."

"Many homeowners fear that they're going to set the system off by mistake," the sales rep said, "but that is actually a rare occurrence. And if it does happen once in a while, it's no different from a child dialing nine-one-one just to see what happens. The police are very understanding about such things." He handed Ann the brochure.

"I see," Ann said.

Sensing that he was dealing with a reluctant customer, the sales rep continued with his pitch. "Each year there are more than two million burglaries in this country. Homes without security systems are three times more likely to be broken into than homes with systems. An added bonus is that you might be able to save as much as twenty percent on your homeowners insurance premiums."

Ann flipped through the brochure.

"Can I answer any specific questions for you?" the sales rep asked.

Ann pursed her lips. She still thought this was a stupid idea, but she also knew Ken was adamant that she go through with it. "How soon would you be able to install the system you've just described?" she asked.

"I could have a team of installers here tomorrow afternoon," the sales rep said eagerly.

"All right," Ann said. "Let's do it." As the sales rep began to fill out the order form, Ann silently chastised herself for allowing herself to be talked into taking this totally unnecessary precaution. It was only because she found Ken's concern for her well-being so utterly charming that she was going ahead with this. Some of the Lambs might be zealots, but she honestly didn't think any of them were going to attack her in her own house—or at least she hoped they wouldn't sink to those depths.

CHAPTER 24

Two days later, the attorneys representing Jenkins and English took Bill Robinson's deposition. The proceeding was held at the office of Patrick Jagoe, Jenkins's counsel, in a new office building on the west side of town.

Ann had spent a couple hours with Bill that morning at her office preparing him for his testimony. "Answer only the question asked," Ann advised. "Don't volunteer additional information. If the defendants' lawyers want more information out of you, they can follow up with more questions."

Bill nodded. "In other words, I shouldn't do their job for them."

"That's right," Ann said. "Also, you should answer the questions to the best of your knowledge but don't guess at anything. If you don't know the answer to a question, simply say so."

"Okay."

"Are you ready for this?" Ann asked, putting her hand on Bill's arm.

"Definitely. I want the case to move forward. After

what happened at my parents' house, I feel more determined than ever to keep going, no matter what happens."

"How are your parents doing?"

Bill shrugged. "As well as anyone can do when they've been the victim of someone's hate. They're just hoping the police will catch whoever was responsible. Unfortunately, after what happened with my case they don't exactly have a whole lot of faith in the legal system. No offense against you," he added quickly.

"None taken," Ann said, smiling. "I understand how frustrated they must feel. I hope the people responsible for setting the fires are caught soon."

In his early questioning, Patrick Jagoe asked Bill Robinson about his activities on the day of the assault.

"I had two classes that morning," Bill explained. "Then I spent an hour in the library doing some research. I had lunch in the cafeteria and then I had another class right after lunch."

"What did you do after that class?" Jagoe asked.

"I went back to my dorm, dropped off my books, and went for a bike ride."

"Were you alone on this bike ride?"

"Yes."

"Where did you ride?"

"About three miles north of town."

"Did you stop anywhere in those three miles?"

"No."

"Did you notice anyone following you as you rode?"

"No."

"Did you speak to anyone along the way?"

"No."

"At some point on this ride you encountered Sam Jenkins and Brad English, is that correct?"

Bill snorted. "Yes, I certainly did 'encounter' them."

"Where did you encounter them?"

"Near the intersection of Stark and Kellner roads."

"What were the circumstances of the encounter?"

"I was minding my own business, riding my bike down the road, when suddenly two guys jumped out from behind a tree and ran at me."

"Do you know who the two guys were?" Jagoe asked.

"Yes. Sam Jenkins and Brad English."

"Did you see them before they jumped out at you?"

"No. I really wasn't paying much attention. I was just watching the road and thinking about a term paper that I had due the next week."

"What happened after you first saw Jenkins and English?"

"With no warning at all, they jumped out from behind a tree. They ran at me and knocked me off my bike. Then they started punching me in the face."

"And this happened with no provocation on your part?" Jagoe said, skepticism obvious in his voice.

"Yes, sir," Bill answered firmly. "With no warning and no provocation on my part, they knocked me off my bike and started beating me."

"Did you fight back?"

"I tried, but I was at a pretty big disadvantage right off the bat, since I was on my back on the ground."

"Isn't it true that you landed punches severe enough to break Sam Jenkins's teeth?"

"Yes."

"And you also dislocated Brad English's shoulder?"

"That's right."

"It was pretty lucky to land punches like that as you were lying on your back on the ground, now, wasn't it?"

"I managed to get to my feet temporarily," Bill explained.

"Oh, you got to your feet," Jagoe said, nodding. "How did you manage to accomplish that as these two boys were beating you?"

"I don't know exactly how I did it," Bill said, his face flushing from anger. "But somehow I did stand up, and it was in the next ninety seconds or so that I was able to land some punches."

"How fortunate that you were able to do that," Jagoe said.

"I suppose it was fortunate," Bill agreed at once. "If I hadn't been able to get up at least temporarily, I very likely would have been killed."

"I move to strike that last remark as nonresponsive," Jagoe said. "And with that, I have no further questions."

Pat Cox's questioning focused on the damages Bill believed he had suffered as a result of Jenkins's and English's actions.

"I went through a lot of pain and suffering," Bill explained. "I was in the hospital for twelve days and in a coma for the first two. After I got out of the hospital, I recovered slowly for the rest of the fall semester."

"Were you able to resume your classes?"

"I had to drop two classes. I finished the other three, although I took all of the exams late."

"Are you completely recovered now from your injuries?"

"I still get tired easily. I am not back to full strength yet."

"Have your doctors told you that you will suffer any long-term effects from the incident?" Cox asked.

"The doctors have said that it's possible I might have problems with my liver in the future, and I will need regular monitoring to make sure it's functioning okay."

"Is that the extent of your injuries?" Cox asked.

"I suffered from depression for several months after the beating," Bill answered.

"Were you treated for that condition?"

"I had a prescription for Prozac."

"Are you still taking Prozac?"

"No, I stopped taking it around the first of the year."

"Do you feel you have suffered any other injuries or damages?"

Bill paused a moment before answering. "I guess I'd have to say that since the assault I always feel suspicious, like I need to constantly look over my shoulder because someone else might be out to get me. In addition, I suffer from fairly frequent nightmares in which I relive the attack."

Ann nodded sympathetically as she heard her client detail his emotional trauma. *I've been there and done that*, she thought to herself. *And it's a real bitch.*

"Thank you," Cox said. "No further questions."

"I have a few things I'd like to follow up on," Ann said. Turning to Bill, she asked, "Did you ever see Sam Jenkins or Brad English prior to the day of the assault?"

"Yes, in the week or two before that I saw them a couple times at the Copper Kettle restaurant near the campus in Mount Pleasant."

"Did Jenkins or English speak to you on either of those occasions?"

"Yes." Bill recounted the antigay remarks that Jenkins and English had directed toward him and Terry Rukeyser.

"Do you feel your quality of life has changed as a result of the assault?"

"Definitely." Bill nodded.

"In what way?"

"I felt that I had to change schools. Because I had to drop the two classes last fall, I'm going to have to go to summer school if I want to keep up with my classes. As I mentioned, I will have to undergo lifelong monitoring of my liver function, and who knows what long-term psychological effects there might be. The doctors have said I might suffer from something like post-traumatic stress syndrome."

"Bill, do you feel your life will ever be the same as it was before the assault?"

"Never," Bill answered firmly. "There is never a day that goes by that I don't remember the attack in vivid detail. I don't think those memories will ever leave me." As he tried to continue, his voice broke.

"I would give anything to go back to the life I had before that day," Bill said, choking up. "I would give anything at all to be the person I was before this all happened." He began to sob uncontrollably and put his hands over his face.

"I have no further questions," Ann said softly. She reached over and squeezed her client's hand, then leaned over and whispered, "It's okay. Everything is going to be all right."

In response, Bill squeezed her hand back so tightly that it caused her to wince.

CHAPTER 25

Ken and his family had long-standing plans to visit Patsy's brother in Minneapolis over Memorial Day weekend. One of Patsy's nephews was graduating from a private high school on Saturday. Ken was taking the girls to the ceremony, and the three of them would be staying at a hotel. Patsy was riding up there with her parents and would be staying with the graduate's family.

Ken was so concerned about Ann's safety that he wanted to cancel the trip. "They won't miss me," he said. "The girls can ride up with Patsy and their grandparents. And Patsy's brother has a huge house, so it would be no problem for him to accommodate the girls."

"You can't back out," Ann said as they sat in her office on Thursday afternoon. "The girls are counting on you to go."

"I just have a bad feeling about this weekend," Ken said insistently.

"There's no reason for you to worry. I have my new home security system now and I am using it religiously. So you just go to Minneapolis and have a good time at the graduation. I intend to have an uneventful weekend catching up on some work here and at home."

"All right," Ken said reluctantly. "But I'm going to leave you a phone number where I can be reached. I want you to promise to call me if anything the least bit out of the ordinary happens."

"I promise," Ann said, giving him a big hug. "Now stop worrying. I'll miss you, but I'll be just fine. The weekend will be over before we know it."

Ken and his brood left town Friday morning. Ann spent a quiet day at the office catching up on some odds and ends. After work she treated herself to a movie, a romantic comedy that lifted her spirits and made her laugh but also made her yearn for Ken's return.

On Saturday she shopped for groceries, had the oil changed in her car, and then spent several hours working in her yard, planting flowers and spreading mulch. She had just come in the house for a cold drink in the late afternoon when the phone rang. It was Gary Carlson.

"Annie, I've got something for you," Gary said.

"What is it?" Ann asked. The excitement in Gary's voice was unmistakable.

"I've been trying to track down the jurors from the criminal trial," Gary explained. "And after making countless calls and getting no farther than you did, I decided to take a different approach."

"What was that?"

"I started trying to find people the jurors knew: family, friends, acquaintances, and then make contact with them to see if *they'd* talk. About an hour ago I hit pay dirt."

"What do you mean?" Ann asked, the hair on the back of her neck starting to prickle.

"One of the jurors was a woman named Crystal Barman."

"Yeah, I've tried to call her numerous times, but all I've ever gotten was an answering machine," Ann said.

"I got the same response when I tried to call her," Gary explained. "But then I located a friend of Crystal's named Patti Majewski. She gave me the cold shoulder at first, too, but after I did a little more talking she recognized my name and said she'd read my book. It seems she's something of a fan," Gary added modestly, "and so she agreed to talk to me."

"How fortunate that your fifteen minutes of fame haven't quite ended," Ann said dryly. "So what did Patti say?"

"I'll get to that if you'd stop interrupting me," Gary scolded. "Patti said she and Crystal used to be fairly close, but after the trial Crystal changed completely. She got very withdrawn and didn't want to socialize with anybody. She particularly didn't want to talk about the trial. If anyone brought it up, she'd leave the room immediately."

"That's weird," Ann said. "I wonder why it affected her to that extent."

"I'm getting to that," Gary said, starting to sound exasperated. "Patti said that about a month ago she picked Crystal up and they went to a bridal shower. On the way home they stopped for a couple drinks and apparently the liquor caused Crystal to lower her guard, because after leaving the bar, while Patti was driving home, Crystal started talking about what had happened at the trial."

"What was it?" Ann asked eagerly.

"Apparently the jury foreman—"

"Claude Furseth," Ann put in.

"Right," Gary said. "According to what Crystal told Patti, Claude pretty much bullied Crystal and some of the other jurors into voting to acquit the two defendants."

"What?" Ann asked incredulously. "How did he do that?"

"With good old-fashioned intimidation and threats, apparently," Gary replied. "Crystal told Patti that while they were in the jury room, Furseth quoted Bible passages supposedly condemning homosexuality, and said anyone who voted to find the kids guilty would be condemned to eternal hellfire. He also made somewhat explicit threats of personal harm to Crystal if she tried to tell what happened once the case was over."

"This is unbelievable!" Ann exclaimed. "How could one person strong-arm an entire jury into voting against their wishes?"

"It sounds like he didn't have to strong-arm the entire jury," Gary replied. "At least some of them were leaning in favor of acquittal anyway. But apparently he was very persuasive in bending the others to do his bidding."

Ann paused for a long moment. "I don't know what to say. I'm absolutely stunned. I've never heard of such a thing happening, outside of movies. What made Crystal spill her guts when she did?"

"It sounds like she'd been racked with guilt ever since the case ended and she just couldn't keep it to herself any longer."

"Has she told anyone else besides Patti?"

"I don't think so. Patti says it was a very emotional experience for Crystal even to tell her. She described Crystal as being very high-strung and emotional by nature, and this has been hell on her. Patti says after telling what happened, Crystal broke down and sobbed for quite a while, then suddenly snapped out of it and became almost hysterical. She insisted that Patti promise she'd never tell another soul about it. Patti has tried to bring the subject up a couple times and Crystal cuts her off immediately. Says none of it ever happened, that she made the whole story up."

"But Patti doesn't buy the recantation?"

"Not for a minute," Gary replied. "She said she'd be willing to bet the farm that everything Crystal said in the car was true but that she's scared shitless that someone will find out she ratted on Furseth."

Ann's head was swimming. "This is dynamite! If it's true, it explains so much about why the verdict came out the way it did. You didn't try to contact Crystal after talking to Patti, did you?"

"No, I was afraid she might get spooked and take off before you had a chance to try to talk to her. Patti said the last time they spoke, Crystal was talking about some vague plan of relocating to a warmer climate. She's a weaver by trade and says she could do that just as easily in New Mexico or Arizona, where the winters are milder. Patti said that was the first time that idea had ever been mentioned. She thinks Crystal is so frightened that she might very well go AWOL."

"I need to try to talk to her right away," Ann said urgently. "My notes about the jurors are at the office. You wouldn't happen to have Crystal's address on you?"

"You betcha. It's 2486 Mill Pond Road. Patti says you go west out of Mount Pleasant on Highway B about three miles. Mill Pond Road will go off to the left. You follow it for two miles and you'll come to a stop sign. Crystal's house is the third place on the right after that."

"Thanks, Gary. I really owe you one for this."

"Are you thinking of going over there right now?" Gary asked.

"Just as soon as I change my clothes," Ann replied. She looked at the clock. It was five-thirty. "If I hurry, I can be there by seven. Maybe I can catch her while she's having dinner."

"Would you like me to go with you?" Gary asked.

"No, I think it'd be best if I went alone. Crystal might get even more skittish if more than one person at a time descends on her. I appreciate the offer, though."

"Let me know how you make out."

"I sure will. I'll call you the minute I get back. And thanks again for your help. This is the first decent lead I've had."

"They don't call me 'Nose for the News' Carlson for nothing," Gary boasted. "By the way, I'm still working on some leads that might be able to tell us something about what Charlie Tremaine did with his life before he blew into our fair metropolis."

"Keep up the good work," Ann said. "If you come up with another great scoop like this, I might just have to reconsider the type of reward I'd be willing to give you."

"Say no more," Gary said. "I'm off to do more sleuthing. Call me when you get back and we'll compare notes."

"It's a deal," Ann said.

As Ann hung up the phone and hurried upstairs to change her clothes, her heart was pounding with excitement. After a long series of disappointments, she was finally hot on the trail of information that could help bring Bill Robinson the victory he deserved. And even the fact that she would have to drive through Mount Pleasant—now the scene of two unpleasant experiences—was not going to deter her from her mission.

Ann hurriedly changed into a pair of black slacks and a white sweater, ran a comb through her hair, and applied a smidgen of lipstick before racing out the front door. She had already opened her car door and was about to get in when she remembered that she had not activated the security system. Her hand lingered on the car door for a moment while she contemplated taking off without performing this task. No, she decided resignedly. She had promised

Ken that she would take extra care for her safety while he was gone, and she would keep her word.

She turned around, sprinted back up the steps, unlocked the door, and set the alarm, then hurried back to the car and headed out for her rendezvous with Crystal Barman.

Ann had briefly considered calling ahead to see if Crystal was home but immediately abandoned the idea. If the woman was as scared as Gary had described, the slightest hint of trouble was likely to send her into hiding. Ann would just have to take her chances that her trip would not be in vain.

During the hour-long drive to Mount Pleasant, Ann silently ran through various opening lines that she might use to introduce herself. She could forthrightly appeal to Crystal's sense of fair play: "Ms. Barman, I'm an attorney representing Bill Robinson in a civil suit against Brad English and Sam Jenkins. I've studied the transcript from the criminal trial and it looks to me like something fishy might have gone on during jury deliberations. Is there anything you'd care to tell me?"

Ann shook her head. That sounded too accusatory. How about, "Ms. Barman, one of the other jurors who served in the criminal case has just come forward and said that the jury foreman, Claude Furseth, threatened her with bodily harm unless she voted to acquit the defendants. Were you aware of anything like that going on, or by any chance did Furseth make such a comment to you?"

Ann made a face. That was an out-and-out lie. As an officer of the court she could probably be subject to discipline if she coerced a statement from a witness under false pretenses. What about, "Ms. Barman, I've read the transcript of the criminal trial and I just don't see how twelve reasonably intelligent people could have found those two young hooligans not guilty. Tell me, what *were* you people thinking?"

That sounded both condescending and downright sarcastic. Ann made a growling sound deep in her throat. She'd be damned if she knew what she could possibly say that might make this woman spill her guts. She guessed she'd just have to wait until she and Crystal Barman were face-to-face and then wing it.

Ann had Gary's directions to Crystal's house on the seat next to her as she drove. It was seven o'clock straight up when she arrived at the Mount Pleasant city limits. With steely determination, she tried to put her last two visits to that fair city out of her mind. She drove across town and found the road Gary had mentioned. Just as he had said, three miles out of town she encountered Mill Pond Road and turned left.

As every turn of the wheels drew her closer to her encounter with Crystal Barman, Ann couldn't help but admire the rustic beauty of the area. The road was narrow and framed on either side by large oak trees. Their branches hung over the road, casting eerie shadows.

The houses in this area were widely spaced and set far back off the road. Ann came to the stop sign Gary had described. After dutifully coming to a halt, Ann pulled across the intersection and began counting the driveways on the right-hand side of the road. One. Two. Three. She braked to a stop and peered up the lane. She could just barely see a dwelling. Taking a deep breath, she pulled into the drive. "Ready or not, here I come," she murmured.

The house was white clapboard. The porch was sagging a bit but the place was well kept and cheerful, with window boxes brimming with flowers adorning the entire front of the residence. Ann could see a light through the front window. There was no vehicle in evidence, but there was a two-car detached garage to the right of the house with the door shut.

Ann cut the car's engine. She sat quietly for a moment, drumming the fingers of her right hand on the leather upholstery. Maybe it was a mistake to have raced all the way over here without a definite plan of action. She still hadn't decided on the best way to approach Crystal Barman. A series of wild thoughts ran through Ann's head. What if Crystal got hysterical? What if she called the police? Worse, what if she called Claude Furseth and told him that Ann was digging up dirt on him?

This is ridiculous, Ann scolded herself. She hadn't come all this way only to chicken out at the last minute. She opened the car door, got out, and walked up to the front entrance of the house.

There was no doorbell, so Ann rapped soundly on the door. She thought she heard some noise inside but there was no response. She knocked again and called out, "Hello? Is anyone home?"

Straining her ears, Ann again thought she heard a sound from within. "Ms. Barman?" she called. She was just about to rap a third time when the door opened a crack. Ann found herself face-to-face with a thin blond woman in her early fifties. "Ms. Barman?" she asked again.

The woman nodded.

"I'm Ann Monroe from Madison. Could I have a few minutes of your time?"

"What do you want?" Crystal Barman's voice was high-pitched and breathy.

Ann hesitated just a moment. Here was the moment of truth. She looked the woman squarely in the eye and said earnestly, "I'm an attorney. I'm representing Bill Robinson in a civil suit against Sam Jenkins and Brad English."

At the mention of these three names, Crystal's mouth dropped open and her chin began to tremble. She began to push the door shut.

"Wait, please," Ann said urgently. "Would you just hear me out?"

Crystal's chin continued to tremble but she made no effort to close the door the rest of the way.

"Bill Robinson didn't get a fair shake at the criminal trial," Ann went on. "I've read the transcript. There was plenty of evidence to convict Jenkins and English, but they walked. I want you to help me understand why."

Crystal stared at Ann some more, a deer-in-the-headlights expression on her face.

"Please," Ann said. "Won't you just give me a few minutes of your time? Then, if you'd like, I'll leave you in peace. Please."

Crystal continued to look at Ann for what seemed

like an eternity. Finally, without uttering a word, she opened the door and stepped back, allowing Ann to enter.

The kitchen was attractively decorated with bird's-eye maple cabinets and a square fruitwood table and four chairs with floral cushions. The walls were covered with hand-loomed tapestries. In the next room, Ann could see a loom and numerous baskets of yarn. Crystal took a seat in one of the kitchen chairs. Ann followed suit.

When Crystal made no effort to speak, Ann said, "Ms. Barman, I've heard rumors that something improper might have occurred while the jury was deliberating."

Crystal immediately tensed up and clutched her hands tightly together.

Ann plunged ahead. "I've heard that Claude Furseth used intimidation tactics in order to talk people into voting to acquit. If that really happened, it's a very serious matter and Mr. Furseth should be prosecuted."

"No!" Crystal's voice came out as almost a wail.

"You needn't worry," Ann assured the frightened woman. "Nothing will happen to you. I just need to know if what I heard is true—"

"No!" Crystal Barman reached across the table and gripped Ann's wrist tightly. "Nothing happened!" she exclaimed, her eyes wild. "Do you hear me? I won't confirm anything because nothing happened. Whoever told you this is lying!"

Ann took a deep breath and slowly pulled her arm free. She looked down at her wrist. It bore the imprint of Crystal's fingers. "I understand that you're frightened," she said soothingly. "I promise that nothing will happen to you. I'll see that you're protected. We can get a restraining order—"

"I said no!" Crystal jumped to her feet and put her hands over her ears. "It's all lies! I don't want to hear any more! I want you to leave right now or I'll call the sheriff!"

Ann also got to her feet and took a step toward the distraught woman. "Ms. Barman, please—"

"Get out!" Crystal screamed. *"Get out now!"* She cowered against the wall next to the refrigerator like a trapped animal.

"All right," Ann said, putting her hands up in a gesture of appeasement. "I'm going." She reached into her purse and pulled out a business card, which she set on the table. "But if you change your mind, would you please call me? People like Claude Furseth need to be taught that they can't get away with manipulating the system, and it's people like you who can do it."

Crystal Barman remained huddled against the wall, making low keening noises.

"Thank you for your time, Ms. Barman," Ann said. "And please remember what I said."

As Ann got back into her car, she felt slightly shaky and sick to her stomach. She had handled it all wrong. She had come on much too strong with the obviously fragile woman. Her chances of finding out what had really happened in that jury room were probably nil.

"I should have let Gary talk to her," Ann grumbled as she turned the car around and pulled out of the driveway. He had an easygoing way about him that made people want to spill their guts. She, on the other hand, in her exuberance to find out the truth, had treated Crystal like a hostile witness.

Ann was still berating her poor judgment when she rolled up to the stop sign down the road from the Barman residence. Dusk had fallen, and with the heavy tree growth in the area, visibility was fading fast. As Ann absentmindedly began to pull away from the stop sign, her headlights picked up something in the center of the road about one hundred feet ahead.

She hadn't noticed anything lying there when she'd passed that spot earlier. It was possible something had fallen off a truck, but she hadn't heard or seen any other traffic passing by. She coasted slowly forward, observing the object and preparing to drive around it, when it suddenly dawned on her what it was. It was a man's body!

"Oh, my God!" Ann gasped. What could have happened? Did someone get hit by a car? Was he sick? Was he passed out? A chill came over her. Was he dead?

As all these ideas ran through her mind, Ann stopped the car about twenty feet from the body. She put it in park and turned on her hazard lights, then opened the door and got out. "Hello?" she called as she approached. "Are you all right?" From the way the body was dressed, it looked like it was a young man, and he was lying facedown on the pavement, his arms over his head.

"Do you need help?" Ann continued. "I have a cell phone in the car. Should I call nine-one-one?"

There was no response.

Swallowing hard, Ann knelt down next to the man and hesitantly reached out and put one hand on his shoulder. "Can you hear me?" she asked, giving the shoulder a little shake. The man seemed to groan a bit in response, and Ann leaned closer and shook him again. "What happened? Do you need help?"

As she silently urged the man to respond, Ann suddenly felt herself being lifted off the pavement by two strong sets of arms. "He doesn't need help," a deep male voice said, "but you sure do."

Ann attempted to kick and struggle against her assailants, but they were too strong. She managed to turn her head and saw that they were both wearing stockings over their faces. As she opened her mouth to scream, a third man, also wearing a stocking, approached. As the first two men held her fast, the third man roughly pressed a cloth to Ann's nose and mouth. She smelled a pungent odor and started to gag. She tried to pull away but the third man only pressed the cloth tighter. Then everything went dark.

CHAPTER 26

Ann's next perception was that she was struggling to awaken from a bad dream. It was strange because she couldn't remember arriving home or going to bed, but she must have done both those things or else she wouldn't be sleeping, would she?

As for the dream itself, she couldn't remember the details but she seemed to recall a bunch of figures dressed in dark clothes dancing around her and then sweeping her off the ground. It was sort of like the scene with the flying monkeys in *The Wizard of Oz*. Maybe she'd better stop looking at that poster in her office. It was starting to give her nightmares. If she weren't careful she'd be dreaming about skipping down the Yellow Brick Road on her way to see the wizard.

As she continued to swim toward consciousness, she had a vague notion that her head hurt and she was thirsty. Maybe she should get up and get a drink and hope for more pleasant dreams after she settled down again. She tried to roll over in bed but something felt wrong. Then all at once her mental haze lifted and she remembered everything.

The man lying in the road had obviously been a decoy intended to get her to stop so the other men could abduct her, she thought as she opened her eyes and struggled to get them to focus. But how had they known that she'd be on that remote country road?

Ann began to shake with terror as she realized that she must have been followed and then abducted. *Oh, God,* she thought. What if these men were connected with the jury foreman, Claude Furseth? Crystal Barman could be in serious danger, too. Ann somehow had to get back to Crystal's house and warn her.

Oh, God! Ann thought again. *I'm going to die.* Breathing hard, she sent up a silent entreaty. *Help me. Please, somebody help me.*

Ann tried to move but found that she could not. Surveying the situation, she discovered that her feet were bound and her hands were tied behind her, lashed to a post. She blinked hard a couple of times and looked around. She must be in an old barn. The place smelled faintly of animals and she was seated on a bale of hay, her back leaning against a wooden gate.

"She's coming to," a deep voice announced.

With some effort, Ann managed to turn her head in the direction of the voice and saw a man with a stocking over his head dressed in jeans and a black T-shirt standing about ten feet away.

"So she is," another male voice answered. Ann looked in that direction and saw another man, similarly attired and also wearing a stocking over his face, walking toward her.

"Hey!" the second man called over his shoulder. "Our guest is back from the dead."

As the second man continued to walk slowly toward her, Ann noticed his watch. It was nine-thirty. She had been unconscious for well over an hour. She ran her tongue around her lips and tried to think of a plan of action, but she was too frightened to come up with anything. She supposed the most important thing was to keep her wits about her and try not to show fear. That was going to be a mighty tall order, since her heart was pounding and she was already shaking visibly.

"Who are you?" Ann managed to ask as the second man came closer still. Her throat was so dry that she could barely choke out the words. She struggled to work up some saliva.

"You're a spunky one, aren't you?" the man said. He stopped directly in front of her. "You weren't talking so smart a while ago. It's amazing what a little chloroform will do." He reached out with one index finger and tweaked her chin.

Ann jerked her head away. "What do you want with me?" she asked again, her voice a bit stronger this time.

"All in good time," the man replied, running his finger sensuously around her lips.

Ann shuddered, trying hard not to think about what the man might have in mind.

The man turned around and called, "Hey, where are you? I told you she's come to life."

As the second man waited for a response from his unseen compatriot, Ann desperately tried to think of what she could do to help herself. There must be at least four men involved in the scheme: the one lying in the road playing possum, the two who had grabbed her, and the one who had administered the chloroform. The first thing she had to do was figure out a way to distinguish them so she could describe them to the police, assuming she got out of there in one piece. She swallowed hard, trying not to think about the alternative.

Concentrate, she told herself as she took some deep breaths. *Try to focus on details.* The man who had touched her was about six feet tall and muscular. His hands were slightly callused, indicating he might be a laborer. He wore brown cowboy boots. Ann would call him Tex.

Turning her head slightly, she glanced at the first man who had spoken, the one with the deep voice. He was a bit shorter and slimmer. Looking more closely, Ann saw that he was wearing a belt with a motorcycle on the buckle. She would call him Harley.

She didn't have to wait long for a glimpse of number three. She heard the footsteps on the cement floor before she could see him. Then he came into view off to her left. He was bigger than the other two, both taller and huskier. His jeans were very tight and he wore black boots. Ann would call him Blacky.

"Well, well," Blacky said as he swaggered up to Ann. "How are we feeling? I hope I didn't do any permanent damage."

"Are you the one who drugged me?" Ann asked.

FINAL JUSTICE

"Yes, ma'am," Blacky replied with a sneer in his voice.

Ann clenched her jaw to keep her teeth from chattering. "Why are you doing this?"

Blacky chuckled. "We just thought you looked like a good-looking girl and we wanted to get to know you better. I'm sure you'd like that, wouldn't you?" he asked, leaning close to her. Ann could smell alcohol on his breath through the stocking.

"Did Reverend Tremaine put you up to this?" Ann asked.

"Who? I don't know anyone by that name. No, you see, in the fall me and my buddies like to do a little hunting. But seeing as how hunting season is still months off, we thought maybe we'd bag us one of the two-legged variety. Didn't you know it was open season on loudmouthed women lawyers?" He pantomimed drawing back a bow and unleashing an arrow. "Bull's-eye!" he chortled. "I always was a damn good shot."

Ann began to shake as the vivid imagery of the Lambs' Web site came rushing back. There was no doubt in her mind that Tremaine's group, if not the reverend personally, was behind her abduction. The bigger question was, What had these men been told to do with her once they captured her? Although she realized that she probably did not want to know the answer, she nevertheless ventured to ask the question.

"How long are you planning to keep me here?"

"Don't tell me you're getting homesick already, sweetheart. We haven't even gotten acquainted yet. You're gonna find that me and my friends are real friendly." Blacky sat down beside Ann on the hay bale and put his arm around her, brashly squeezing one of her breasts.

The indignity of his actions made Ann cry out boldly in spite of her fear. "Don't touch me!"

"You are a lively one, aren't you?" Blacky laughed. He squeezed her breast again, harder this time. "I can see where we're gonna have to teach you a little respect. Isn't that right, boys?"

"You bet," Harley said.

"Sure thing," Tex chimed in.

Blacky glanced off to his right. "What's taking the kid so long?" he asked. "He ought to be back by now."

Ann's ears perked up at the mention of the fourth man. He must be the one who had been lying in the road. She wondered where he had gone. She supposed she didn't dare hope that he'd gotten cold feet about the whole operation and gone to fetch help.

"I don't know," Harley replied. "You want me to go look for him?"

"Maybe you'd better," Blacky answered. "I thought it was a mistake to get him involved in this. I swear he could screw up a wet dream."

"Oh, he's okay," Harley said. "He's just inexperienced."

"Guys like him can royally fuck up operations like this," Blacky said.

"I'll find him," Harley said. He turned and walked off.

Blacky turned his attention back to Ann. "Now, where were we? Oh, yeah. We were talking about how long we're going to keep you here. Now, the answer to that question could very well depend on whether you're a fast learner or not. Ain't that right?" he asked his remaining compatriot.

"Yes, sirree," Tex replied cheerfully as he walked over to them. "Shove over a little, sister," he said. He sat down on the other side of Ann and put his hand on her knee. She was now squeezed in between the two men so tightly that she couldn't move. She had to force herself to keep breathing evenly in order to keep from getting faint.

"Let me ask you something," Blacky said, leaning over so his stockinged face was nearly touching Ann's. "Do you really like perverts or is representing them just a job for you?"

Ann gritted her teeth and remained silent.

"I was wondering that, too," Tex said, sliding his hand up Ann's leg. "Why would a nice-looking woman like you want to waste her time hanging around with queers?"

"The same thing goes for taking sides with those baby killers," Blacky said. "How can a woman do that? You look like a nice person. Don't you have any maternal instincts?"

Ann forced herself to look at the floor.

"Hey!" Blacky said, grabbing Ann hard by the hair and forcing her head up. "I'm talking to you. The first thing you better get straight here is, when I ask you a question, I expect an answer. Got that?"

"Go to hell," Ann spat at him.

Blacky slapped her hard across the face. Ann winced but did not cry out.

"It's not fair that you have all the fun," Tex said to his partner. "The rule here is share and share alike." He slapped Ann even harder, then pulled on her ears until she thought her eardrums would burst. In spite of her best efforts to remain silent, she found herself making low whimpering sounds.

"She's a tough one!" Tex announced admiringly. "It'll be interesting to see just what it takes to make her cooperate."

"We've got all night," Blacky said leisurely.

Ann felt her stomach lurch as visions of the possible atrocities to come flew through her head.

"Hell, yes," Tex said. "We're just getting warmed up." He slapped Ann again. Within seconds Blacky followed suit.

Ann's head was pounding and her feelings of doom were rapidly mounting when she heard two sets of footsteps approaching.

"There you are," Blacky said, looking up. "What the hell was going on?"

"We've got a problem," Harley announced. He sounded out of breath. "The kid says there's somebody up at the house."

"Shit!" Blacky exclaimed, jumping to his feet. He marched over to the fourth man and grabbed him roughly by the arm. "You told me you checked the place out and everybody was gone. How the fuck do you explain this?"

"I don't know," the young man they'd called "the kid" stammered. "There was no one there before. They must've just come back. I'm sorry."

"You're sorry!" Blacky spat. "I ought to shoot you

and skin you out like a deer. Then you'd know what sorry was." He addressed Tex and Harley. "Come on. We gotta get out of here."

The three men started to walk off.

"Wait!" the kid exclaimed. "What about her?"

"What about her?" Blacky asked. "Somebody will probably find her in a day or two."

"You can't just leave her here," the kid protested. "She might starve to death or a wild animal might get her."

"That's her problem," Blacky said. "Come on, fellas. Let's get to the truck. If Mr. Softy wants to stay behind and keep the bitch company, that's his problem." He strode over to Ann and leaned down so that she could feel his breath on her face. "You were warned, sweetheart. You should have taken the hint and cleared out while you could. Now you're going to be sorry." Then he turned around and rapidly walked out of the barn, followed by two of the other men. The kid stood there for a moment; then he, too, started for the door.

"Please help me," Ann said urgently.

The kid stopped, then turned back.

"Untie me," Ann implored.

The kid looked back in the direction his companions had gone, then turned back to Ann.

"Please," Ann begged. "You seem like a good person. This is your chance to prove that you're not like them."

The kid hesitated a moment, then hurried over to Ann's side. He pulled a jackknife out of his pocket and exposed one of the blades, walked behind her and deftly cut the ropes that were securing her wrists, then came around the front and freed her ankles.

"Thank you," Ann said gratefully as she shook her hands to try to restore the circulation. "I'll never forget your kindness."

"Wait for about ten minutes to make sure the coast is clear, then walk to the right when you leave the building," the kid said. "Stay on the gravel road for about a half mile. Your car is parked down there. The keys are in it."

"Thank you," Ann said again. "If you tell me your name, I'll see that you get a reward."

"They'll kill me if I tell you my name," the kid said, fear evident in his voice. "They might kill me anyway." He paused a moment, then said, "I'm real sorry about all this. Good luck." Then he turned and sprinted outside.

Ann waited for about seven minutes, then decided she couldn't stand to be cooped up in that building a moment longer. She stood up and tried to take a step but immediately found that she was so dizzy she nearly fell. She steadied herself by clinging to a post and took more deep breaths. After a minute or so she tried again to walk. Moving slowly at first, then a bit faster, she made her way outside and, following the kid's directions, reached her car in about twenty minutes, stumbling along the rutted gravel road in the moonlight.

As the kid had promised, her keys, as well as her purse, were in the car. She started the engine and locked the doors. She considered calling 911 but decided there was little point in doing so from that remote location. She wouldn't be able to explain where she was, and she didn't think the police would be able to track her by her phone signal. Since her abductors had apparently fled, it seemed to make more sense to wait until she came to some landmark.

She drove back to the barn where she'd been held captive. From there she continued on the gravel road and in about three quarters of a mile she came to a paved road and a farmhouse with the lights on. This must be the reason her captors had fled.

Locked safely in her car, Ann called the Jasper County Sheriff's Department, explained what had occurred, and then sat back and waited to be rescued.

CHAPTER 27

"Make that gag good and tight," Jesse Greer directed. "I don't want to hear a single peep out of her."

Denise Riley threw her head around violently but there was little she could do to resist. The four men who had attacked her as she walked through a park near her home had already bound her hands and feet, so it was not much of an effort for one of the thugs to tie a handkerchief tightly across her mouth.

"Bastards!" Denise cursed through the gag. Cowards, too, all wearing dark stockings over their faces.

"All right," Jesse said, "now blindfold her."

One of the men wrapped heavy duct tape around Denise's head, over her eyes.

"Now carry her over to the shelter house."

Denise tried not to panic as she felt herself roughly being picked up and carried a short distance by two of the men.

"Okay. That's far enough," Jesse said.

The men unceremoniously dropped Denise. The

FINAL JUSTICE

back of her head hit the cement floor. The pain was intense and she groaned aloud.

"Not acting so smart now, are you, bitch?" Jesse taunted. He spat at the helpless woman. "You might think you're high and mighty, but you're nothing but a baby killer. Isn't that right, boys?"

"Yeah," one of the others echoed. "Godless baby killer."

"Worthless bitch," another added.

In her cocoonlike state, Denise tried hard to think of some way to help herself, but she was completely helpless. She couldn't get away and she couldn't even describe her captors, except perhaps by voice.

"Worthless fucking abortionist," the one with the Southern accent jeered close to her ear. His proximity made Denise shiver. He was obviously the leader of the group. And he was clearly the most dangerous.

"I think this bitch needs to be taught a lesson," Jesse said. "What do you all think?"

"Yeah."

"You bet."

"Fuck, yes."

Denise tensed, wondering what form the lesson would take. She got her answer a moment later when someone kicked her hard in the side.

"All right!" the Southern boy drawled. "Everybody join in."

Suddenly all four men were kicking Denise, in the side, in the legs, in the head. The punishment seemed to go on endlessly, and the pain was so intense she was sure they were going to kill her. Then the blows ceased just as quickly as they'd begun.

"Are we having fun yet?" The Southern boy whooped. "Boys, I think it's time to move on to plan two."

The bile rose in Denise's throat as she wondered what fresh hell lay in store for her.

Two squad cars containing five Jasper County deputies pulled up alongside Ann's car within minutes of her phone call.

Ann immediately told the officers about her concerns for Crystal Barman's safety, and two of them were dispatched to Crystal's house, which was some five miles away. They returned in about twenty minutes, reporting that Crystal was not home, her car was gone, and it appeared she had left in a hurry.

Although the last thing in the world Ann wanted was to ever have to set foot in that barn again, the deputies insisted that she accompany them back to the structure. Even in the presence of five brawny, armed men, Ann found herself shaking with fright the entire time she remained in the building.

While the other deputies actively searched for evidence that might reveal the identity of her abductors, Ann gave a lengthy statement to a detective named Jon Wilson.

"Your descriptions of the four men are great," Wilson praised Ann. "It must have been tough for you to concentrate on remembering that many details, considering what was happening to you."

"And here I always thought my good memory and

my eye for detail were completely worthless traits," Ann said. She rubbed her hands wearily over her eyes. "I just wish I could give you something more concrete to go on. I realize that those physical descriptions probably match at least a quarter of the people in the county."

"No, you did great," Wilson reassured her. "The little details like the boots and the belt buckle could prove very useful. Do you think you would recognize their voices if you heard them again?"

Ann nodded. "Definitely. I don't think I'll forget those voices as long as I live."

"Good," Wilson said. "That could come in very handy."

Another deputy walked into the barn and made his way over to where Wilson and Ann were standing. "I talked to the old couple living in the farmhouse," the new arrival said. "Their names are Dirk and Irene Swenson."

"What did they have to say?" Wilson asked.

"They had been visiting their son and daughter-in-law in Illinois the past two days. They'd been planning to stay down there another day, but Mrs. Swenson started feeling a little under the weather tonight and decided she wanted to sleep in her own bed, so they headed back. They said this barn hasn't been used in years, and they were shocked to find out that criminal activity had taken place on their property."

"They don't have any idea who any of the men who abducted Ms. Monroe might have been?"

The officer shook his head. "No clue at all. They're

quite concerned for their own safety. They wondered if they should drive into Mount Pleasant and spend the night with Mrs. Swenson's niece."

"You tell them I don't think they have anything to be concerned about," Detective Wilson said. "Unless I'm badly mistaken, the four men who pulled this caper are long gone, and this farm is the last place on earth any of them are likely to set foot."

"I'll tell 'em that, sir," the officer said. "I know that will really ease their minds."

In spite of the evening's excitement, Ann could feel fatigue overtaking her, and she still had nearly an hour's drive back to Madison. "If you don't need me for anything else right now, is it all right if I go home?" she asked.

"Of course," Detective Wilson replied. "I'll probably be in touch tomorrow. I'm very sorry for what happened, but I want you to know our department will do everything in its power to catch the men who did this to you. And we'll also try to locate Ms. Barman."

"Thank you," Ann said. "I appreciate everything you're doing."

"Drive carefully," Detective Wilson said as Ann walked out to her car.

It was three in the morning when Ann got home. She pulled her car into the garage and shut the door behind her. After deactivating the security system, she walked into the house. She had left a light on in the kitchen, and her black cat came sauntering out of the dining room and brushed against her leg.

Ann reached down and picked up the cat, rubbing her face in its soft fur. She felt weak and numb, and her face stung from being slapped. She set the cat down, opened a cupboard door, and took out a bottle of cognac. She removed the stopper and took a long drink right from the bottle. It wasn't very ladylike, but after all, it *was* three in the morning and she had just been held hostage and beaten up and was lucky to have escaped with her life. So under the circumstances good manners and protocol could go to hell in a handbasket for all she cared.

After taking another long swallow of booze, she noticed the light on her answering machine blinking. She hit the play button.

"You have three messages," the machine announced.

The first two were from Gary Carlson. The first was friendly and nonchalant. "Hi, Ann, it's Gary. It's about ten o'clock. I was just anxious to hear how you made out with Crystal, but I guess you're not home yet. Give me a call when you get back."

The second was more urgent. "Hi, it's Gary again. It's now eleven-thirty and I'm starting to get a little worried about you. Call me as soon as you get home."

When the third message started to play, Ann fully expected to hear Gary's voice again, but instead a highly distraught woman came on the line. "Ann, this is Marcia Inkster, Denise Riley's assistant. I'm calling from University Hospital. It's about two-thirty. Denise was brought to the emergency room here about a half hour ago. She was found in a park near her house. She'd been severely beaten. She's in a coma." Marcia's voice broke at this point and as she paused, Ann set the cognac bottle down on the counter with a loud thud.

"I'm really sorry to bother you at home," Marcia went on, "but if you get this message, could you please come to the hospital? Thanks."

"Oh, God!" Ann moaned, her own weariness and fear and pain vanishing. She scooped up her car keys and purse and raced back to the garage.

CHAPTER 28

"I knew I should have gone with you to talk to Crystal Barman," Gary Carlson said. "If I had gone along, you might not have been attacked."

"There's no way to know that," Ann said.

It was early Sunday afternoon, and Ann and Gary, along with Marcia Inkster and Denise Riley's daughter, Maureen, were keeping vigil in a waiting room at University Hospital, where Denise was undergoing surgery to remove bone fragments that had been driven into her brain by her attackers.

Ann and Gary were seated on one vinyl couch while Maureen and Marcia were seated on an adjacent couch.

"Who knows?" Ann said. "Maybe if you'd been with me, things could have gotten even uglier. We might have both been killed." She gingerly touched her face, which was badly bruised and very tender.

"Are you doubting my ability to protect you?" Gary asked, feigning hurt.

"No, I'm just being practical," Ann said. "After all, four to two still isn't great odds, especially when the four had the advantages of both surprise and chloroform."

"I still feel responsible for putting you in danger," Gary said.

"Don't worry about me," Ann said. "I came through okay. It's Denise we need to think about now." She paused a moment and added, "And also Crystal Barman. I just hope those thugs who ambushed me didn't grab her, too."

Just then a female doctor stepped into the waiting room and everyone fell silent.

The doctor walked over to Denise's daughter. "Ms. Riley?" she asked.

Maureen nodded.

"I'm Mary Jo Lanska. Your mother is out of surgery, and I'm happy to report that things went well."

"Oh, thank God!" Maureen exclaimed, clasping her hands over her mouth.

Marcia Inkster began to weep.

"We were able to remove the bone fragments without incident," Dr. Lanska said. "Your mom has just been taken to the recovery room."

"What's her prognosis?" Ann asked.

"She's still in critical condition," Dr. Lanska said, not mincing words. "We'll be monitoring her very closely for the next forty-eight hours."

"Will she have brain damage?" Maureen asked, her voice quavering.

"I'm afraid it's too early to know that," the doctor said. "We'll be better able to assess her cognitive function once she comes out of the coma."

"But you think she *will* come out of it?" Gary asked.

"We're certainly hoping for that," the doctor said. "At this point there's no reason not to be cautiously optimistic about her chances for a good recovery."

"When can I see her?" Maureen asked.

"In about half an hour," the doctor replied kindly. "There's a small waiting room closer to recovery. If you'll follow me, I'll take you there."

"Thank you," Maureen said. "Can Marcia come, too?"

"Of course," Dr. Lanska replied. "You'll only be able to be with her for a few minutes, though."

"Just so I can see her," Maureen said eagerly. "I need to see for myself that she's still alive."

"I understand." The doctor patted Maureen's arm. "Come with me."

Several minutes later, as Ann and Gary sat silently contemplating Denise's fate, Ann sensed a movement off to her left. Looking up, she saw Ken rushing into the waiting room.

"Thank God you're all right!" Ken said, hurrying over to Ann. She stood up to meet him and he hugged her tightly. "I've been so worried."

"I'm fine," Ann replied, hugging him back.

"It's really swell how all you Mishler and Stettler lawyers get on so well together," Gary said jovially, looking from Ken to Ann and back to Ken. Although the true nature of Ann and Ken's relationship was quite apparent, Gary said no more. "How goes it, Counselor?" he asked Ken.

"That's the longest five hours I've ever spent," Ken said ruefully as he and Ann sat down. "I was on the road within fifteen minutes of the time Ann called me this morning, but there's road construction almost the entire way. I was seriously thinking of pulling into an airport and chartering a plane. How's Denise?" he asked.

Ann filled him in on Dr. Lanska's recent comments.

"Who found her?" Ken asked.

"A man with insomnia who was walking his dog through the park saw her and called for an ambulance," Ann explained. "It's a good thing he did, because if she'd lain there until morning it probably would have been too late."

"And how are you doing?" Ken asked, gently touching Ann's cheek. "Did you get checked out by a doctor?"

Ann shook her head. "I'm just bruised," she said. "There's no lasting damage—at least not physically. It may be a while before I take any solitary evening drives down lonely country lanes—or, for that matter, before I go anywhere near Mount Pleasant," she added ruefully.

"I've been on edge ever since I first saw that damn Web site," Ken said, standing up and starting to pace. "And this is my worst nightmare come true." Turning to Ann, he asked, "Did the men who held you give you any idea what they'd been told to do to you?"

"Not really," Ann said. "They were just starting to slap me around when the youngest one reported that the elderly couple who lived in the farmhouse on the property had come home. They all hightailed it out of there pretty fast after that."

"Thank God the old couple's plans changed unexpectedly," Ken said, sitting down next to Ann again. "Did any of the men mention Tremaine or the Lambs?"

"No," Ann replied. "I brought up Tremaine's name and they played dumb. One of them did tell me I'd been warned. I took that to mean these guys were somehow connected to the two I encountered in Mount Pleasant—the ones I think sent me those two notes."

"Did any of their voices sound familiar—maybe like one of the picketers at the clinic?"

Ann shook her head. "No."

"Tremaine or someone high up in the Lambs' organization must have ordered this," Ken said. "Is the sheriff's department going to interview the reverend?"

"The deputies I talked to said they would. I gave them Ravenswood's name, too. He's probably filing a slander and defamation lawsuit against us as we speak."

"Let him," Ken said in a growl. "I'll get the judge to declare it frivolous and have costs assessed against the Lambs and Ravenswood personally."

"I've been trying to come up with some background on Tremaine," Gary said. "I've got some feelers out down in his old stomping ground in Tennessee. I haven't come up with anything yet, but I'll see if I can't turn up the heat a little bit. It could prove helpful on this end if we could find some dirt from his past."

"At this point, anything would be helpful," Ken said. He looked at his watch and then turned to Ann. "Do you mind if I desert you for a little while? I want to go to the office and draft another supplemental motion asking Judge Bies to order the images of you and Denise removed from the Web site immediately. Obviously the fact that you were both abducted and assaulted lends great credence to my argument that your inclusion on the Web site served no purpose but to incite violence."

"Go ahead," Ann said. "I'll be fine here."

Turning to Gary, Ken asked, "Will you stay with her until I get back?"

"It would be an honor," Gary replied.

"I don't need a chaperon here," Ann protested. "What could possibly happen to me in a hospital waiting room?"

"I'm not going to allow you to take any more chances," Ken said. "Now, either Gary stays here with you or you're coming down to the office with me. I'm not going to leave you here alone."

While Ann was touched by his concern, she did not cotton to the idea of being treated like a helpless waif. "Oh, all right," she said grudgingly.

"While Ken's gone we'll work the phones and see if we can track down some info on Crystal Barman's whereabouts," Gary suggested.

"Okay," Ann agreed. "I'm concerned about the Robinsons, too. What if they're the next targets?"

"You should call and warn them about what happened," Ken said.

"I tried," Ann said, "but I couldn't reach them.

I left messages at Bill's apartment and at Tom and Laurie's house."

"We'll keep trying to raise them, too," Gary said.

"I'll be back in a couple of hours," Ken said. "Call me at the office if any news breaks here." He headed out of the waiting room, then turned back. "Oh, one more thing. I'm going to arrange for a bodyguard for you." Ann opened her mouth to protest but Ken cut her off. "Don't even think about trying to talk me out of it. You're getting a bodyguard whether you want one or not."

CHAPTER 29

Ken spent Sunday night at Ann's house. He had hired a bodyguard to start work the following day but insisted on spending the first night after the attack alone with her.

"What if the girls try to call you at home?" Ann asked as they sat on the couch in her living room.

"They're still with Patsy and her family in Minneapolis. I already called them and explained what happened. I told them if they need to reach me I'd either be at the hospital or at your house, and I gave them both numbers."

A sudden chill went through Ann, and she shivered.

"Are you okay?" Ken asked.

Ann snuggled closer to him. "I think what happened is just now starting to sink in, and I'm feeling a little spooked."

"You're probably experiencing a form of post-traumatic stress syndrome," Ken said, holding her tightly. "They say it's common for a person who has undergone a traumatic event not to be able to truly process it for a while. You're in shock and denial at first, and it's not until sometime later that you begin to feel the impact of what's happened. It's a coping mechanism. It's perfectly normal."

"I don't feel normal," Ann said. She was starting to shake. "I feel very weird all of a sudden, like I'm going to get hysterical."

Ken gently stroked her hair. "It's okay. You're safe. I'm going to make sure of that."

Ann took a deep breath. "I was afraid something like this was going to happen to me. I've never admitted this to anyone, but I've been afraid ever since I got hit by that brick at the abortion clinic riot. For months I had nightmares that someone was going to kill me. They'd finally started to go away in the last year, but as soon as I heard Reverend Tremaine was back in the area I started to panic again." She covered her face with her hands and began to weep. "And now I'm fine and Denise Riley is in a coma, fighting for her life. I'm so ashamed at myself for being such a baby."

"You are *not* acting like a baby," Ken assured her. "What you're feeling is perfectly normal. Why don't you let me get you a glass of wine, and then I think you should try to get some sleep. You're going to need to keep up your strength. Something tells me this is going to be a tough week."

Although in the early part of the evening Ann had trouble dozing off, shortly before dawn she fell into a sound sleep and did not awaken again until after nine o'clock. After she showered and dressed, she went downstairs, where she found Ken sitting at the kitchen table reading the morning paper. He had made a pot of coffee and fed the cats.

"I could get used to having you wait on me like this," Ann said, pouring herself a cup of coffee and sticking a bagel in the toaster oven.

"It would be my pleasure," Ken said. "How do you feel this morning?"

"A lot stronger emotionally than I did last night."

"How about physically?"

Ann touched her cheeks. "The skin on my face feels like it's going to burst open, but I suppose that's to be expected, considering what happened. Any word on Denise?"

"I called the hospital and spoke to Marcia," Ken said. "There's been no change."

Ann felt her stomach churn at the thought of her friend lying in a coma. "I want to go back to the hospital for a while," she said. "I doubt that I'll be able to see her, but at least I can give Marcia and Denise's daughter some moral support."

"We'll go as soon as you've had something to eat," Ken said. "Tom Robinson called about an hour ago," he said as Ann took her bagel out of the toaster oven and put it on a plate.

"I didn't hear the phone," Ann said. "I must have really been dead to the world. Are he and Laurie and Bill all okay?"

"They're fine," Ken replied. "They're very upset about what happened to you and Denise. Tom assured me he'd take extra precautions to make sure his family remains safe."

After Ann had eaten and changed her clothes, she

and Ken drove to the hospital. They ended up staying there until lunchtime. Denise's daughter seemed to be holding up well under the strain.

"Dr. Lanska is still optimistic that Mom will come out of it," Maureen Riley explained as they all sat in the waiting room. "She said the fact that Mom had a quiet night was a good sign, and there's no particular timetable for people who've suffered serious head injuries to start coming around. She says we just have to be patient."

After seeing how worried Ann was, Maureen got permission for Ann to spend five minutes alone with Denise. Although Ann was happy to be able to see for herself that Denise was really still alive, the first glimpse of her friend and client left her physically shaken.

Denise's head was swaddled in bandages and there were tubes and IV lines running everywhere. "Hang in there, Denise," Ann said, trying to sound upbeat. "You're going to pull out of this and be as good as new. Don't you even think about giving up. You've got a lot of people rooting for you, so I want you to concentrate on getting well."

Ann squeezed her friend's lifeless hand. "I'll be back tomorrow to check on you." She turned and fled the room before she dissolved in tears.

After grabbing a bite to eat at Applebee's, Ann and Ken went back to her house. Detective Wilson called and asked Ann some additional questions about her abductors.

"I was just wondering if you've thought of any other details that might help us identify your abductors," the detective said. "For instance, did they refer to each other or any other people by name? Did they mention any place or business name, anything like that?"

"No, I'm sorry," Ann replied. "I'm quite sure I told you everything I heard and observed. Did you find anything on the Swensons' property that might be helpful?"

"Very little," Detective Wilson admitted. "We found some tire tracks that were made by a four-wheel-drive truck, but I'd be willing to venture that two out of three households in that area have a vehicle like that, so that's not much to go on."

"Has Crystal Barman surfaced?" Ann asked.

"No, she hasn't," Wilson replied.

"I'm really worried about her," Ann said.

"We've checked out her house and there's no sign of foul play," the detective said. "The indications are that she just jumped in her car and took off on her own."

"I hope you're right," Ann said warily, "but it seems like too much of a coincidence to me. Have you talked to Reverend Tremaine?"

The detective made a snorting sound. "Yes, and to his lawyer as well. How can I put this? Those conversations were not exactly a high point in my day."

"But they couldn't shed any light on who might have attacked me or Denise Riley?"

"Let me put it this way: If either of them knows anything, they're not talking."

"Well, somebody knows something," Ann said in frustration. "If we can just get them to come forward."

"We're working on that, ma'am. And you be sure and let me know if you think of anything else, no matter how trivial."

The bodyguard Ken had retained came over to her house in the late afternoon. Jeff Steiner was a tall, muscular man in his early thirties. He was businesslike but had an easygoing way about him. Ann liked him at once.

As Ann showed him around and explained what had happened to her and Denise, as well as her past history of animosity with Reverend Tremaine, Jeff corrected her designation of his job title. "We prefer 'personal security consultant,'" he said. "It's a little more modern than 'bodyguard.'"

"That's fine by me," Ann said. "You know, I have to level with you: I feel a little silly about your being here, like it's an over-the-top yuppie reaction to the situation."

"You were kidnapped and beaten!" Ken, who was tagging along behind on the house tour, exclaimed. "Denise is still in a coma! How can you call taking precautions against a repeat occurrence an overreaction?"

"He's right, you know," Jeff chimed in. "These days it just makes good sense to be cautious."

They had finished the house tour and were back in the kitchen. "I suppose you're right," Ann said. She looked at Jeff closely. "Can I ask you something?"

"Sure," Jeff replied.

"Do you carry a gun?"

"Yes," Jeff answered. "Would you like to see it?"

"No," Ann replied immediately.

"Does it bother you that I'm armed?"

"A little," Ann admitted.

"I don't anticipate having to use it," Jeff said. "But like I told you, it's better to be prepared."

Ann nodded slowly. "If both you and Ken think this is a good idea, I'll go along with it, even though I'm a little uncomfortable with the whole scenario."

"Believe me, this is a good idea," Ken said.

"For what it's worth, I agree with him," Jeff put in.

"Okay," Ann said. "You guys win. I'll trust your judgment."

"I don't think you'll regret it," Jeff said.

The following day was Memorial Day, so Ann and Jeff spent a rather quiet day at home. Jeff spent the night downstairs in her house, keeping watch. The next morning he established Ann's new routine. He followed her to work, walked her from the parking ramp to her office, and then returned to her house to catch some shut-eye. He instructed Ann that when she was ready to leave the office, she was to call and he would drive downtown again, come inside the office to escort her to her car, and follow her home.

Ken's first order of business that morning was to file the supplemental motion detailing the weekend's violent occurrences and urging Judge Bies to order the Lambs to remove all references to Ann and Denise from their Web site.

FINAL JUSTICE

Late that afternoon, Ken burst into Ann's office waving a sheaf of papers. "Judge Bies issued her ruling!" he said triumphantly. "We won!"

"We did?" Ann jumped up from her desk and walked over to where Ken was standing. "What did she say?"

"There are fifteen pages of factual findings, but I won't bother with those," Ken said, flipping through the document. "Here are the conclusions of law. 'Based on the foregoing findings of fact, I conclude that plaintiffs have proven with clear and convincing evidence that the defendants acted with specific intent and malice in a blatant and illegal communication of true threats to kill, assault or do bodily harm to the plaintiffs.'"

"That's wonderful," Ann said. "What else?"

Ken continued reading. "'I reject the defendants' attempts to justify their actions as an expression of opinion or as a legitimate and lawful exercise of free speech. I find that plaintiffs are entitled to permanent injunctive relief because they lack an adequate remedy at law. Defendants are hereby immediately and permanently enjoined and restrained from publishing, republishing, reproducing, and/or distributing anywhere, either directly or indirectly, the likeness of either of the plaintiffs. Defendants and their agents shall promptly submit to the custody of the court all materials in their possession, custody, or control that are not in compliance with the provisions of this permanent injunction.'"

"Hip hip hooray!" Ann said, clapping her hands.

"Wait," Ken said. "There's more. 'The court shall

retain jurisdiction of this action for all purposes. The court holds open the issue of monetary damages and will order further briefing on that matter at a later date.' "

"Thank you, Judge Bies!" Ann exclaimed. "She must have worked like a demon to get that out today." She put her arms around Ken. "And thank you for keeping the faith and for all your work on this motion. I couldn't have done it without you."

"You know I'd do anything for you," Ken murmured, holding her close.

They had broken their clinch and Ken was about to head back to his office when there was a brief knock at the door.

"Come in," Ann called.

The door opened and Kari burst in. "Great news, guys!" she exclaimed. "Marcia Inkster just called. Denise woke up about thirty minutes ago!"

CHAPTER 30

"It's so good to see you," Ann said, squeezing Denise's hand. "We were all so worried."

"I'm sorry to have kept you in suspense," Denise replied in a voice that was soft but clear. "If it had been up to me, I would've come to much sooner."

It was early Tuesday evening, and Ann and Ken had stopped at the hospital to visit their friend.

"Well, we're certainly glad to see that you're on the mend," Ken said.

"I'm glad, too," Denise said. "How are you getting along, Ann?" she asked.

Before Ann and Ken went in to see Denise, Denise's daughter had informed them that Denise had been told about Ann's abduction. Ann was aghast. "Are you sure that was wise?" she asked with concern. "She's had such a terrible shock herself. She's still in a fragile state. Hearing what happened to me must really upset her."

"Believe me, if Mom had found out that I'd been holding out on her, she would never have forgiven me," Maureen Riley answered firmly. "She was very concerned about your well-being, of course, but once she heard that you hadn't been seriously hurt, she took it all quite calmly."

Ann smiled at her friend. "Now that you're on the mend, I'm doing just fine. Did I mention that I have a good-looking bodyguard staying with me?"

"Only about three different times," Denise said.

"He's not a bodyguard; he's a personal security consultant," Ken joked.

"Whatever his title is, I think I'm going to be glad he's around," Ann said. "When Ken first proposed the idea I wasn't wild about having someone in the house, but I must admit I've slept much easier the last two nights knowing he's downstairs."

Denise nodded. "It's better to play it safe until the police figure out who was responsible for ruining our weekends."

"Have you talked to the police yet?" Ken asked.

Denise sighed. "Yes. They left just before you came. I wish I could be more help, but the truth is, I can't remember many details."

"It's probably just as well that you can't," Ann said gently.

"I know; they tell me amnesia is the brain's way of coping with trauma," Denise said. "But believe me, if it would help catch the bastards who did this to me and the ones who attacked you, I'd gladly remember every horrible detail."

"Sometimes after an accident memories come back in stages," Ken said.

Denise closed her eyes and tried to will herself to recall what had happened. "It was such a nice night that I'd gone for a walk. I often did that in the evening. It was getting dark, so on my way back I cut through the park. I often did that, too. I was listening to my Walkman and not paying a lot of attention to the world around me when suddenly I was grabbed from behind." She paused and took a couple of deep breaths.

"I'm not sure how many men there were. I think there were at least three or maybe four. I tried to fight, and I tried to scream, but they were too strong. They got me down on the ground and bound and gagged me. Then they wrapped duct tape over my eyes. Before that happened I was able to see that they all had stockings over their faces and they were all wearing dark clothing."

"Exactly the same as the guys who got me," Ann said.

"Then they carried me into the shelter house and threw me on the ground," Denise went on. "That's when things start to get hazy. I know for a while they taunted me and called me names. 'Godless bitch.' 'Baby murderer.' Over and over."

"Maureen said you recall that one of them had a Southern accent?" Ann said.

"Yes." Denise nodded. "I definitely remember that. He was the ringleader. The really nasty one."

"It couldn't have been Reverend Tremaine, could it?" Ann asked hopefully.

Denise shook her head. "I would dearly love to say it was him, but it sounded like a much younger person."

"Still, that's a lead that might help the police find who did it," Ken put in.

"I hope so," Denise said, her thoughts again drifting back to the attack. "I think at first they each kicked me a few times, like that was some kind of a warm-up. Then the last thing I remember was the sound of a heavy metal object, like a crowbar, clinking on the cement floor of the shelter house."

Denise stopped and looked at Ann. "Would you hand me that glass of water, please?"

"Sure," Ann said.

After she'd taken a few swallows of water and handed the glass back to Ann, Denise went on. "I suppose that's what they used to smash my skull in. And that's the last thing I remember until I woke up today feeling like my head had been split open—which, of course, it had."

"You don't remember any of the men calling each other by name or saying anything else that might help identify them?" Ken asked.

Denise shook her head. "Nothing. I've tried so hard to remember, but there's just nothing there."

"If the Lambs haven't complied with the terms of Judge Bies's injunction and removed our pictures from the Web site by tomorrow, Ken is going to haul them back into court," Ann said.

"The judge's ruling is certainly good news," Denise said. "Now if we could just get a hefty money judgment against them. Not that I think we'll ever collect a red cent, you understand. Just for the enormous satisfaction it would give me. Marcia tells me that the Lambs are still picketing at the clinic but that their numbers have dropped off."

Ann nodded. "They're down to about twenty people a day now."

"Maybe the dropouts are either in hiding or home washing out their stockings and dark clothes," Denise said drolly.

Ann smiled. "Maybe so. Anyway, it looks like they're running out of steam. Maybe in a couple more weeks they'll give up the ghost entirely."

"They'll just move on to the next target," Denise said. "Those people obviously see tormenting others as an endless crusade. Why don't they just wear hair shirts and flog themselves? It would make life so much more pleasant for the rest of us."

A nurse stepped into the room. "I hate to be a grinch, but Denise needs her rest. And it's also time for her pain medication."

"It sure is," Denise agreed. "My head feels like it's the size of a bushel basket."

Ann stepped over to the bed and gave her friend a big hug. "Sleep well," she said. "We'll be back to visit again tomorrow."

Ken leaned down and kissed Denise's cheek. "Hang in there, champ."

"You're damn right I will," Denise replied. "I'll be ready to go fifteen rounds before you know it."

As Ann and Ken walked down the hall toward the elevator, Gary Carlson came sprinting toward them. "There you are!" he said. "I'm glad I was able to catch you here."

"What's up?" Ann asked.

Gary leaned close and said, "I found Crystal Barman!"

"What?" Ann exclaimed. "Where is she? Is she all right?"

"She's fine," Gary replied. "Your visit spooked her so much that she packed up and ran. But after she heard about the attacks on you and Denise, she did a lot of heavy-duty thinking and she says she's ready to talk."

"When? Where?" Ken asked eagerly.

Gary put one arm around Ann and Ken and steered them toward the elevators. "I've got it all arranged," he said with a wink.

CHAPTER 31

Late the following afternoon Ann, Ken, and Gary met Crystal Barman at a motel near Wisconsin Dells. In a series of phone calls over the past twenty-four hours, Gary had seemed to establish a rapport with Crystal, and the frightened woman had insisted that he come along to the meeting.

Crystal refused to reveal the exact location of the rendezvous until they were en route. She had instructed Gary to wait in a phone booth at two P.M. at a specified rest stop, where she would call him and reveal their final destination.

"Got it!" Gary said triumphantly as he walked back to the vehicle waving a piece of paper. "Now begins phase two of the journey."

"Stop posturing and get in!" Ann ordered. "I'm afraid if we don't get the lead out, Crystal will have changed her mind and bolted."

"This is awfully cloak-and-dagger," Ken agreed. "Intrepid sleuths rendezvous with frightened witness in secret location. Where are we going, Sherlock?"

"Get back on the interstate," Gary directed. "The

exit we want is about another twenty-five miles north."

"Okay, now where?" Ken asked twenty minutes later as he pulled the Navigator onto the exit Crystal had identified.

Gary looked at his notes. "She said to stay on this road for a mile and a half and then turn left on Falls Drive."

Ann, who was sitting in the back, asked anxiously, "Do you think she's really going to be there?"

"I think she'll be there," Gary replied. "There's no doubt she's scared, but she sounded like she genuinely wants to help. Slow down," he directed Ken. "Here's our road. Another mile and we should see the place on the right. It's called the Sherwood Motel. She's in room two-ten, around the back."

The Sherwood Motel was a rather run-down establishment whose best days were at least three decades in the past. The brown paint on the sign was peeling and the grass in the yard was full of brown spots and dotted with weeds.

"If Crystal wanted privacy, she certainly came to the right place," Ann commented as they drove around the back of the building. "It's the beginning of tourist season. All the major hotels are packed, and there are only four cars in the lot here."

Ken parked the Navigator and they got out. The Sherwood Motel was the older, cheaply built sort of establishment in which each room had its own outside entrance. The trio climbed a rickety stairway to the second level and located room 210.

"The moment of truth has arrived," Gary said dramatically. He knocked sharply on the door. "It's Gary Carlson," he called out.

A moment later the door opened a crack and Crystal Barman peered out at them warily.

"May we come in?" Gary asked.

Crystal hesitated a moment, as if she were trying to decide, then nodded mutely, opened the door, and stepped aside to let them pass.

"This is Ken Devlin," Gary said, "and I believe you've already met Ann Monroe."

Crystal nodded again and walked the short distance across the room to take a seat in one of the straight chairs placed next to a scuffed-up round wooden table. Ann followed her and claimed the other chair, while Gary and Ken sat down on the bed.

"Thank you for seeing us," Ann said.

"I didn't want to get involved in this," Crystal said in her high-pitched voice as she fidgeted with the hem of her blouse. "I didn't want to be on that jury in the first place. I tried to get out of it. When I got the summons, I called the clerk and told her I was claustrophobic. She said I'd need a doctor's excuse and that I could be fined if I shirked my civic duty. I should have let them fine me. Then none of this would have happened."

"We've been worried about you," Ann said in an attempt to calm the woman's nerves. "With what happened after I left you last Saturday night, well . . ." Her voice trailed off. "I was afraid my visit might have caused something to happen to you as well."

Crystal clenched her jaw and shook her head rapidly back and forth. "You frightened me. Hearing what you had to say brought back too many bad memories. As soon as you left I had a panic attack and I knew I had to get out of there. I threw a few things in a bag and headed out."

"Has anyone other than Ann spoken to you about the criminal trial since it ended?" Ken asked.

"No," Crystal replied.

"Can you tell us what happened?" Ann asked gently. "Had you ever met Claude Furseth before the trial?"

At the mention of the jury foreman's name, Crystal's fidgeting increased in intensity. "No. I'd never met the man before."

"The trial lasted several days," Ken said. "Did Furseth make any comments early on that indicated he might have prejudged the case?"

"No," Crystal answered, "but from the beginning it was clear that he had a very strong personality."

"How so?" Ann asked.

"Whenever we took breaks he would always dominate the conversation. He's a big man and he has a rather loud voice, so you couldn't help but pay attention to him. There was never really any doubt that he was going to be the foreman of the jury." She paused a moment and said, "And that's exactly what happened."

"Did you vote for him as foreman?" Ann asked.

Crystal nodded. "He seemed like a born leader. He was elected unanimously." There was another long pause.

"What happened then?" Ann gently prompted her.

Crystal took a deep breath, then exhaled. "That's when he started to press his agenda." She nervously smoothed back her hair with her hands before going on. "As soon as he was chosen to be the foreman, he said something like, 'Well, do any of you think they're guilty?' I remember thinking that was an odd way of putting it, but I was the first one to raise my hand, and that's when he started belittling me."

"What did he do?" Ken asked.

"He slammed his fist down on the table and said, 'What are you, some kind of bleeding heart? Don't you know that homosexuality is a sin? The Bible says so. That faggot got just what he deserved.'"

"Did you say anything to that?" Ann asked.

"I just sat there for a minute. I was completely taken aback, and I think most of the others were, too. Eventually I said something like, 'I thought we were told to follow the instructions the judge gave us, and I don't recall him reading the Bible.' That only made Furseth angrier."

"Didn't anyone else speak up in your defense?" Gary asked.

Crystal nodded. "Yes. Two other women and one man indicated that they also thought the defendants were guilty. At that point Furseth jumped up and acted like he was preaching. He waved his arms and spouted Bible verses a mile a minute and said anyone who voted to find the defendants guilty would be condemned to eternal damnation."

"Did you have any indication while the trial was going on that Furseth was religious?" Ann asked.

"Not really," Crystal replied. "Once during a

lunch break it looked like he was maybe saying a prayer over his food but I didn't really pay much attention. I've always felt that a person's faith or lack of it is their own business."

"Didn't anyone else on the jury try to turn the discussion around to the evidence and whether the prosecution had proven its case?" Ken asked.

"Several of us tried," Crystal replied, "but Furseth would hear none of it. With every comment that was made challenging him, he became more belligerent. It wasn't long before he had intimidated everyone in the room."

"Was a vote ever taken?" Gary asked.

"Yes, several votes," Crystal replied. "After Furseth's initial outburst one of the other women suggested that we vote in writing, by secret ballot. We did that and there were four of us who voted guilty."

"How did Furseth react to that?" Ann asked.

"He flew into a rage. He spouted more Bible verses and stomped around the room. After a while we cast another secret ballot. This time the guilty votes were down to three."

"Did you ever consider summoning the bailiff and reporting what was going on?" Ann asked.

"Of course I did," Crystal replied. "After forty-five minutes or so of him humiliating us, I said I had to go to the bathroom. I intended to report what was happening. I got up quickly and walked over to the door and he was right there, breathing down my neck. As I started to open the door, he leaned in real close and whispered, 'You'd better keep your mouth shut, missy, or I'm going to make you wish you'd never met me.' After I heard that, I got all flustered and I chickened out. I couldn't say anything."

"What happened after that?" Ann asked.

"Well, it was a few more hours before Furseth wore everyone down. A couple of the men started saying that even if Jenkins and English had gotten too rough, maybe Bill Robinson had it coming, and anyway Bill had recovered nicely from his injuries so maybe it wasn't all that bad."

"How horrible!" Ann exclaimed.

"How long did this go on?" Ken asked.

"It seemed like forever," Crystal replied, "but I guess it was three or four hours. We took another vote and only two of us were still voting guilty."

"Were you the last holdout?" Ann asked gently.

Crystal nodded. "Eventually some of the others started getting on me, saying, 'Let's get it over with and go home. What's the big deal about letting those kids off? They've already been punished with all the bad publicity the case has generated. Even if they were convicted, they don't have a prior record, so they'd probably just get a slap on the wrist.' By this time I was feeling so claustrophobic that I knew I was going to have a panic attack if I stayed in that room any longer, so I finally gave in, too. I am so sorry I didn't have the guts to resist." She put her hands over her face and began to sob.

Ann reached over and patted the woman's arm. "We can understand how intimidated you must have felt," she said. "Did Furseth say anything to you after you agreed to change your vote?"

Crystal took a moment to compose herself, then

nodded. "He said, 'It's about time you saw the light.' Then, when we told the bailiff we'd reached a verdict and were just going to file back into the courtroom, he whispered to me, 'I hope you understand that what happened here is not to leave this room. If I ever hear that you've been shooting your mouth off, you will be very sorry.'"

"But you told your friend Patti about it, didn't you?" Ken asked.

"She sort of pried it out of me after I'd been drinking, but I needed to tell somebody. I'd been keeping it bottled up and it was just eating away at me. I'm so ashamed of myself." She began to weep again.

"While he was quoting the Bible and spouting off, did Furseth ever indicate what denomination he was?" Ann asked.

Crystal wiped her eyes. "No, I don't believe he did," she said. After thinking for a moment, she added, "But he did mention his minister's name once."

Ann took a deep breath and asked—although she was sure she knew the answer—"What was his minister's name?"

Crystal answered without a moment's hesitation. "Reverend Tremaine."

CHAPTER 32

"So Reverend Tremaine is connected to Bill Robinson's case, too," Gary said as they headed back toward Madison. "Isn't it a small world?"

After discovering that Claude Furseth was apparently a member of the Lambs, the trio had expressed their profound gratitude to Crystal Barman for her courage in admitting what had happened in the jury room.

While Crystal had agreed to help Ann in any way she could, both with Bill Robinson's civil suit and in identifying the people responsible for the assaults on Denise Riley and Ann, she was still very wary about returning home and perhaps facing Furseth's wrath.

"I think I'm going to stay out of sight for a while, but I'll keep in touch," Crystal promised as they said their good-byes. "And if you need to reach me, we can use Patti Majewski as a go-between."

"I suspected that someone connected with the Lambs set the fires at Planned Parenthood and the Robinsons' home," Ken said, "but I figured they hit the Robinsons only because Ann was Bill's lawyer. It never dawned on me that there might be an independent connection between the Lambs and Bill's case."

"This is so bizarre," Ann said, rubbing her palms over her cheeks as she tried to puzzle it out. "What are the odds that one of Tremaine's disciples would not only find his way onto the Jenkins and English jury but would end up as the foreman and control the outcome of the case?"

"Is there any way Furseth could have been planted on that jury?" Gary asked.

Both Ann and Ken shook their heads.

"I don't see how that would have been possible," Ann said. "Potential jurors are identified randomly from all kinds of places: voter-registration lists, Department of Transportation records, things like that."

"And even when a person is summoned to serve as a juror, there's still no way to guarantee what case they might serve on," Ken added. "Most counties set aside one day to pick all the juries that will be needed for the entire week. Everyone reports to one big room and from there the group is split into smaller groups by juror ID numbers."

"That's right," Ann said. "So unless you're suggesting some sort of vast conspiracy that encompasses the entire Jasper County court system——and I just can't believe that happened——it would have been very tough for someone to plant Furseth in the initial large jury pool, and it would have been even harder to get him slotted into the group of people from whom the Jenkins and English jury would be chosen."

"Still," Gary said, "it's a hell of a coincidence that

the foreman of the jury in Bill Robinson's case just happens to be a member of the congregation headed by a man who has publicly denounced Ann and has organized protests at another of her clients' businesses. There has to be some common bond connecting him to both cases."

"Oh, there's something there, all right," Ken agreed. "The problem is going to be figuring out what it is."

"I don't suppose there's any point in trying to talk to Furseth," Gary said.

"No," Ann said at once. "For the time being we don't want him to know that Crystal told us what happened. I think our next step should be trying to talk to the other three jurors Crystal identified as initially wanting to convict Jenkins and English."

"Didn't you say you already tried to contact all of the jurors and nobody would talk to you?" Ken asked.

"That's true," Ann answered.

"So what makes you think they'll talk to you now if they wouldn't talk a few weeks ago?"

"Well, for one thing I know what I'm looking for now," Ann said. "Maybe if I'm up front with the jurors about what I know they'll be more willing to admit what happened."

"Getting them to talk to you is still going to be a long shot," Ken said.

"I know that," Ann agreed, "but without corroboration from at least one of them Furseth could dismiss Crystal's allegations as the product of a warped mind."

"What would you need to do to bring this to the court's attention?" Gary asked.

"It's a delicate situation," Ken answered. "The very nature of the jury system mandates the sanctity and privacy of juror deliberations, and only in the most extreme circumstances can that process be invaded. This makes sense because if jurors' discussions and thought processes could be made public it would have a chilling effect on free-ranging discussion, and it would also make jurors vulnerable to outside influences. In other words, they might not vote the way they really felt because of fear of retaliation or public ostracism."

"But in an egregious situation like this surely there must be a way to get around that general rule," Gary said.

"There is," Ann said. "You can delve into the jury's deliberative process in cases where juror prejudice regarding race, religion, or sexual orientation is of such magnitude that it constituted an obvious denial of justice or fundamental fairness."

"Crystal's description of Furseth's behavior should certainly meet that standard," Gary said. "So assuming you can get corroboration for what Crystal told us, what's the procedure for making a claim of juror misconduct?"

"We'd have to file affidavits from Crystal and hopefully one or more other jurors setting forth exactly what Furseth did," Ken said. "The court would then hold a hearing at which it would hear testimony from those witnesses."

"Would Furseth have to testify?" Gary asked.

"Yes," Ann said. "And I'm sure he'd deny everything."

"What would the result be if the court believed Crystal's version of events? Since Jenkins and English were acquitted, they can't be tried again, can they?"

"No, but Furseth could be charged with jury tampering," Ann replied. "And the whole sordid incident could be made public, which in itself would be some consolation to Bill Robinson."

They had arrived back in Madison, and Ken dropped Gary off at his house.

"I'll keep nosing around and see what I can find out about Tremaine," Gary said as he got out of the Navigator. "I've got some solid leads on people who knew him before he moved up here, and I'll press them a little harder to see what I can turn up. I'll also nose around and see what I can find out about Furseth, his ties to the Lambs, if he's a big financial contributor, how tight he is with Tremaine personally. I have the feeling we're real close to a breakthrough here."

Once again, Ann's efforts to speak to the jurors from the Jenkins and English trial ended in frustration. She was unable to reach two of the people Crystal Barman had identified, and the two she did contact refused to cooperate.

"That case is ancient history," Harriet Bacon said testily. "After it was over, the judge made it very clear that we didn't have to speak to anyone or explain what we did, and I am sticking to that."

"I understand your wanting to maintain your privacy," Ann said sympathetically, "but if the verdict rendered was the result of intimidation or scare tactics, then justice was not served and the person who did the intimidating should be held accountable."

"I don't know what you're talking about," Harriet said, her voice taking on a shrill tone. "I have nothing to say to you—not now and not ever—and I'll thank you not to call me again."

Ann heard a click indicating that the woman had hung up on her. She fared no better with Patricia Loomis.

"No comment," the juror said after Ann asked if she would be willing to help unmask what had really happened at the Jenkins and English trial.

"But Ms. Loomis," Ann said, almost pleading now. "I know something happened in that jury room. Why is everyone afraid to talk to me about it? Have you been threatened?"

"I just don't want to talk about it," Patricia replied.

Ann could sense that this woman, too, was about to hang up, so she hurried on. "Another juror has already told me what happened at that trial. The impact the improper conduct had on the verdict is disturbing enough, but it looks like what happened in that case could have contributed to a good friend of mine being brutally attacked. Now if everyone insists on maintaining this veil of silence, what's to stop more innocent people from being abducted and beaten—or worse?"

Ann could hear the juror take a deep breath, as if she were perhaps going to volunteer something. But she merely exhaled and said curtly, "As I told you before, I have no comment. Good-bye." The phone clicked in Ann's ear.

"Shit!" Ann cursed as she slammed down the receiver. Why couldn't she get any breaks?

That night, Ann and Ken went to the hospital and made their way up to Denise's room. The moment they walked through the doorway, Ann knew something was wrong. The bed was empty, and the room had been stripped.

"Something must have happened to her," Ann said, panic evident in her voice.

"Stay calm," Ken urged. "We'll find out what's up."

As they walked back out into the hall, Ann spotted a nurse going into another patient's room and sprinted down the hallway to intercept her. "Excuse me," she said. "Can you tell me what happened to Denise Riley? She was in four-fifteen but it looks like she's been moved."

"What was the name again?" the nurse asked, consulting her chart. "Oh, yes. She was moved back to intensive care a couple of hours ago."

"Oh, no!" Ann gasped. "What happened?"

"I'm afraid I don't know that," the nurse replied. "You'd have to check with the people in intensive care."

Ann felt herself growing faint, and she slumped against Ken. He immediately put his arm around her. "Come on," he said soothingly. "Whatever it is, I'm sure Maureen could use some support."

They found Maureen Riley and Marcia Inkster in

the waiting room outside the intensive care ward. Maureen jumped up from her seat and embraced Ann the moment she saw her.

"I'm so glad to see you!" Maureen said. "I feel like I'm falling apart."

"What happened?" Ann asked.

"Mom was just fine until early afternoon, when all of a sudden her speech got garbled. Within a few minutes she was making no sense at all, so I went and got a nurse. She took one look at her and called Dr. Lanska right away. By the time the doctor arrived Mom had slipped into a coma again!"

Maureen paused a moment to fight back the tears. "They tell me Mom has fluid on her brain. They just took her up to surgery to try to drain it off. I just don't know how much more of this I can stand!" The distraught young woman began to sob.

Ann hugged Denise's daughter tightly. "Does the doctor think she'll be okay?"

Maureen wiped her eyes and nodded. "She said this type of complication is not unexpected, given the sort of injury Mom suffered. She's hoping once the pressure on her brain is relieved that Mom will come out of the coma again."

"Well, that sounds promising, doesn't it?" Ann asked.

"I guess so," Maureen said, her voice quaking. "But how much can one person go through?"

"Your mom is one tough broad," Marcia Inkster spoke up. "If anybody can come through this, she can. We all just have to think positively and keep our spirits up, because that will help her, too."

"How long will Denise be in surgery?" Ken asked.

"They said she should be coming back down within the hour," Maureen replied.

"Can I get either of you anything?" Ken asked. "A cup of coffee or a soda?"

Maureen shook her head. "No, thank you."

"Not right now," Marcia said.

Ken turned to Ann. "Why don't you and I go get a cup of coffee and then come back up here in a little bit?"

Ann hesitated a moment. She wanted to be there so she'd hear the moment there was an update on Denise's condition, but she had to admit she was still feeling rather woozy, and she knew it would not exactly bolster Maureen's spirits if she had a fainting spell.

"All right," she said to Ken. Turning to Maureen, she said, "We'll be back soon."

Maureen nodded. "Thank you both so much for coming. It means a lot to me—and to Mom, too—to have you here."

Ken patted Maureen gently on the back. "See you in a little bit."

As Ken steered her toward the elevators, Ann clutched his arm tightly. She waited until they had rounded a corner and Maureen and Marcia were out of earshot before she spoke. "Denise was doing so well that I thought it was just a matter of time before she'd be as good as new, and now this has to happen! She could still die."

"She's not going to die," Ken said, putting his arm around her.

"You don't know that!" Ann exclaimed. "She could very well die, and the police are no closer to finding a suspect than they were the night she was attacked. And we're no closer to figuring out the connection between Bill Robinson's case and Reverend Tremaine. Nothing is working out the way it's supposed to, and unless we get a break soon I feel like I'm going to explode!"

"Ann—" Ken began, but she pulled away from him and rushed into the women's rest room. Allowing the full force of her emotions to overtake her, she sank down onto the floor and wept.

CHAPTER 33

Denise's attack, as well as the fire at the Planned Parenthood clinic, was being featured on the "Crimestoppers" public announcements broadcast on local radio and television stations. Ann heard the spots several times a day.

"I'm Madison police officer Angie Stelter," the segment began. "On May twenty-first, a fire was set at the Planned Parenthood clinic on Regent Street. Then, on the evening of May twenty-ninth, the executive director of Planned Parenthood was savagely beaten by several men as she walked in Madison Park. The victim remains in critical condition in a local hospital. The perpetrators of both these crimes remain at large. If you have information about this crime, or any crime, please call Crimestoppers. Callers can remain anonymous and may be eligible for cash rewards."

Ann had just arrived at work two days after Denise had lapsed back into a coma when her direct phone line rang. Picking it up, she found Gary Carlson on the other end.

"Good morning, Annie," he said brightly. "Did you have a pleasant evening?"

"Not particularly," Ann replied truthfully. "How about you?"

"I'll have you know that I spent several blissful hours engaged in prayer and meditation," Gary said.

"I don't follow you."

"In an effort to help you out, I attended Reverend Tremaine's traveling salvation show."

"You did what?" Ann asked.

"I saw a poster advertising a good old-fashioned religious revival at Tremaine's church, so I thought I'd check it out. As an event, I guess it was about what you'd expect from a man whose idea of culture is wearing navy slacks and white buck shoes. But the most interesting part about the evening was not so much the content of the program as who else was in attendance."

"Now you've really lost me," Ann said. "Who was there?"

"Well, for starters, Claude Furseth, jury foreman extraordinaire."

"For *starters*? Who else did you see?"

"A drumroll, please. None other than your favorite district attorney and mine, Ted 'hang my client and the state both out to dry' Lawrence!"

"You're kidding!" Ann exclaimed. "Ted Lawrence was at a Lambs of God revival?"

"Yes, indeed, and he was sitting next to Furseth."

"Unbelievable!" Ann said. "Did they arrive together?"

"No, Furseth was there first and then Lawrence came in and sat beside him."

"Did it look like they were friendly?"

"Quite," Gary replied.

"Well," Ann said, "I suppose since Jasper County isn't that heavily populated, and since Lawrence has been in office forever, it's not that surprising that they'd know each other. But the bigger question is, What the hell were they both doing an hour away from home at a fundamentalist revival?"

"The plot gets even thicker than that," Gary said. "One of the things I researched when I got home was contributions Lawrence received in his last campaign. Did you know all that stuff is available on-line now? This new technology is truly amazing, but I digress. Would you care to hazard a guess as to who might have contributed a few shekels to Lawrence's coffers?"

"Claude Furseth," Ann said at once.

"To the tune of two hundred and fifty dollars. And who else's name do you think showed up?"

"Reverend Tremaine."

"Right, for five hundred dollars. Guess again."

"I've run out of possible suspects," Ann said.

"Oh, no, you haven't," Gary replied. "Why not try Daniel Jenkins for three hundred."

"Sam Jenkins's father gave money to Lawrence's campaign?"

"Yes, Jasper County must truly be an incestuous little area," Gary said.

"None of the contributions you've identified are very large," Ann said.

"True enough, but doesn't it strike you as just a little suspicious that the jury foreman and the father of one of the defendants in your criminal trial both contributed to the DA's campaign? And doesn't it strike you as odder still that the DA and the jury foreman would both happen to show up at a revival meeting hosted by a controversial minister whose gay-bashing ideas are well known?"

"Sure, the whole thing stinks," Ann said. "But what's the connection between all these people? And more important, how does it tie into either Bill Robinson's civil case or the attacks on Denise and me?"

"I'm still working on all of that," Gary replied. "I've got some feelers out in Jasper County about the relationship between Furseth, Lawrence, and the Lambs. In fact, I've got to leave pretty soon. I'm going to drive over there and talk to a few people in the flesh. But while I'm gone I have an assignment for you, if you choose to accept it."

"What is it?" Ann asked.

"I think I told you I had some leads on Tremaine's past in the glorious South. Well, as luck would have it, one of my contacts left a message last night while I was gone. It sounds promising and I thought you might want to follow up on it."

"Is it a lead about why Tremaine moved up here? I tried to find that out when I first locked horns with the reverend a couple years ago. I know he had a church in southern Tennessee for about eight years before moving to the Midwest, but the people I spoke to in the South seemed rather reluctant to tell me why he left."

"I have some information that might help you out," Gary said. "Actually, it's not about Tremaine; it's about his son. Or, more correctly, his stepson. His wife's boy, Jesse Greer. My source indicated that Jesse, who'd be in his early to mid-twenties now, got in some trouble back home shortly before the entire family migrated north."

"What kind of trouble?"

"I don't know exactly, but I got the impression that it could have been serious enough to cause the whole family to relocate. I'd be happy to follow up on it myself, but as I said, I need to head over to Jasper County and I thought it'd be the most efficient use of time if you'd run down the skinny on young Master Greer."

"I'd be glad to," Ann said. "Where do I start?"

Gary gave her the name of the Tennessee town where the Tremaines had previously lived, along with the phone number of the clerk of court and the local sheriff's department.

"I'll see what I can find out," Ann promised.

"Great," Gary said enthusiastically. "I'll probably be back in touch later in the day, following my triumphant return from Mount Pleasant."

"Be careful, Gary," Ann said soberly. "Remember that my last trip over there didn't exactly end in triumph. And the two before that weren't any picnic either."

"Young woman, have you forgotten that danger is

my middle name?" Gary asked brashly. "Yours truly knows how to keep one step ahead of the bad guys. Never fear, I shall return safe and sound and hopefully bearing useful information."

"Thanks again for all your help," Ann said. "It means a lot to me."

"I never turn down a chance to help a damsel in distress," Gary said before he rang off, "even if she does have the misfortune of being a lawyer."

After finishing her conversation with Gary, Ann decided she should start making inquiries about Jesse Greer.

Her first call was to the courthouse in the town where the Tremaine family had lived. After explaining who she was and what she wanted three different times, Ann was finally transferred to a deputy clerk.

"What was the fellow's name again?" the female clerk asked in a pleasant Southern drawl.

"Jesse Greer," Ann replied.

"We just recently computerized all our closed files," the clerk explained. "This will be a good test to see if the system works. If you can just hang on for one moment, I'll enter Mr. Greer's name and see what turns up."

Ann could hear the sound of keys clacking; then there was a pause.

"Well, well," the clerk said pleasantly. "It does work. I show quite a number of entries for Mr. Jesse Greer."

"Can you tell me what type of cases they were?" Ann asked.

"I surely can. Would you like me to start with the oldest one?"

"That would be great," Ann said.

"All righty. Eight years ago, as a juvenile, Mr. Greer was convicted of disorderly conduct and placed on six months' probation."

"How old was he at the time?" Ann asked.

"Let's see if I can find a birth date. Oh, yes. Here it is. He would have been sixteen at the time. Then the following year he was arrested on a weapons violation. That charge was dropped. Then the year after that, when he would've been eighteen, he was charged with assault and battery. He entered a nolo contendere plea and got one year of probation on that one."

As the clerk related the criminal history of Tremaine's stepson, Ann scribbled notes on a piece of paper. While she took a sort of perverse pleasure in knowing that the reverend had raised—or been saddled with—a problem child, she still didn't know what the kid's record had to do with Bill Robinson's case or the attacks on Denise and herself. But just as Ann was wondering if Gary's hunch had been mistaken, the clerk recited the next entry from the log.

"And then five and a half years ago, at age nineteen, Mr. Greer had a whole bunch of charges filed against him. Criminal damage to property, arson, accessory to assault with a deadly weapon, hit and run."

Ann's ears perked up. "Was he convicted of all those things?"

"It looks like the hit and run was dropped," the

clerk answered. "But Mr. Greer entered a plea of nolo contendere to the other two."

"And his sentence?" Ann asked.

"Six months in the county jail," the clerk replied.

Although Ann wasn't sure why, she now had the feeling she was onto something. "Can you tell me the name of the prosecuting attorney who was assigned to the case?"

"Yes, ma'am, I can. It was Ruth Ruf."

"Is she still working as a prosecutor?"

"Yes, ma'am. I can give you her phone number if you'd like."

"I'd like that very much," Ann said. After taking down the phone number and also obtaining the court's file numbers for the cases in question, Ann asked, "Is that the last entry you have for Mr. Greer?"

"Yes, ma'am, it is."

"Well, thank you very much for all your help. In case I should need to ask you to follow up on something later, could I have your name?"

"Certainly. It's Betty Ortman."

"Thanks again, Betty."

"No problem at all. You have a nice day."

Things might be looking up, Ann thought as she dialed Ruth Ruf's number. Ann asked for the prosecutor and found that her luck held: Ruth was in the office.

When Ruth came on the phone, Ann identified herself and briefly explained her conversation with Betty Ortman. "I was just wondering if you had any recollection of the case," Ann said.

"When did you say this was?" Ruth asked. "Over

five years ago? Honey, if you knew how many dirtbags I've dealt with in the past five years you wouldn't expect me to remember each of 'em by name."

"Of course," Ann said. "Would it help if I gave you the case number?"

"Yeah. If you don't mind holding on, I can go pull the file."

"Sure," Ann said. She read the case number Betty had given her.

"Okay," Ruth said. "Chill out for a few minutes. I'll be back as soon as I can."

"I'll be here," Ann said.

When the prosecutor came back to the phone, Ann detected a change in her demeanor. "I *do* remember this case," she said.

"You do?" Ann asked.

"You bet. I just didn't remember Greer's name specifically. A whole group of young hoodlums was charged in that particular case. Greer happened to be one of the lesser players."

Ann could feel her pulse rate increasing. "What kind of case was it?" she asked.

"A bunch of guys who belonged to an Aryan Brotherhood–type organization went on a spree one night and did some really low-down and dirty stuff."

"Such as?"

"First they defaced a Jewish temple and attacked two Jewish men. Hurt 'em pretty badly, too. One of them has permanent brain damage. Then later in the evening they set fire to a black family's house. Fortunately no one was home at the time."

"Do you remember the details of the assault on the two men?" Ann asked, involuntarily holding her breath.

"They were beaten over the head with a lead pipe," Ruth replied.

Ann immediately thought of the attack on Denise. "I understand Greer was also charged with hit and run. What was that all about?"

"He was driving one of the getaway cars," Ruth explained. "As he was rounding a corner after his buddies set the fire at the black family's house, he ran into an old lady pulling out of a driveway."

"For being involved in something that serious, it seems as though Greer got off very lightly," Ann commented. "The court clerk I spoke to said the hit and run charge was dropped and he got only six months in jail."

"I would've liked to see him get a lot stiffer penalty," Ruth said, "but my boss had other ideas."

"Why?"

"The two Jewish men who were attacked weren't able to ID the perps. My boss was afraid that without some help from one of the insiders, our case might be in trouble. So in exchange for his testimony against the four guys who actually carried out the beating, Greer got a sweetheart deal."

"Did Greer deliver on his part of the bargain?"

"Oh, sure, he got up on the stand and said what he was supposed to. But to tell you the truth, I didn't like the kid one bit and I didn't trust him."

"Why is that?" Ann asked.

"Call it woman's intuition," Ruth said a bit sarcastically. "Whenever I talked to Greer, I always had the feeling that just below the surface he was smirking at me. No, I take that back. He wasn't just smirking at me. He was thumbing his nose at the whole damn system, like he was trying to let me know he'd pulled one over on us."

"What made you think that?"

"His four buddies all claimed that Greer actively participated in the beatings and that he personally set the fire. I tended to believe them, but like I said, my boss thought it was better to make sure we could nail four of them than hold out for all five and maybe get nobody."

"So you think it's possible Greer downplayed his role in the crimes and sold his buddies out?"

"Very possibly," Ruth said.

"Did you know Greer's stepfather?" Ann asked.

"Refresh my recollection," Ruth said. "Who was that?"

"Rev. Charles Tremaine."

Ruth groaned. "Oh, God, I'd forgotten he was Greer's stepdad. Yes, I knew him. If you lived in this part of the state, you couldn't help but know him. That man was positively made for the age of mass media. He could play to a crowd like an Oscar winner. Good old Charlie Tremaine. I haven't heard that name in a while. What happened to him?"

"He's up here playing to the crowds now," Ann said.

"Lucky you," Ruth said.

"I wouldn't exactly put it that way," Ann murmured.

"I vaguely remember that the reverend left here rather abruptly," Ruth said. "Do you know why that was?"

"I'm beginning to wonder if it didn't have something to do with his stepson's criminal problems."

"You could be onto something there," Ruth said. "The timing was about right, wasn't it?"

"What happened to the guys Greer testified against?" Ann asked.

"They're still in prison," Ruth replied with obvious satisfaction. "And by the time they get out they'll hopefully be too crippled with arthritis to be wielding any more lead pipes or setting any fires."

"I hope so," Ann said. "Say, thanks so much for taking the time to talk to me. You've been very helpful."

"May I ask why you're checking into Greer's background?" Ruth inquired.

"There have been some things going on up here that are quite similar to the incidents you described."

"What kinds of things?"

"A hate crime against a gay man. An innocent woman beaten over the head with something like a lead pipe. A couple of fires set. And Reverend Tremaine hovering around the fringes of it all."

"And Jesse Greer?" Ruth asked.

"I don't know how he fits in," Ann admitted. "Until this morning I didn't even know he existed. But like most lawyers, I gave up believing in coincidences a long time ago. So my gut—or maybe it's *my* woman's intuition—is telling me that it's possible that Jesse might be involved in this, too."

"Good luck," Ruth said. "Dealing with slippery eels like that, you're going to need it."

"I'm afraid you're probably right there," Ann said.

Ann hung up the phone, then sat quietly at her desk pondering what she had just learned. Reverend Tremaine's stepson had been part of a crime spree that involved setting fires and beating people over the head with a lead pipe.

Denise Riley had been beaten with something like a lead pipe. And one of the few clues Denise could give about her attackers was that one of them was a young man with a smooth Southern accent.

Just like Jesse Greer.

CHAPTER 34

"I assume you heard about the vicious attack on Denise Riley, the director of Planned Parenthood, that took place the Saturday before Memorial Day," Detective Andy Lowell said conversationally.

Jesse Greer settled comfortably into the plush sofa in the living room of his stepfather's home and nodded. "Yeah, it'd be hard to miss it," he drawled. "It's been in the news a lot lately."

"It's been in the news a lot because it was a particularly vicious attack that's left Ms. Riley in a coma," Detective Lowell, who was seated in a chair across from Jesse, responded dryly. "You wouldn't happen to have any idea who might have attacked Ms. Riley, would you?"

Jesse threw up his hands. "No idea at all. What makes you think I'd know something about it?"

"Do you recall where you were that night?" the detective asked, ignoring Jesse's question.

"The Saturday before Memorial Day?" Jesse

pursed his lips and pretended to be struggling to remember. "I was right here."

" 'Here' meaning in this house?"

"That's right."

"Can anyone verify that?" the detective asked.

"My mother," Jesse answered at once. "Thelma Tremaine."

"Your mother will be able to verify that you were here in the house with her the entire evening of Saturday, May twenty-ninth?"

Jesse smiled. "Yes, sir. She most certainly will be able to verify that."

"Was your stepfather home that night as well?" Detective Lowell asked.

"No, I believe he was out of town that weekend," Jesse replied sweetly. "He was at a religious revival in Minnesota."

"Is either your mother or stepfather home now?"

"No, sir, but I expect them back in an hour or so."

"Does anyone else live here besides the three of you?"

"No."

"Did you leave the house at all that Saturday night?"

"No."

"Do you recall if you made or received any telephone calls?"

"I can't remember. It's possible."

"Were you anywhere in the vicinity of Madison Park at any time over Memorial Day weekend?"

Jesse shook his head. "No, that's clear on the other

side of town. I'd have no reason to go way over there."

"Do you recall if you did anything special that Saturday evening?" the detective asked.

Jesse shrugged. "Not specifically, but if it's like most nights I watch TV for a few hours after dinner. Sometimes I rent a couple movies."

"Did you eat dinner with your mother that night?"

"Yes, sir. I believe I did."

"Do you recall what you ate?"

Jesse smiled. What a boob this policeman was. "Not specifically, but my mother is a fine cook, so I'm sure whatever she prepared, it was delicious."

"Do you recall any television programs you might have watched that night?" Detective Lowell asked.

"Not really."

"Would you have watched TV with your mother or by yourself?"

"Sometimes she and I will watch a show together. Other times I'll go to my room and watch something alone. I don't remember which I did that night." Jesse leaned forward and rested his elbows on his knees. "So tell me, Detective, is there a particular reason for your interest in my activities the night that woman was attacked? Surely you don't think I had something to do with that." Jesse smiled engagingly.

"I told you at the beginning of our conversation that I've been talking to a lot of people," Lowell replied. "And I also told you that you are not a suspect at this time and that you are under no obligation to talk to me at all. Would you like to terminate our conversation, Jesse?"

"No, I am thoroughly enjoying our little talk, Detective Lowell," Jesse answered truthfully. Showing off his superior wiles always pleased him. "Please continue with your questions."

"You are a member of the Lambs of God, are you not?"

"Of course. With my stepfather being the head of the congregation, how could I not be a member?"

"Have you participated in the picketing that's gone on outside of Planned Parenthood the past few weeks?"

"I've been at the clinic a few times for an hour or so, joining in the peaceful protests against the abomination of abortion."

"And that's been the full extent of your participation in the demonstrations?"

"Yeah. With my work schedule I really don't have a lot of time to devote to public-service activities like picketing," Jesse said condescendingly.

"Where do you work?" the detective asked.

"I'm a sales manager at Barker Sporting Equipment at West Towne Mall."

"What hours do you work?"

"It varies," Jesse said. "Usually ten to six, Monday through Friday, and then either a couple of nights or one weekend day. I usually put in about fifty hours a week."

"How long have you worked at the store?"

"Three months."

"Who's your supervisor?"

"Jerry Bostwick."

"Where did you work before that?"

"Before that I worked at a sporting goods store in Des Moines, Iowa, for about a year and a half."

"During the handful of times you joined in the demonstration outside of the Planned Parenthood clinic, did you ever see the director, Ms. Riley?"

"I think I might have seen her once," Jesse replied noncommittally. "I'm not sure."

"Did you ever hear any of the other picketers talk about physically harming Ms. Riley?"

"No."

"Are you aware that there was a fire set at the clinic a few weeks before Ms. Riley was attacked?"

Jesse shrugged. "I might have read something about that in the paper. I don't really remember."

"Did you ever hear any of the people picketing at the clinic mention the fire?"

"No, I did not."

"You never heard any rumors about who might have started it?"

"Nope."

"And you never heard any rumors about who might have attacked Ms. Riley?"

Jesse shook his head. "Sorry. Wish I could help you."

"I'm sure you do," Detective Lowell said. "You got yourself into some hot water down in Tennessee five or six years ago, didn't you, Jesse?"

"Yes, sir," Jesse answered without hesitation. "I got in with a bad crowd. It was a dark chapter in my life, but I paid my dues, and with the Lord's help I've become a better person for the experience."

FINAL JUSTICE

"I'm a little hazy on the details," Detective Lowell said, fixing his gaze on Jesse's face. "Maybe you can refresh my recollection about what happened. Weren't a couple of Jewish men severely beaten over the head with a tire iron or a crowbar?"

"That's what I heard," Jesse replied with a straight face. "But I wasn't there when it happened. I was waiting around the corner in a car."

"You were just the driver of the getaway car?"

"Right."

"Not an active participant in the attack?"

"That's correct."

"In exchange for your testifying against the active participants of the crime, the charges against you were substantially reduced, weren't they?"

"Yes," Jesse admitted. "But my primary motivation in agreeing to testify was that I realized the great error of my ways and I wanted to make amends to the victims and to society."

"That was very altruistic of you," Detective Lowell said. "Did those two Jewish men recover from their injuries?"

"I do not know the answer to that, sir, but I certainly pray that they made a fine recovery."

"I hope so, too," the detective said. He got to his feet. "Thank you for your time, Jesse."

"I'm sorry I wasn't able to be of more help," Jesse purred as he walked the detective to the door. "Good luck in your investigation, Detective. I hope you catch whoever it was who beat that woman."

Detective Lowell paused in the doorway and

looked Jesse straight in the eye. "I will catch the person responsible," he said firmly. "You can count on it." He turned and walked down the steps to his car.

"Dumb fucker," Jesse murmured under his breath as he went back into the house.

Moments later the front door opened and Reverend Tremaine burst into his living room.

"Who was that who just left?" Tremaine demanded, walking over to where Jesse was sprawled on the sofa.

"Some policeman," Jesse replied.

"Get your goddamn feet off that sofa and sit up when I'm talking to you!" Tremaine hollered, slapping Jesse's legs.

The younger man glowered at his stepfather but sat up.

"Why did a policeman want to talk to you?"

Jesse shrugged. "Because he's too damn dumb to track down any real criminals so he has to waste his time talking to innocent people."

Tremaine lashed out and slapped Jesse hard across the face. "Don't give me any of your double-talk, boy," he warned. "What did that policeman want to talk to you about?"

"The fire that was set at Planned Parenthood," Jesse replied, rubbing his cheek with his hand.

"And why would he think you might know something about that?"

"I don't know. I guess he figured just because you were the head of the Lambs of God and you're married to my mama that I might have heard somebody threaten to burn the clinic down."

"You don't know anything about that fire, do you?" Tremaine asked, his brows furrowing together.

"Of course not," Jesse replied, avoiding Tremaine's gaze.

"You look at me when I'm talking to you, boy!" Tremaine commanded. "Do you or do you not know anything about that fire?"

Jesse looked directly at his stepfather. "No, sir. I do not."

"Did the police ask you about anything else?" Tremaine asked.

Jesse shook his head. "No, they just asked about the fire."

"You'd better be telling me the truth," Tremaine said.

"I am. I am," Jesse insisted.

"I am damn sick and tired of your lies," Tremaine blustered. "And I am sick and tired of bailing you out of one scrape after another. Don't you ever forget that I saved your sorry ass back in Tennessee."

Jesse hung his head.

"I'm the one who talked that prosecutor into giving you a sweetheart deal in exchange for your testimony against those other criminals," Tremaine expounded. "Even though I knew damn well that your testimony was perjured, I bailed you out because it would have killed your mother if you'd gone up the river along with your friends. But I am not going to do that again, so let me warn you that if I find out you got yourself into more trouble, you'd better hope the police catch you before I do . . ." Tremaine paused ominously. " 'Cause the police and the legal system are honor-bound to give you a fair trial before they find you guilty and exact their retribution. I, on the other hand, am under no such restraints. In spite of the fact that your mama thinks the sun rises and sets on you, if I find out you've fucked up again, you are going to be mighty sorry you were ever born."

Jesse flushed scarlet with anger, then got up and stormed out of the house, thoughts of patricide running through his head.

CHAPTER 35

Just before noon the next day, Ann's phone rang. It was Gary. "I've got a lead," he said excitedly. "The owner of a restaurant on the outskirts of Mount Pleasant says that Ted Lawrence and Claude Furseth are buddies. They've been in there together at least half a dozen times in the past year—both before and after the trial." He gave her the contact's name and address.

"That's great news!" Ann said. "So Lawrence *did* know Furseth before the trial, and presumably was aware of his conservative mind-set and should have known he wouldn't be a sympathetic juror in Bill's case. Good job, Gary! You've really brightened my day."

"Glad to be of service. Just promise me you won't go rushing over to Mount Pleasant alone to interview this guy."

"Don't worry. I don't plan to go to Mount Pleasant alone ever again."

She was just about to rush down to Ken's office to tell him the good news when the phone rang again.

For a long moment after she answered it, there was nothing but silence on the other end of the line.

"Hello?" Ann said.

"Ahh . . ." a voice stammered.

"May I help you?" Ann asked rather impatiently.

"You're the lawyer for Planned Parenthood, aren't you?" a soft male voice asked.

"Yes," Ann replied.

"I'm calling because I heard the Crimestoppers ad on the radio."

Ann drew in her breath. She knew she had heard that voice before, but she couldn't quite place it. "Why are you calling me?" she asked. "You should call the phone number they give in the ad."

There was a pause. "Well . . . the thing is . . . I'm sort of afraid to call the police."

All at once Ann knew where and when she had heard the voice: It was the night she was held hostage in the barn. She would bet her life on the fact that the caller was the young man who had untied her—the one she had nicknamed the Kid.

Ann took a couple of deep breaths to stop herself from shaking. She knew she had to handle this conversation very delicately or the Kid would get scared and hang up. "So you're saying you feel more comfortable talking to me than to the police?" she asked, trying to sound casual.

"I guess so, yeah."

"That's fine. What did you want to tell me?"

"Well, first, I wanted to say I'm really sorry to hear that the Planned Parenthood lady is still critical. I hope she gets better. She didn't deserve to have that happen to her. That wasn't right."

"Do you have some information about what happened to my friend?" Ann asked gently. "Is that why you called?"

There was another long pause.

"Look," Ann said, "If you know anything at all about what happened to Denise, please tell me. The police have talked to a lot of people and they've gotten nowhere. Unless someone comes forward and helps out, the people who hurt my friend are most likely going to get away with it."

Another pause. "Is she going to die?" the Kid asked softly.

"I don't know. She suffered a brain injury. She's in a coma, and her doctor doesn't know if she's going to come out of it."

"I didn't think anybody would get hurt. They said they were just going to scare her." The Kid now sounded as though he were talking to himself as much as Ann.

"Who said that?" Ann asked urgently.

"If they knew I was talking to you, they might kill me," the Kid said. He sounded frightened now.

"No one will hurt you," Ann said. "I promise. Please tell me. Who was behind the attack on my friend? Was it someone connected with the Lambs of God?"

"Yeah."

"More than one person?"

"Yeah."

"Can you tell me their names?"

"I'll be dead meat if anyone finds out!"

"I promise no one will find out. Please. It's very important. Can you give me just one name?"

The ensuing pause was so long that Ann was afraid the Kid had hung up. Finally, in a voice barely above a whisper, he said, "Jesse Greer."

Ann gasped. "Jesse Greer was one of the people who planned the attack on Denise Riley?" she asked, hoping her voice didn't betray the great emotion she was feeling.

"Yeah."

"Was he one of the people who actually beat her?"

"I think so."

"You think so but you're not certain because you weren't there when my friend was attacked, were you?"

"No."

"You were at the Swenson farm with me."

"I gotta go," the Kid said. He sounded frantic now. "I shouldn't have called."

"Wait!" Ann exclaimed. "Don't hang up, please. You helped me that night. If it hadn't been for you I could have ended up in the same condition as Denise. You might very well have saved my life."

"They said no one would get hurt," the Kid repeated.

"Are you a member of the Lambs of God?"

"Not really. A couple of guys I hang out with are, though."

"You said you heard the Crimestoppers ad. Is that why you decided to call me?"

"I felt terrible about what happened to you, too,

but I didn't know that other lady was hurt that bad until I heard it on Crimestoppers."

"If you'd tell the police what you just told me, you could get a reward," Ann suggested.

"I don't want to talk to the police," the Kid said at once.

"You're really afraid of them, aren't you? Jesse Greer and the others?"

"They're not people you mess with," the Kid said.

"The police would protect you," Ann assured him.

"No!"

"Will you tell me your name?"

"No," he said adamantly. "And you can't trace this call either, because I'm calling from a pay phone."

"At least tell me your first name so I know what to call you."

"Well . . . okay. It's Ben."

"Ben, do you know who planned the attacks on Denise and me?"

"Jesse Greer was one of the main ones."

"Were the attacks planned before or after our pictures were put on the Lambs' Web site?"

"After."

"Did Reverend Tremaine know about the attacks in advance?"

"I never heard one way or the other."

"If you're not really a member of the Lambs, how did you get mixed up with them?"

"A guy I know named Roy Meyer told me he was into something real exciting and he asked if I wanted in on it."

"Is Roy a member of the Lambs?"

"Yeah. His parents are, too."

"What did you think Roy meant when he said he was into 'something exciting'?"

"I didn't know."

"When did you find out?"

"I went to a sort of planning meeting with Roy one night behind the American Legion Hall in Mount Pleasant."

"When was that?" Ann asked.

"About a month ago."

"How many people were at this meeting?"

"About fifteen."

"Who was in charge?"

"Jesse and some older guy."

"Do you know the older guy's name?"

"Furseth."

"Claude Furseth?" Ann fairly shouted.

"I think so."

"What was discussed at the meeting?"

"How to make trouble for the people running the Planned Parenthood clinic. The Lambs wanted to put the clinic out of business."

"Did Jesse Greer think attacking Denise and me would accomplish that?"

"Well, at that meeting they didn't discuss attacking anybody. They discussed setting the fires."

"The fire at the clinic?"

"Yeah, and the one at those people's house."

Ann's mouth dropped open. "The Robinsons?"

"I guess so. The gay guy who filed the lawsuit."

"Did Jesse Greer set those fires?"

"Yeah."

"Are you sure?"

There was another long pause. "I'm positive. I was with him."

Ann fought to control her excitement at hearing this revelation. "Was anyone else with you?"

"No, it was just the two of us."

"When was the idea of attacking Denise and me first mentioned?"

"There was another meeting about ten days after the fires."

"Were the attacks Jesse's idea, too?"

"Yeah. He was real mad that the fire hadn't put Planned Parenthood out of business. But like I said, the word 'attack' was never used. Jesse just said he wanted to scare you and the other lady."

"Did Jesse ask for volunteers for the job?"

"Yeah. He said something like, 'So who's with us?' And most of the guys raised their hands."

"Did anyone explain to you exactly what was going to happen?"

"No. Jesse said, 'We need to show those bitches who's boss. We'll put the fear of God back into them.'"

"There was no talk about physically harming either me or Denise?" Ann asked Ben.

"Not that I heard. Jesse just said the operation would go down on the Saturday before Memorial Day."

"When and where did you meet that Saturday?"

"At the Target store on the west side of Madison around five o'clock."

"How many people showed up at Target?"

"Eight."

"Did Jesse seem to be in charge of the operation?"

"For sure. He split us up into two groups, one to go after you and the other to go after your friend. Then we headed out."

"Did you learn the names of any of the other guys?"

"Yeah. As we were leaving Target, Jesse slapped one of the guys who was in his group on the back and said, 'So are you up to this, Jenkins?'"

Ann's mouth dropped open. "Jesse called one of the guys with him Jenkins? What did this Jenkins look like?"

"He was young, maybe eighteen or twenty. Tall and on the heavy side. You know, built like a football player."

Although Ann's head was spinning, she forced herself to concentrate on the conversation. "Was Furseth there that day?"

"No."

"Then what happened?"

"Four of us went to your house. A guy named Carter Strom drove us in his truck. Your car was in the driveway, so Carter said you must be home. We went around the block a couple times and saw you come out of the house like you were in a big hurry. So we just followed you. Carter joked that if we'd known you were going to Mount Pleasant we could've saved ourselves the drive into Madison. When you got to that house in the country, Carter got the idea about taking you to the Swensons' place. He's familiar with the property and he'd heard the Swensons were out of town for a few days, so he figured it'd be the perfect place to take you."

"Did he or the other two guys ever say what they intended to do to me?"

"Not to me they didn't. They just made like they wanted to talk to you and then they'd let you go."

"Did they tell you they were going to use chloroform on me?" Ann asked.

"Not until it happened. That's when I really started to get cold feet. I told Carter I didn't like the way things were going. Once they got you inside the barn, Carter must've decided it'd be best if I weren't there to see what they did to you, because he told me to run up to the Swensons' house and make sure nobody was around."

"It was lucky for me that you saw the Swensons had come home," Ann said.

Ben drew in his breath, then exhaled. "To tell you the truth, I had a bad feeling about what might be going on in the barn, so I'd already decided that when I got back I'd tell Carter the Swensons were back even if they weren't."

Ann was touched. "Thank you, Ben. You're a very kind person."

The young man snorted. "If I were any kind of a man I would have found a way to stop the whole thing. Then maybe your friend would be okay."

"You can't blame yourself for that," Ann said firmly. "You did what you could, and I'm so grateful.

But there is something you can do for my friend." She paused a moment, then said, "You know what it is, don't you?"

"I don't think I can," Ben said in a voice barely above a whisper.

"You must," Ann urged. "If you don't tell the police what you've just told me, Carter, Jesse Greer, Jenkins, Furseth, and the others are going to get away with very serious crimes. Jesse Greer is a bad person. He was convicted of similar attacks down in Tennessee. One man was left with brain damage. If he isn't stopped, the next victim could end up dead. You don't want that to happen, do you?"

"No," Ben choked out.

"Well, the only way to stop that from happening is to go to the police."

"You promise I could get protection?"

"I promise."

Ben hesitated, thinking it over. "Would you go with me?"

"Of course I would."

"Okay," the young man said decisively. "I'll do it."

"Should I meet you at the police station?" Ann asked.

"Can we meet somewhere else first and maybe talk a little about what'll happen?"

"Sure. Why don't you come to my house tonight around seven." She gave him directions. "Then we can go to the police station together."

"Okay."

"One more thing," Ann said. "Would you mind telling me your full name?"

There was a pause; then the young man said, "Ben Kowalski."

"How old are you, Ben?"

"I'm nineteen."

"Do you go to school?"

"No, I just got a job working at the English Landscaping Company. I like growing things and the boss seems to like me. He says if I do a good job he'll pay for me to take some landscaping classes."

Through her discovery in the Robinson case, Ann knew that the English Landscaping Company was owned by Brad English's father. "That's nice that Mr. English thinks that highly of you," Ann said, amazed at how there was yet another connection between Denise's attack and Bill Robinson's case. "Well, then, thanks so much for calling, and I'll see you tonight around seven."

"Yeah," Ben said. "See you then."

CHAPTER 36

"Going somewhere?" Jesse Greer asked with a sneer as he stepped in front of Ben Kowalski.

Ben, who was walking to his car, about to drive to Madison for his meeting with Ann, recoiled in horror when he saw Jesse. Hoping he might be able to run back to the safety of his house, Ben wheeled around, only to find one of Jesse's staunchest supporters, Al Hubble, blocking his way.

"I asked you if you were going somewhere," Jesse said. "When I ask somebody a question, I expect an answer."

Ben turned back to face Jesse and nervously ran his tongue around his lips. "Yeah, I'm going to the grocery store," he stammered.

"Why don't you let me and Al give you a ride?" Jesse said. "We need some groceries, too. Don't we, Al?"

"Damn straight, Jesse," Al said.

"I don't need a ride. But thanks anyway." Ben took a step toward his car, wondering if he might be able to make a mad dash for it, but Jesse reached out and put a hand on Ben's chest.

"It would be our pleasure to escort you," Jesse said. He roughly grabbed hold of one of Ben's arms. By this time Al was standing next to them and he grabbed Ben's other arm. Although Ben tried to struggle, he quickly found himself being dragged to Jesse's Jeep Cherokee, which was parked around the corner.

Jesse opened a rear door and unceremoniously shoved Ben into the backseat. Al got in next to him. Jesse opened the driver's-side door, reached under the seat, and pulled out a handgun. He passed the weapon back to Al. "If he gives you any trouble," he said, grinning at his friend, "shoot him."

Ben cowered against the seat as Jesse drove several miles north of Mount Pleasant. From the moment Jesse had appeared, Ben had known there was a very real possibility he might be killed, but his spirits sank even farther when he saw the remote area to which he was being taken.

Jesse pulled the Jeep onto a gravel lane. At the end of the lane was an abandoned building. There was very little traffic within several miles. It was the perfect location for whatever torture or horrors Jesse might have in store. Ben knew that even if he were to scream at the top of his lungs, no one would hear him. He started to shake from fright.

Jesse and Al hauled Ben inside the building and ordered him to sit down on the cement floor. While Jesse held the gun on the helpless young man, Al bound Ben's hands and feet with strong rope.

"Some soldier you turned out to be," Jesse said to Ben disdainfully. "I'm going to have to have words with your friend Roy and tell him he should find himself some more masculine companions. Why, I've seen girls a hell of a lot braver than you."

"Maybe he's a homo," Al jeered.

"I asked him that once and he denied it," Jesse said. "No, I don't think he's a homo. I just think he's a coward and a damn bleeding heart. But one thing I know for sure is that he's a fucking traitor. Isn't that right, boy?"

"I don't know what you mean," Ben said, his teeth chattering.

"Sure you do," Jesse said. "You're fixing to rat me out, aren't you?" He paused and stared down at Ben. "Or have you done it already?"

"No, I haven't!" Ben protested his innocence.

"You're a liar," Jesse said calmly. Then he kicked Ben hard in the abdomen with his steel-toed shoe.

Ben screamed in pain.

"Who have you been talkin' to?" Jesse yelled.

Ben could only groan in response.

"I asked you a question!" Jesse screamed. He kicked Ben in the face. Blood poured out of the young man's nose and mouth.

"You answer me when I ask you somethin'," Jesse roared, giving Ben another vicious kick in the gut. *"Who have you been talkin' to?"*

Ben made a small sound.

"What'd he say?" Jesse asked Al.

"I dunno," Al replied. "Sounded like 'mama' to me."

"Are you begging for your mama, boy?" Jesse

FINAL JUSTICE

asked in a softer tone. "You really are a sissy. I've hardly gotten started and already you're crying out for your mama." Jesse squatted down close to Ben's battered face. "Now you listen to me, boy. Why don't you make this easy on yourself? I will get the answers I'm lookin' for out of you, no matter how long it takes me and no matter what I have to do to you to get 'em. But I'm warning you, the longer you make me work for it, the harder it's gonna be on you. So to keep what's left of your pretty face in one piece, why don't you do yourself a big favor and tell me what I want to know right now? What do you say, Ben? Have we got a deal?"

Ben was in excruciating pain. It seemed that every nerve ending in his whole body was throbbing in agony. It was an effort to breathe. He felt as if he were drowning in his own fluids. He swallowed hard, trying to work up enough saliva to form words. He opened his mouth and tried to speak.

"Don't mumble like that, boy," Jesse scolded. "Say it again, nice and clear this time. Who have you been talkin' to?"

The words came out in a whisper. "Ann Monroe. I'm supposed to meet her at her house at seven."

Jesse got to his feet and grinned. "Did you hear that, Al? Ben's been talkin' to Ms. Monroe. Thank you, Ben. I'm proud of you."

Ben managed to take a deep breath and relaxed just a bit. He didn't want to think about what might happen to Ann. He certainly didn't want her to be hurt, but he had found that his instinct for self-preservation was stronger than his heroic instincts. In his muddled mental state he was sure Ann would understand.

Just as Ben was contemplating his good fortune in negotiating with his enemy rather than offering further resistance, he heard a strange clanging sound. Opening one eye, the young man saw Jesse standing over him brandishing a crowbar.

Seeing the look of stark terror and disbelief on Ben's face made Jesse laugh. "Oh, Ben, you really are a half-wit, aren't you? Did you really believe my bullshit story about letting you off easy if you told me what I wanted to hear? Well, let this be a lesson to you, boy. Most people are lying most of the time. And I'm afraid I am no exception." With a broad grin on his face, Jesse raised the crowbar over his head and swung it down toward Ben with all his might.

CHAPTER 37

Ken arrived at Ann's house at six o'clock. He and Ann shared a pizza while they awaited Ben Kowalski's arrival.

"Would you like a piece?" Ken asked Jeff Steiner.

"No, thanks," Jeff replied as he leaned against the kitchen counter. "I had a sandwich a little while ago." He walked toward the living room. "I'll be right back. I'm just going to run out to the truck and get something."

As Jeff went out the front door, Ann wrapped the few remaining slices of pizza in plastic and put them in the refrigerator. "I think the poor guy is bored out of his mind on this job," she said. "I'll bet he'll be glad when this assignment is over."

"I wouldn't be so sure about that," Ken said. "I doubt he gets too many clients as attractive as you."

Ann leaned down and kissed him. Just then the doorbell rang.

"The kid's early," Ken said.

Ann nodded and got to her feet. "I wonder what happened to Jeff?" she asked.

"Maybe he locked himself out," Ken suggested.

The doorbell rang again.

"I'm coming, I'm coming," Ann said, hurrying to answer it.

She opened the door from the living room and stepped into the foyer. From there she could see a good-looking, dark-haired young man standing on the front stoop. Opening the storm door, she said, "You must be Ben."

The young man grinned shyly.

"Come on in," Ann said, holding the door open. "I hope you don't mind, but my partner, Ken Devlin, is here," Ann said as she led the way to the kitchen.

They had reached the kitchen. Ken was standing and extended his hand. "Ken Devlin," he said. "And you must be Ben Kowalski."

The young man merely grinned again and shook Ken's hand.

"A man of few words, eh?" Ken said, sitting down again.

"Could I get you a soda or a glass of water or something?" Ann asked.

The young man shook his head.

"Nothing at all?" Ann asked. Then she gasped when an all-too-familiar voice behind her announced, "There is one thing you could do, sweetie—"

Time stood suspended as the owner of the voice stepped into view, carrying a large-caliber pistol that he pointed directly at Ann. It was the fellow who had accosted her on the street in Mount Pleasant. "You could sit your pretty ass down in that chair right there against the wall."

As Ann meekly did as she was told, the young man she and Ken had thought was Ben Kowalski bent down and removed a small handgun from an ankle holster. He pointed the weapon at Ken.

"It would seem that introductions are in order," Ken said, his voice amazingly calm. "I'm Ken Devlin and I assume you already know that this is Ann Monroe."

The first man grinned and said in a slow Southern drawl, "Jesse Greer and Al Hubble at your service. Now, I suggest that if the two of you keep your mouths shut and do as you're told you'll experience minimal discomfort. But should you choose to disobey me"—he reached into his belt and pulled out a large hunting knife and ran his index finger lovingly over the blade—"well, then, things could get rather unpleasant."

"What do you want with us?" Ann asked, hoping that she did not sound quite as frightened as she felt.

"I want to finish what my no-account friends started Memorial Day weekend," Jesse replied. "My end of the operation turned out just fine, and theirs got all fucked up. That just goes to show what happens when you leave an important job to amateurs like Ben Kowalski."

This answer did not exactly lift Ann's spirits. "Ken's not involved in this," Ann said. "Why don't you let him go?"

Jesse grinned, displaying even, white teeth. "I don't think so, sugar," he drawled. "He might just come in handy." He waved the gun at Ken. "Stand up."

Ken slowly got to his feet.

"You, too, sugar," Greer said, pointing the gun at Ann.

She reluctantly complied with the order.

"Now walk toward the front door," Greer ordered.

"Why?" Ann asked.

"Because we're going for a little ride."

Where the hell is Jeff? Ann wondered, looking furtively toward the front door.

"If you're looking for your muscle-bound friend, why, he's taking a little nap in the bushes," Jesse said, chuckling.

Ann's eyes widened.

"Don't worry, sugar," Jesse said. "He shouldn't have any permanent brain damage. Now let's get moving."

Ann and Ken traded a quick glance. Ken looked remarkably calm, Ann thought. She wished she could think of something to do, but her mind was a blank.

"Quit dawdling," Jesse said. "Let's go." He gave Ann a rough shove.

"Don't hurt her!" Ken shouted, grabbing Jesse's arm.

Jesse's reaction was instantaneous. He slammed the butt of the gun down on the side of Ken's head.

Ken sank to his knees, clutching his head. Ann screamed and tried to reach for Ken, but Jesse grabbed her by the arm and roughly pulled her forward. *"I said, Let's move out,"* he shouted. Addressing Al, he said, "Bring that piece of shit along."

Al grabbed Ken under the arms and hauled him toward the front door.

FINAL JUSTICE

As Jesse pulled her out onto the sidewalk, Ann desperately tried to concoct a way to leave some sort of clue for someone to follow. But when she hesitated briefly on the steps, Jesse slapped her sharply on the back of the head.

"Ouch!" she exclaimed.

"Get the lead out!" Jesse ordered, pulling her along. Al, with Ken in tow, was close behind.

A late-model Jeep Cherokee was parked in the driveway next to Ken's Navigator. "You get in the rear passenger seat," Jesse directed Ann. Turning to Al, he said, "You put him in the front."

Jesse climbed in the back of the vehicle next to Ann, while Al heaved Ken into the front passenger seat and then settled himself into the driver's seat. As Al fired up the engine, Ann spotted a pair of legs sticking out from under the arbor vitae next to the house. She gasped. *Jeff!*

"Don't worry about him, sugar," Jesse laughed. "He'll probably live."

For the first time it really sank in for Ann that perhaps she and Ken would not survive. Then in a flash Al was backing out of the driveway. Away from home and hearth. Away from help. Perhaps away from life itself. *No, mustn't think like that*, Ann scolded herself. But what else was there to think when she was being driven off to parts unknown by two armed men?

After Jesse's companion turned off of Ann's quiet residential street, he headed north. After a couple of miles, he turned west onto a major highway leading out of town. At this point Ann fought to suppress a feeling of utter doom. Although no one had spoken, she already knew their destination: They were headed toward Mount Pleasant. And judging from what had happened on her last visits there, that was *not* a good sign.

In the front seat, Ken was beginning to regain his senses. "So what happened to the real Ben Kowalski?" he asked in a slightly slurred voice.

"Oh, he won't be bothering anybody for a while," Greer said with a sneer.

"What do you mean by that?" Ken asked.

"What I mean is that at the moment Ben's all tied up." Jesse and the driver began to chuckle at their little joke.

Ann felt sick to her stomach, recalling how she had promised Ben that he would be safe, that the police would protect him. She should have gone to the police right after Ben's call and let them step in right away. If she had done that instead of trying to play Miss Marple, Ben would be safe, Jesse would be in jail, and she and Ken would be home enjoying pizza and a few beers. *Stupid. Stupid. Stupid*, she chastised herself.

"Did your stepdad put you up to this, Jesse?" Ken asked.

"Nobody puts me up to anything," Jesse retorted. "I'm my own man."

"So the reverend doesn't know you've been a bad boy?" Ken persisted. "I'll bet he wouldn't be too happy if he knew what you've been up to. You're the reason he had to clear out of Tennessee, aren't you? Were you behind the move to Iowa, too? How old are you now, twenty-four? You've got a long life of crime ahead, don't you? If you keep doing things like this, and your stepdad has to keep moving, eventually he'll run out of places to go. Then maybe he'll let you take your lumps."

"Shut up!" Jesse said in a snarl.

"I suppose it's hard living under the same roof with a charismatic leader like Reverend Tremaine," Ken went on. "Is that why you started doing hate crimes, to get some recognition for yourself?"

"I told you to shut up!" Jesse yelled. He again lashed out angrily and slammed Ken in the back of the head with the butt of his pistol.

Ann screamed.

"You shut up, too," Jesse said, gripping her arm so tightly that she winced in pain. "I'd like some peace and quiet in here."

Ken was hunched over in his seat, cradling his head in his hands and moaning slightly. Ann desperately wanted to ask if he was all right but she was afraid of infuriating Jesse even more, so she remained silent.

They continued their trek west. The sun was still shining, and the countryside was lush and green. *What a horrible day this would be to die*, Ann thought, trying hard to fight back her feelings of doom.

Before they reached Mount Pleasant, Al headed north. After several miles, he turned off on another country road. Al drove a half mile then pulled onto a gravel lane almost obscured by the underbrush and slowly continued another hundred yards until he brought the Jeep to a stop next to a run-down building.

"All right. Everybody out," Jesse ordered. He

opened his door and deftly jumped out, then roughly dragged Ann out across the seat, all the while waving the gun menacingly. Ann anxiously looked to see how Ken was doing. He was getting out under his own power, but it looked as if he was in considerable pain, and his gait was unsteady.

"Come on," Jesse said. "Around this way." He grabbed Ann roughly by the arm and half dragged her over to a side door. He yanked the door open and shoved Ann inside. Al unceremoniously gave Ken the same treatment.

After they'd come in out of the sunlight, it was dark inside the building and it took a moment for Ann's eyes to adjust. She thought she detected some movement to the right, so she turned and looked in that direction. When she saw the source of the movement, she gasped. A young man was lying on the dirt floor of the building. He was bound and gagged, and blood was pouring out of a large wound on his forehead.

"Ben Kowalski, I presume," Ken said in a low voice.

The young man on the ground thrashed around and groaned in response.

"He's badly hurt!" Ann exclaimed. "He's losing a lot of blood. He needs medical attention." She started to move toward Ben, but Jesse pulled her back.

"Where do you think you're going, Florence Nightingale?" Jesse chided her. "You come over here and keep me company." He roughly pulled Ann toward the other side of the shed. Addressing his colleague, he said, "Tie them up."

Al picked up some lengths of rope off the ground

and approached Ann. "Sit down," he said. Ann reluctantly obeyed. Al efficiently tied her hands and ankles with the rope.

"Now you," Al said to Ken. Within moments he was similarly restrained.

"Now it's time to teach you a little respect," Jesse said, his voice taking on an even more sinister tone. Walking over to one side of the shed, he stuck the revolver into his waistband, then bent down and picked something up off the floor. When he turned around again, Ann felt her stomach constrict. It was a crowbar.

"Your friend from Planned Parenthood had a very hard head," Jesse said as he approached Ann. "I had to hit her quite a few times before her skull finally cracked. Maybe I'll have better luck with you."

"Leave her alone!" Ken shouted.

"Or maybe I should start with you instead," Jesse said, walking over to Ken.

"Tell me what you think you're going to accomplish by beating us both senseless—or even by killing us?" Ken challenged. "Are you really naive enough to believe that by wiping out a few people here and there you're going to be able to halt freedom of speech or put places like Planned Parenthood out of business? Unless you've got an atomic bomb in your little bag of tricks you're just spitting into the wind."

"No, I'm not," Jesse retorted. "I am making a statement."

"What kind of statement?" Ken persisted.

"A statement that I don't like your pathetic, liberal ideas."

"And you think that getting rid of us is going to wipe those ideas off the face of the earth? There will be more people to replace us before you've even got the blood wiped off your weapon."

"Shut up!" Jesse ordered.

"I don't feel like it!" Ken shot back.

"I've had enough out of you," Jesse said in a growl. He threw the crowbar down on the ground and pulled the gun back out of his waistband. Walking slowly over to Ken, he said, "Want to shoot your mouth off again, smart guy?"

"Sure, what have I got to lose?" Ken retorted.

"Ken, be quiet," Ann said softly.

"I don't feel like being quiet," Ken said. "Getting slugged in the head has made me quite garrulous. In fact, I think I feel a song coming on." And sure enough, he burst into a loud and very off-key rendition of "The Marine's Hymn."

"From the halls of Montezuma . . ." Ken shouted.

Oh, my God, Ann thought. What was wrong with Ken? The blows to his head must have caused brain damage. How could this be happening? *I'm going to throw up*, she thought. *I'm going to die and my last conscious memory is going to be of the most god-awful caterwauling I've ever heard in my life.*

"I told you to shut up!" Jesse screamed.

". . . to the shores of Tripoli," Ken continued.

"*Shut up!*" Jesse gripped the pistol in both hands and pointed it at Ken's face.

"We will fight our country's battles . . ."

Ann closed her eyes, waiting for the gunshot. It

came a moment later, followed by a scream of pain, followed by the sound of scuffling.

"No!" Ann yelled. Her eyes flew open and she turned toward Ken, but he was still calmly sitting next to her. To his left, Jesse lay writhing on the ground, clutching his shoulder. And ten feet away, in the middle of the dirt floor, Jeff Steiner and Al Hubble were locked in a struggle for a gun.

It took only thirty seconds for Jeff to get the upper hand. Using his superior weight and strength, he pinned the younger man under him, wrenched the gun away, and delivered several sharp blows to the man's head. Al went limp.

As Jeff got to his feet, half a dozen uniformed Jasper County sheriff's deputies burst through the door, their weapons drawn. Gary Carlson was right behind them.

"It's nice to see you fellows," Ken said dryly, "but you're a little bit late." Nodding his head toward Jeff, he said, "The marines already landed."

As two deputies attended to Ben Kowalski and the others cuffed Jesse and his buddy, Jeff rushed over to Ann and, using his Swiss Army knife, cut the ropes that were binding her.

"Thank God you found us!" Ann exclaimed as Jeff turned his attention to Ken. "How can we ever repay you?"

"No problem," Jeff replied modestly as he untied Ken. "I'm just glad that I was finally able to do something in my job description."

CHAPTER 38

"Are you all right?" Ann asked Jeff. "I was afraid Greer had killed you. And how did you ever find us?"

Ann, Ken, Jeff, and Gary were at the Jasper County Sheriff's Department. They had each given statements about the incident.

Ben Kowalski and Jesse Greer had been taken to a local hospital for treatment. Ben's head wound had required forty stitches, and he was being treated for a mild concussion, but the doctors said he would be fine.

Jesse was in surgery to remove a bullet from his shoulder. His companion, Al, was already in a jail cell. Jesse would join him as soon as he was released from the hospital.

"You can thank Gary for that," Jeff explained. "He pulled into your driveway a moment after you left. In fact, he saw Greer's Jeep turn the corner as he pulled up. I had just come around and was trying to stand up when he got there. At that point I wasn't in any shape to drive, so Gary loaded me into his car and took off after them like a bat out of hell." Jeff clapped the reporter soundly on the back. "Let me tell you, this guy could give Rusty Wallace a run for his money."

"Thank you, Gary," Ann said, giving her friend a big hug. "You're my hero."

"Oh, go on," Gary said. "It was nothing."

"So how did you find us?" Ken asked.

"That was a real stroke of luck," Gary admitted. "I had a gut feeling that they might be heading toward Mount Pleasant, so I took off in that direction. But I didn't actually spot the Jeep until you were a few miles out of town."

"So you followed us right to the shed," Ann said.

Gary nodded. "By the time you got there, we were right behind you. In fact, Jeff said I was following a little too closely and made me drop back so we wouldn't be spotted. We followed you up that gravel road. As soon as we saw them dragging the two of you outside, I got on the phone and called the sheriff's department and told them to get over there pronto."

Jeff picked up the narrative. "Fortunately my adrenaline kicked in on the drive, so by the time we got to the building I was feeling pretty pumped. While Gary called the authorities, I got out of the car and stood outside the door so I could monitor the situation. I would have preferred to wait for reinforcements to arrive rather than charging in on my own, but from the way Greer was talking, I figured I didn't have the luxury of waiting."

"I'm so glad you didn't wait," Ann said, hugging

him. Turning to Ken, she asked, "Did you know they were following us?"

"I was hoping they might be," Ken replied. "But I didn't know for sure until Greer walked over to pick up that crowbar. Then I glanced over at the door and saw a slight movement and I was pretty sure our saviors had arrived."

"Is that why you started singing?" Ann asked.

Ken nodded. "I was trying to create a diversion to allow Jeff time to get inside. Singing was the only thing I could think of."

"But why 'The Marine's Hymn,' of all things?" Ann asked.

Ken laughed. "I guess fear has a strange effect on the brain. It was the first thing that came to mind."

Ann leaned over and kissed Jeff, then bestowed the same treatment on Gary. "Thanks, guys. We wouldn't have made it through this without you."

"Aw, shucks," Gary said. "Does this mean I get an exclusive on this story?"

"You've got an exclusive on all stories within my control for the next millennium," Ann assured him.

"How did Greer know that Ben Kowalski was ratting him out?" Gary asked.

"Al Hubble told the deputies that Greer had been worried Ben might spill the beans ever since he heard how Ben had turned yellow the night I was abducted," Ann explained. "So he had Al, who lives in Mount Pleasant, watching Ben very closely. Al suspected something was up because Ben had been acting a little strange the past few days. So he and Greer confronted Ben just as he was about to drive to Madison to meet me. They had to beat the truth out of him, but Ben finally admitted that he had talked to me. After hearing that, Greer went nuts. He took a crowbar to Ben and decided it was high time that I be eliminated."

Just then one of the deputies who was working on the case came into the room. "You're all free to go now, folks. Sorry we had to keep you so long."

"No problem," Ken said, standing up and shaking the deputy's hand. "If you need any additional statements, just let us know."

The deputy nodded. "The DA's office will be in touch as the criminal cases proceed. Have a safe trip home."

Gary clapped Jeff on the back. "Come on, partner; let's head out. See you back at the ranch, kids," he called over his shoulder.

"What a night this has been!" Ken said, enveloping Ann in his arms. They held each other for a long time; then Ken looked into her eyes and asked, "Are you ready to go home now?"

Ann gave him a dazzling smile and nodded. "Absolutely," she said. "After all, there's no place like home."

EPILOGUE

"I can hardly believe this day is finally here!" Ann exclaimed. "I thought it would never come."

Ken nodded, then leaned forward in his chair and put his elbows on Ann's desk. "In about an hour Denise will be coming home from the hospital."

"It's about time," Ann said.

Three weeks had passed since Ann and Ken had been abducted by Jesse Greer and his companion. Five days after that incident, with no forewarning, Denise Riley had stunned everyone by awakening from her coma. She woke up completely lucid and had made steady progress ever since.

Dr. Lanska had no explanation for her patient's marvelous recovery. "I had almost given up hope," the doctor admitted. "We'll never know what caused her to come out of it. You can call it an unexplained event or you could call it a miracle." The doctor had paused a moment and grinned. "My money's on the latter."

Based on the statement Ben Kowalski had given to police, Sam Jenkins and his father had both been arrested in connection with the assaults on Ann and

Denise, Sam for participating in the assault on Denise and the elder Jenkins for aiding and abetting the attacks.

In exchange for his promise to testify against Jesse Greer, Sam had given a full confession confirming that Greer had been the mastermind behind both assaults as well as the man who had wielded the weapon that had smashed Denise's skull.

After spending two nights in the hospital for treatment of his gunshot wound, Greer had been transferred to the county jail. He had refused to give a statement to police and was facing trial on four counts of attempted murder.

To Ann's disappointment, there was no evidence linking Reverend Tremaine to the assaults. Although the reverend's wife was also refusing to cooperate with police, it was clear that she had lied when she claimed that Jesse had been with her the night Denise was assaulted. The reverend had issued a statement expressing his profound sympathy for what had happened to Denise and Ann, and asking the community to pray for his family.

As soon as word of Greer's latest crimes became public, Crystal Barman overcame her fears and came out of hiding in order to personally prevail on other jurors who had served at the criminal trial to come forward and tell what had happened. Two of them had heeded her call, and Claude Furseth had been charged with jury tampering. If convicted, he faced a lengthy prison term.

It was purely coincidence that Furseth had ended up on the Jenkins and English jury pool, but it was

DA Ted Lawrence's inaction that had allowed him to actually serve on the jury. In an effort to obtain a better deal for himself, Furseth admitted that Lawrence was a personal friend and that Furseth had talked Lawrence into letting him remain on the jury even though Lawrence knew that would probably mean Bill Robinson's assailants would get off scot-free. As soon as Furseth's allegations became public, Lawrence resigned his position, citing ill health and personal reasons.

The attorneys representing the English and Jenkins families in the civil case had offered Bill Robinson a hefty settlement. Bill and his parents were thrilled that their long ordeal was now at an end. Bill intended to donate a portion of the money to Lifelines, the gay and lesbian organization at UW, Mount Pleasant, in the hope the group might be able to prevent future acts of violence.

"We'd better get going," Ken said, looking at his watch, "if we want to be there when Denise comes out the front door of the hospital."

"I'm ready," Ann said, getting up and coming around her desk. "Why don't we stop on the way and pick up some flowers for her?"

"Good idea," Ken said.

"What's our schedule for tonight?" Ann asked, leaning down and putting her arms around Ken's neck.

"The girls are both spending the night with friends," Ken said, pulling Ann down onto his lap. "So it looks like we're going to have a rare evening alone. What would you like to do?"

Ann pretended to be pondering her options. "Well, first I think we should have a leisurely dinner."

"That sounds good," Ken said. "Then what?"

"Then I think we should take your dog for a long walk. She really doesn't get enough exercise."

"I agree. Frannie is much too sedentary. Then what?"

"Maybe there'll be something good on TV," Ann said, teasing him. "Is there anything you especially feel like watching?"

"There is one thing," Ken admitted.

"What is it?"

"You. In bed. Au naturel."

Ann leaned close and said seductively, "I think that can be arranged."

"I was hoping you'd say that." He gave her a lingering kiss. "I know you doubted it, but I kept telling you all along that the good guys would win," he said.

"You're right. The good guys did win," Ann said, nuzzling her head against Ken's head. "And I've got the best one of all. Now let's go welcome Denise home."

SIGNET   ONYX   (0451)

HOT CRIME WRITING

THEY CALL THEM GRIFTERS by Alice McQuillan.
It's not easy to track a mother-and-son con team who steal everything from identities to mink coats, but journalist Alice McQuillan effectively manages to pin down the elusive Sante and Kenneth Kimes in *They Call Them Grifters*.
(409078)

DEATH SENTENCE: *The True Story of Velma Barfield's Life, Crimes and Execution* by Jerry Bledsoe.
In 1984, Velma Barfield became the first woman since 1962 to be executed in the United States. Her crimes were unusual: Barfield was convicted of the 1978 arsenic poisoning of her fiancé, Stuart Taylor, and she admitted killing three other people with poison, including her own mother. But her path to execution was circuitous, involving appeal after appeal to various high courts, a grassroots movement to prevent her death, a jailhouse spiritual epiphany, and subsequent "recollections" of childhood abuse and torment that she claimed eventually led to her abuse of prescription tranquilizers, which in turn clouded her judgment and enabled her to perform murderous crimes.
(407555)

TRACE EVIDENCE: *The Search for the I5 Strangler* by Bruce Henderson
Some books about serial killers are dramatic and emotional. Trace Evidence, by contrast, has a steady relentlessness that allows the reader to become fascinated by the characters of the investigators and the facts of how the evidence was assembled. This killer specialized in picking up his victims along Interstate 5, near Sacramento, California, and he had an odd penchant for snipping at their clothes with scissors.
(408780)

To order call: 1-800-788-6262

⊘ **SIGNET**   ⊜ **ONYX**
(0451)

TRUE CRIME AT ITS BEST

MY LIFE IN THE NYPD
by James Wagner and Patrick Picciarelli (Contributor)
(410246)

James "Jimmy the Wags" Wagner takes readers behind the badge and into the daily drama of working New York City's toughest job in New York City's toughest precinct. It's the NYPD as no one has ever seen it before—from a street cop who walked the walk through the turbulent '60s, the violent '70s, and the drug-fueled '80s. Unbelievable war stories from a man who's seen it all.

JIMMIE THE WAGS: *Street Stories of a Private Eye*
by James Wagner w/ Patrick Picciarelli
(409272)

These are the true life stories of a real private eye. This book is tough, hilarious, and streetwise. It is a fascinating glimpse into a life lived on the rough edge of the law.

FATAL VISION   by Joe McGinniss
(165667)

The writer Joe McGinniss went to visit Dr. Jeffery MacDonald, with the intent of writing a book that would help clear his name. But after extensive interviews and painstaking research, a very different picture emerged. This is the electrifying story of a Princeton-educated green beret convicted of slaying his wife and children. "A haunting story told in detail." –*Newsweek*

A KILLER AMONG US:
A True Story of a Family's Triumph over Tragedy
by Charles Bosworth, Jr.
(408543)

Here is the incredible story of a small town crime that made national head-lines, of three explosive trials, of a seething hotbed of adultery and abuse, and of a stunning verdict that ignited a legal minefield of child-custody battles and a chilling final retribution.

To order call: 1-800-788-6262

TrueCrime/O387

PENGUIN PUTNAM INC.
Online

Your Internet gateway to a virtual environment with hundreds of entertaining and enlightening books from Penguin Putnam Inc.

While you're there, get the latest buzz on the best authors and books around—

Tom Clancy, Patricia Cornwell, W.E.B. Griffin, Nora Roberts, William Gibson, Robin Cook, Brian Jacques, Catherine Coulter, Stephen King, Ken Follett, Terry McMillan, and many more!

**Penguin Putnam Online is located at
http://www.penguinputnam.com**

PENGUIN PUTNAM NEWS

Every month you'll get an inside look at our upcoming books and new features on our site. This is an ongoing effort to provide you with the most up-to-date information about our books and authors.

Subscribe to Penguin Putnam News at
http://www.penguinputnam.com/newsletters